An Unlikely Arrangement

BRIDES OF BILTMORE
BOOK ONE

CINDY PATTERSON

EDITED BY
LESLEY ANN MCDANIEL

Springbrook Press

Brides of Biltmore

1

An UNLIKELY ARRANGEMENT

CINDY PATTERSON

For information contact: www.cindypattersonbks.com

Cover design by: Roseanne White Designs

Editor: Lesley Ann McDaniel

Published by Springbrook Press, NC

ISBN:978-1-64669-043-5 Paperback

ISBN:978-1-64669-044-2 Hardback

ISBN:978-1-64669-045-9 Ebook

Library of Congress Control Number: 2024902757

Printed in the United States of America

For you, Mama
I love and miss you everyday.
Thank you for always being my biggest fan.

"Mema"
Pamelia Baines Gardner
September 26, 1951-February 6th, 2022

Chapter One

Nearly sliding off the vanity bench, Abigail Dupree twisted away from her mother. "I refuse to be bartered like a prize pig."

"You will do as I say." Catherine Dupree's grip tightened on a lock of Abigail's hair as she tugged the comb through it with more force than necessary. "And stop fidgeting. It's not ladylike."

Instead of yelping out in pain, Abigail clenched her jaw. "I do not like him, Mother. He's twelve years my senior. And he's—"

"He's what?" Through the mirror, her mother punctured her with a glare, her long, cold fingers still working in the same area. "Rich? Handsome? Single?"

"He's arrogant, pushy…" Abigail pressed on, though the sound of her mother's indrawn breath gave her pause. "Why is it so important to you that I marry?"

"I need to know you'll have someone to care for you. Your father and I won't be around forever."

William Arendell did not care for her. Not the way a man

1

should care for a woman he intended to marry. Abigail trailed the intricate edges of her mother's vanity chest. "I want to explore the world and write about every place that I visit and fill multiple books with all the details."

"Daydreaming is a waste of time. No decent man would ever allow such a thing."

Ignoring her mother's thought, Abigail continued. "Of course, I would prefer to travel alone."

"It isn't proper. Nor is it safe." Mother yanked through another strand. "Traveling is only suitable for men."

"I know, I know. Because a woman's place is at home with her husband." She had never made any progress with changing her mother's way of thinking. Even if her own father did not always agree with Mother's notions. "Perhaps if the woman loved the man." But she would never feel anything toward William Arendell. Even the thought of him made her physically ill.

Mother eyed her skeptically. "There is more to marriage than love."

"But it is the foundation." Abigail exhaled a full breath. "I wish not to marry if I cannot have a man who will love me as Father loves you."

Mother shook her head. "It's not that simple, dear."

"Why don't you just say it, Mother? I know what you're thinking." Abigail sniffed, probing her mother's pitiless eyes, her own begging for affirmation—an affirmation she would never receive. No decent man would ever have her. Much less love her.

"Mr. Arendell's qualities will serve you perfectly. No one else has made any offers. Face it dear, you do not have the advantage other girls have."

Nor would she ever. The very reason she needed to take matters into her own hands.

Her mother fluffed a few gray streaks framing her own weathered cheeks. "Rose should be able to take it from here."

Abigail's mistakes had always lurked beneath the surface, but never had her mother voiced the flaw of her immoral choices aloud. She drew in a deep breath before she burst into tears and ran from the room. When she reached her bedchamber, she slammed the door, hoping the sound echoed along the hardwood floors, all the way to her mother's ears.

Abigail sprawled across her bed and stroked the white-laced quilt as knots coiled in her belly. Fancy dresses hung in the wardrobe, French-carved-walnut furniture surrounded her, and porcelain dolls stared back with pity. None of it had ever made her happy.

After only two minutes, she took a deep breath, squared her shoulders, and moved to her closet.

Abigail's cheeks flamed with regret.

Why had she allowed her temper to flare again? It had accomplished nothing. Her tantrums would only serve to widen the wedge between her and her mother. And forfeiting the love of her parents was the last thing she needed.

Abigail thumbed through her dresses slowly, barely absorbing the styles or colors as Rose, her lady's maid, entered. Abigail's gaze traveled to the young woman's face.

Rose's dark brown eyes assessed her, altering her attentive smile into a frown. "Good heavens, miss. Why are you crying?"

"I am destined to live a lonely, miserable life under the careful watch of my mother."

Rose bent her thin frame over the bed and straightened the quilt. "Oh, no, miss. You will find a wonderful man who will love you dearly."

Abigail expelled a lungful of air. "Not if I am to marry that despicable Mr. Arendell."

"The Lord has a way of working these things out. You must trust in Him."

Rose was right, of course. But it didn't seem Abigail's mother was allowing the Lord to work in this particular situation.

Instead, Catherine Dupree had taken things into her own hands. Perhaps Abigail could talk her father into allowing her to stay home this evening.

"I'll be right back." Before Rose could question her, Abigail hurried from the room.

As Abigail took the back stairs, a prickle of unease wormed down her back, but she had to at least try to make her case.

Abigail stepped into her father's office, stomach fluttering. "Hello, Father."

Her father lifted his head from the stack of paperwork before him, and then leaned back in his chair and clasped his hands. "Why Abigail, what a lovely surprise. How are you this fine evening? I pray you are having a good day?"

"Yes, Father." She scanned the room, her focus darting over the stacked containers that lined the walls and the mass of paperwork on the corner of his desk. "What is all this?"

"I have decided to start doing some of my work here."

Abigail eyed her father, who was intent on the folder he held. Why ever would he choose to work from here? But then hope stirred within her. If Father was around more, maybe that would help smooth the constant tension between herself and her mother. "Oh? I pray there was no issue with your office uptown."

"No, no dear. It's nothing like that. Did you have something on your mind?" he asked without looking up.

"Nothing of great importance." Pausing to think of the best way to plead her case, she peeked out the doorway to make sure her mother wasn't within hearing range.

He lifted his head, his eyes glazed over with a flicker of worry. "Is your mother all right?"

"Yes, sir." Her optimism waned a bit. When had he ever not taken Mother's side? It would be better to ease into the topic of skipping the ball than to blurt her request. Especially since her father was obviously preoccupied. "She is fine."

His apprehension seemed to dissolve just as quickly as it had

4

appeared. So abruptly in fact, that she almost believed she must have imagined the whole thing.

"Wonderful. I do appreciate you stopping by, darling, but now is not the best time for a visit. I have an important project to tend to and I am running out of time." He rose and came around the desk to lay a kiss on her cheek. "I shall see you later at the ball."

Dismissed. A hard lump of distress formed in the back of Abigail's throat. "You are attending?"

"Yes, of course, my sweet." He wrapped an arm around her shoulder. "Your mother insists on going, and I must accompany her."

Not willing to outright lie to him or proceed with her argument of all the reasons she should not attend, she allowed her father to shuffle her from his office.

She would simply have to find another way.

Over the next ten minutes, Rose curled Abigail's long, wavy locks and pinned them into a loose bun.

Rose clasped her hands together. "There, Miss Abigail. You look just lovely."

"You've done an exquisite job as always." Regarding her reflection in the mirror, Abigail scrutinized the fair shade of her skin tone. "Maybe I can help myself by convincing Mr. Arendell that I am all wrong for him." Giving that man the wrong impression would indeed be advantageous to her plight.

Rose chuckled as she examined her work. "Good luck with that, miss."

Abigail powered her nose, daubing her face with a bit of color. "I daresay, I do adore this hairstyle. You are very talented, Rose."

The young woman's cheeks flushed as she adjusted a loose

pin. "You may not have success in convincing Mr. Arendell tonight, nor any other night for that matter."

Abigail fixed her gaze on Rose, who had been blessed with a complexion half a shade darker than her own. "Maybe if I chose a different dress, one less suitable for a ball, he may think me undesirable. Or maybe all of my hair will escape its pins. That would be easy, since my head is always rejecting them."

"It might have the opposite effect. Besides, your mother would never allow you to leave the house." Rose went to the armoire for the dress Abigail's mother had chosen, then lugged it across the room.

Meanwhile, Abigail mentally composed a believable argument as to why she wasn't the best match for Mr. Arendell. There were beautiful, more affluent women who would better suit a man of his potential. Women who would fancy a life of wealth and status—the very thing she had come to despise.

Women who had saved themselves for their future husbands.

After Rose hung the lavender gown on a hook, Abigail pulled on her stockings. She then adjusted her silk ribbon garters as her mind wandered in another direction. "If only I could see him once more."

The woman's green eyes dimmed a shade. "Who do you mean, Miss Abigail?"

Abigail bit down on her treacherous tongue. Why had she blurted that? Yet, a part of her was relieved it was out. A bigger part than she'd realized. For too many years, she had buried her feelings. Pretended that nothing had happened. Though secretly, she had counted the days since she'd left Asheville. Left him behind. And today just so happened to be the five-year anniversary of their departure. A pang twisted in Abigail's stomach. She had wasted a full sixty months wishing for a man to come for her, who in all likelihood did not even remember her name.

Abigail lifted her attention to her lady's maid, who still

waited patiently for a response. "Randall Thorne." His whispered name fell from her tongue.

Rose assisted Abigail into her petticoat. "Oh? Wasn't he the young man from your youth?"

Her youth, indeed. Abigail nodded and lifted her arms so that Rose could lace her corset as Abigail's remembrance of the man filled her weary heart with a strange sense of hope.

It had been 1,825 days since she had last seen Randall, and still the grief of his abandonment would surface often without warning. The pain of his rejection, harsh as it had been, had never completely diminished. Not with her mother's constant reminders of how she had ruined any hope of gaining another marriage prospect.

No longer classified as a youth, and creeping dangerously to two decades was the very thing that had Abigail in this perilous predicament. Though she shouldn't complain. The Lord had been generous to her and sheltered her in His protection at the most critical moments of her life. Had spared her of an even worse fate by removing her from pitying glances and careless whispers, even though all her tribulations had been self-inflicted. Surely, He wouldn't abandon her now. Though her fear of living her whole life without love strangled her feelings on the matter. If only there were a way to rewrite certain moments in her own history.

Abigail shook her head. Nurturing regrets only muddied the waters to any hope of a fresh start. Something she could desperately use.

An idea struck. "Mother can't make me go, if I'm not here." As Rose lifted the heavy dress and lowered it carefully over her head, Abigail cast a glance at the bolted bedroom door. It vanished behind a curtain of flounces. When the skirt fell to her waist, she twisted it into its proper place.

"You are speaking nonsense, Miss Abigail. You must go." Rose huffed her objection as she adjusted a loosened pin at the back of Abigail's head. "Just imagine, tonight could be the very night you meet the gentleman who will steal your heart. There will be so many men at the ball. Surely one will turn your head. Besides, your mother—"

"The gentlemen in attendance will be the same men that I have already encountered." Abigail began fastening the countless buttons. "And even if a new gentleman emerges from the shadows, then he most likely delights in this high society nonsense. Therefore, I shall have nothing in common with him." Though none of that mattered. Even if she were wrong and one of them captured her attention, she had forfeited her privilege to a happily-ever-after.

"If you feel so disapproving of them all, how will you ever find your true love?" Rose gave her a starry-eyed look.

Heaven be praised for Rosalind Whitmore. How would Abigail have managed without the young woman's ability to find rays of hope within clouds of ash.

Abigail almost felt sorry for her maid. Rose had always been a romantic. Even if her situation were not so dire, no man would ever again be given a chance to break Abigail's heart.

"I do not intend to." Abigail dabbed a finger to each side of her neck with her favorite Victorian spiced rose oil. "And for heaven's sake, Rose, call me Abigail."

Rose lowered her head. "I apologize, but your mother—"

"Yes, I know. She insists. But when she's not here, it is truly not necessary to include the 'miss." She took Rose's arm and led her to the door. "I would like a few moments to myself. I shall see you later."

Ignoring Rose's frown, Abigail closed the door and advanced to her only window. She pushed one heavy curtain to the side. After lifting the window carefully, she leaned forward and shuddered at the distance to the ground. Tree limbs swayed in the wind, brushing against the house. The lantern's low light flickered from the sudden breeze as the drape shifted back into place.

After contemplating the best avenue of escape, she decided to leave right under her mother's nose.

Stretching out her fingers, she slipped her hands into a pair of sleek gloves, grabbed her wrap and hat, then left her bedchamber and closed the door behind her. Her mother stood sentinel at the bottom of the stairs. Waiting for Abigail's descent, no doubt.

"The dress is beautiful. Turn around," her mother demanded the moment Abigail took the last step. Mother yanked on the bow at the back, redoing the knot to her satisfaction. "I knew this dress would suit you perfectly. Wait until Mr. Arendell sets his eyes on you."

Abigail fashioned out a smile, masking her disgust at merely hearing the man's name, and curtsied.

Mother walked away, rattling on about having the carriage brought around, and Abigail slipped out the front door. A grin wedged across her lips at how easily that had worked.

She wandered down the lane and within thirty minutes had reached the crossroads in town. The streetlamp glowed down on her, the light shielded by her hat. She held her back straight, though her courage diminished with each step she took farther into town, farther away from home. It hadn't occurred to her that more people than she could count would be milling about. Why weren't they home preparing for tonight's gala? Maybe there *were* others who had not succumbed to the nonsensical society demands of their fellow peers? Though most weren't polite and darted curious glances her way as if she were the odd one out.

Then the shriek of a yowling cat made her jump. What had she been thinking walking out there alone at this hour? And in these dancing shoes? Her feet were aching and a blister had cultivated. And worsened with each step. As she lifted her skirt to reach for her foot, the thundering of hooves split the silence.

A carriage closed in on her.

Chapter Two

A bigail took a wobbly step back, her heel turning onto its side.

From behind her, strong arms steadied her before she tumbled. "Oh!"

"Pardon me, miss, but perhaps those shoes aren't made for this cobblestone street."

Startled at the sound of the deep voice far above her head, she skittered from his hold.

After putting more distance between them, she straightened her skirt. "You are correct. But what shoes would you expect a lady to wear with a formal gown? I certainly can't allow my hem to drag the pavement, now can I? Besides, these were imported and very expensive." What had prompted her to say such a thing? Especially since the item in question had her feet begging for mercy. And if she'd had any say so in the matter, she would have chosen a more sensible pair and no one would have been the wiser. Except perhaps, her mother. Of course, this stranger had taken notice and that fact did not sit well with her.

Then her rescuer stepped into the streetlamp's radius, and she wished she had held her tongue.

He tapped the brim of his hat. "Garrett Barringer, ma'am."

The man's attire captured her attention first. Well-dressed in a crisp white shirt, black suit and tie. No doubt he would be attending the ball. Then her head lifted. He was younger than she had expected. At the very most, a few years older than her. Her mistake, though, was meeting his eyes. Abigail collected her breath as she stared into the deepest brown eyes she had ever seen. Her mind raced, then went completely blank under his steady gaze.

His lids creased in confusion as if waiting for the conclusion of her attack. When she said nothing else, he glanced about. "Where is your escort?"

At the same rate that her cheeks flamed, her foolish nature kicked in. "I do not have an escort."

Why had she readily admitted that? What if he meant her harm? No, he couldn't. Not this man. There was something about his demeanor. Perhaps it was the way he looked at her. Of course, she had always been taught not to judge a book by its cover. And his particular cover had been perfectly chiseled. With his knight-in-shining-armor characteristics, she imagined him sweeping her away on his white horse and rescuing her from a marriage to that vile man waiting at the ball this very moment. A smile curved her lips.

He quirked a judging eyebrow. As if he could read her scandalous thoughts.

A wave of mortification swelled within her. Her eyes slid closed. What was wrong with her? Had she not learned anything from her mistakes? No knight would ever show up to rescue her. And even if he did, she would be foolish to trust his intentions.

The hum of his deep exhale unbolted her eyelids. "Where are you headed?"

Abigail snapped him a look. That was none of his business. But that was not the only reason she gave no answer. For even she did not know. She cleared her throat. "Thank you for—" *Catching me?* She could never say that aloud. "Preventing my fall. I do, appreciate your assistance. Now, if you will excuse me."

The stranger tilted his head, grooves etching his brow. "You should not be out here alone at this time of night. And if I may, it would be better to wear a shoe that wasn't imported or expensive if it kept you from twisting an ankle. Even if they do not match the extravagant dress." He took another deep breath, and his lips turned downward, yet the concern in his eyes remained.

"I suppose you also believe a woman is not capable of traveling alone." She had not meant to speak that aloud.

"I'm not certain I understand quite what you mean."

Abigail shook her head. "Nor do I."

"Please, allow me to assist you to your destination. My carriage is just around the corner."

As tempting as resting her weary feet and legs sounded, Abigail took a tentative step back. Clearly her judging skills needed polishing. "I beg your pardon, but I do not make it a habit to accompany strange men to their buggies."

Blowing out a slow breath, the man crossed his arms. "And you shouldn't. But I could only assume you were heading in the same direction as I and thought…Well, I assure you, I mean no harm."

Out of the corner of her eye, Abigail caught the man taking a measured step back.

"May I at least walk you to safety?"

Avoiding the temptation of a yes, she turned a bit more. "Thank you." She offered a brief smile, though she had no intention of accepting the man's offer. "But no, I am perfectly fine."

"And I am late. But it isn't safe to roam the streets this time of night unescorted. As you can see, the respectable parts of the city are shut down for the evening, so in the event that you should need further assistance, there would be none." She detected no smugness in his tone, only concern. As if she were a helpless woman incapable of defending herself. "Please, pardon me, miss, but I cannot in good conscience leave someone like you out here alone."

She rotated and her chin lifted with a heavy dose of defiance before she met his dark eyes straight on. "Someone like me?" Whatever was that supposed to mean? Even if he were correct, she refused to let this man push her around. "Not every woman requires a man for protection."

"Are all women pig-headed?" he muttered under his breath. "If you are determined not to use the good sense God bestowed upon you, I will leave you to it. Good evening, Miss…"

She flattened her mouth, not about to offer a complete stranger her name. Using her lack of experience or, more so, lack of judgment for once to her advantage, Abigail lingered in the shadows.

"Have it your way. I pray you make it to your destination intact. Good evening, ma'am." He tipped his hat before walking on.

She aimed her body in the opposite direction and rested on the bench beneath the street lantern. Rubbing her ankle, she steeled herself against the acknowledgment that he had been right. And she was irritated at herself for admiring his strength. His courtesy.

Her heart did an irrational leap in her chest, forcing her to stand.

It didn't matter that the depth of his eyes dizzied her emotions. Or that his character, in the insignificant time she had to ascertain, seemed agreeable. More agreeable than any man she had acquainted of late.

She would never see him again. Besides, he had insulted her. *Pig-headed.*

To be fair, he hadn't been wrong—for even *she* couldn't deny how difficult she could be. But who did he think he was? Like a wind-storm lifting loosened shingles, irritation gusted up and carried off her approval.

She stared at his diminishing form, livid that he would speak to her in such an audacious way. Lifting her skirts, she watched out for ruts as she walked farther down the street, her courage suddenly stronger than before. "Extravagant?"

If he only knew.

"What on earth are you doing here?" Her mother's shrill voice echoing through the starlit sky brought Abigail's confidence to a halt and replaced it with a sudden chill. "Climb in and take care not to wrinkle your dress."

"I am not going to the ball, Mother. Tell Mr. Arendell I am unwell." Abigail turned, and her skirts shifted.

Mother was out of the buggy within seconds, her gold dress glittering beneath the street lamps, her lips pinched in tight lines. "Yes, you are attending the ball. Now climb into the carriage this minute, young lady, before I order the driver to pick you up and carry you. Hurry, or we will be late."

The command bucked her pride, but Abigail obeyed.

"How can you be so ridiculous as to presume I would let you skip the ball? How did you even get here? Do you not know how dangerous it is for a little girl to be out in the middle of town at this hour?"

A little girl? Abigail stared at her mother. It wasn't the first time her mother had referred to her in that way. It was almost as if her mother's mind had transported to another period of time where she actually envisioned Abigail younger. Much younger. "I am perfectly capable of walking down the street alone. And I am not a child. I am nearly twenty."

Mother averted her focus toward the bench where Abigail had just been sitting and cleared her throat. "Well, it would seem to me if you wanted to be treated like a twenty-year-old, you would start acting your age."

A realm of accusation lingered behind her mother's statement. "What is that supposed to mean?"

"Well, just look at you. Your hat is crooked, your hair has come loose, and more importantly, you are unmarried."

Her mother's stern tone cut through the confusion of being referred to as a child, and vanquished Abigail's sympathy. "Mother, I am afraid I will not be able to attend."

Her mother harrumphed. "Of course, you will attend. Do you not realize the significance of your presence this evening?"

Abigail trailed a gloved hand along the arc of her ankle. "It is of no importance to me."

Her mother's harsh intake of breath forced Abigail's head upward. "Mr. Arendell has specifically inquired of your attendance at this event and I will not allow you to disappoint the gentleman."

She was no more than wasting her breath arguing with her mother.

"But my feet hurt." Abigail pushed a fallen curl into a pin, wishing to expunge her spoken words, as she heard her own whiny voice in them. "Can we at least return to the house so I can exchange these shoes for a more comfortable pair?"

"There is no time for that. Because of your frolicking about, we will be late. I had to send your father on ahead. You have no idea how hard it was to convince him to leave me behind."

She suddenly regretted her decision to sneak out. "You didn't have to do that, Mother." Having Mother disappointed was one thing, but Father? That was unbearable.

"Well, of course, I did. He is under enough pressure. The last thing he needs is to catch wind of another one of your outlandish attempts to avoid William."

Abigail gasped. "You and Mr. Arendell are on a first-name basis?"

"What? No. I didn't mean…Well, surely you can see my nerves have been overworked and I am not thinking clearly." Her mother glanced at her with a sheepish frown. "Mr. Arendell is expecting your presence tonight, and I, for one, have no intention of being the cause of his disappointment."

"I have no interest in Mr. Arendell, or anyone else. I am perfectly happy by myself."

"I refuse to argue with you. I know what's best. You will simply have to trust me."

Abigail sighed. It was useless. Mother wouldn't give up until she had her married off to the wealthiest man in North Carolina. But how could she agree to marry someone else when her heart still ached for the man who had forsaken her five years ago?

"I am truly sorry, Mother. I do not know what came over me." Though her apology was sincere, one thing was certain. Her mother couldn't force her to fall in love with William.

For one instant, Abigail's thoughts roamed back to the tall, broad-shouldered man who had prevented her fall.

The man had been a distraction of the worst kind. The kind that at one time would have had her swooning over those dark, protective eyes. Those muscled shoulders. But she was no longer a naive girl powerless to the flattering charms of a handsome man. Though she could hardly label that man charming.

He had all but called her incompetent. And pig-headed. Even still, an annoying tingle whirled through her middle.

She may see him again.

Garrett Barringer stepped into the grand ballroom, his hands stuffed into his pockets, the scent of spiced roses slowly fading from his jacket.

"Garrett!" The high-pitched voice of his best friend's sister pierced his ears. "I'm so happy you made it." Elizabeth Madden curtsied. "Unfortunately, my brother has been detained."

"It's quite all right. I have my own matters of business to attend to."

Elizabeth offered her hand and Garrett lifted it to his lips.

She blushed a deep pink, and it was obvious his kindness had been mistaken as a personal gesture. Elizabeth had more than once made herself available, and he didn't want to hurt the young woman by giving her false hope.

"If you will excuse me," Garrett said as he detected a bit of heartbreak in her smile.

"Yes, of course," Elizabeth said, as she let him pass.

Walking further into the room, Garrett spoke to several acquaintances he'd met while doing business here in Charlotte. The city differed from the vast, mountainous countryside of Asheville, but he determined to make the most of it. He had no choice. This opportunity was his only chance to escape a past that no longer wanted him, and couldn't have come at a better time.

Garrett was turning to shake a gentleman's hand, when he caught another scent of the spiced roses. He searched the area until his view settled on the young lady who'd faltered unexpectedly into his arms earlier this evening. She stood motionless near an older woman. The same one who had thankfully forced the pig-headed woman into her carriage. If the older woman hadn't arrived, he might still be waiting in the shadows, ensuring no harm would come to the young lady.

In the room's light, he found her even more beautiful, but that was of no consequence. It didn't matter that something about her made it hard to look away. She would never catch him staring.

He was speaking with an acquaintance when the young woman walked directly by him, and he caught a stronger scent of those spiced roses. His head lifted without consent.

"Miss Abigail, how nice to see you!" Garrett's acquaintance spoke and the young lady stopped. "My daughter hoped to see you tonight."

17

CINDY PATTERSON

Garrett watched as her eyes glistened with sincere delight. *Abigail.* Subconsciously, he tucked her name away.

"I must find Marguerite immediately." Abigail smiled. "Enjoy your evening, sir."

Her overly polite tone was nothing like the snap and bite he'd witnessed earlier. She curtsied, and her lips curled upward, revealing perfectly straight teeth. She looked in his direction as if she'd known he would be staring, and then without acknowledging his presence, she started to walk away.

"Wait, Miss Abigail. I wanted to introduce you to the newest member of our board. Garrett Barringer, allow me to introduce Miss Abigail Dupree."

Dupree? Anthony Dupree's daughter?

She curtsied again, and Garrett took her offered hand. He laid his lips to the silky material of her white glove and inhaled that same delicate fragrance clinging to it.

"Garrett is our newest lawyer. You'll save a dance for the young lady, I trust."

Abigail Dupree's agreeable smile weakened by a millimeter. Something he was sure only he noticed—but noticed he did. Garrett enjoyed watching her squirm. She needed to be taken down a few notches, and it would honor him to oblige. "It would be my pleasure to accompany you in a dance later this evening, Miss Dupree."

A hint of pink enhanced the cream of her cheeks. She then turned, her long lavender skirts hanging from her slim waist, her expensive dancing shoes clinking against the floor—the ones responsible for landing the beauty in his arms.

He laughed out loud, unable to control the deep satisfaction building within him.

And it felt good.

Chapter Three

A bigail hissed. "Of all the nerve." Why was he laughing? Was it at her? Because of her slight limp? Something she had been consciously trying to improve. But it was impossible. Not with her sore ankle and the insole irritating the flaming blisters on her toes with each stride. If only she could remove her shoes and sit down.

Glancing over her shoulder at the man she had clearly misjudged, she grunted. Every person in this room considered themselves her superior. And he was just like them.

Foolish woman. She'd thought the pitying glances and whispering gossip of her neighbors would be the source that festered old wounds. Never would she have imagined that a complete stranger could inflict such torment.

She turned to the right, anxious to be removed from the dandy's line of sight, and something solid struck the heel of her shoe from behind her. Biting back a yelp, she forced herself to not reach for her ankle. The chatters would not receive an additional offering of ammunition against her.

"There you are. I have been looking for you." A male voice said, guiding her thoughts away from the arrogant man to an even worse matter she had feared from the moment of her arrival.

Abigail rotated. Too quickly, for she nearly fell into the man. "Oh, Mr. Arendell. You startled me."

The unintentional collision brought even more penetrating pain to the blister that was taking its toll with each step. Ignoring the urge to kick her shoe off and rub her heel, she curtsied and concealed her sour response. She had hoped to avoid the man until near the close of the evening. But because of her concern over Mr. Barringer's opinions, she had not paid attention to her surroundings, which prevented her from dodging this unavoidable encounter with William Arendell. Adding one more negative mark against the new lawyer.

"How lovely to see you." Only a little fib.

"Are we still being formal then?" Arendell held out a hand, a sneer darkening his features. "Would you care to dance?"

It would be rude to say no to a gentleman, even if he wasn't a true gentleman. She accepted his arm, her blood curdling at the touch. "If you wish."

He led her across the floor to the exact area she'd hoped to avoid. In perfect view of that Garrett Barringer man. With each encounter she disliked him more. Laughing at her and her inability to walk across the room with grace. *How dare he?*

"Did you say something, my darling?"

Mr. Arendell had not permission to use such endearments. In her opinion, her Christian name was not tolerable for his lips.

He held her at a respectful distance at first, but with each twirl, he inched closer. And with his rancid breath grazing her nostrils, her stomach twisted tighter with repugnance.

Out of fear of gossip and her own discomfort, she reprimanded him. "A little too close, do you not agree?"

He whispered into her hair. "Not nearly close enough for me."

A spasm cinched her muscles, and she searched the room.

Only one person seemed to be paying attention—her mother, who was standing on the opposite side of the room.

The instruments faded, and she sighed with relief until he spun her around at the announcement of the next dance. She realized with a pang of frustration that William didn't follow the rules.

Any of them.

A new ache radiated up her leg as she leaned back as far as she could. "Mr. Arendell, a little more space, please?"

"If I must." The man grumbled but complied by shuffling back a few inches.

She had hoped to explore and visit with Marguerite, to remove her insufferable shoes and sit, just sit. Instead, she had to endure more unbearable pain until another agonizing song ended.

"Excuse me, sir. May I cut in?"

The sound of his familiar tone pierced through the beginning prelude of woodwinds and strings.

Her eyes lifted upward to find Mr. Barringer waiting for a response. When Mr. Arendell did not give his permission, the stranger pressed on. "I do believe, sir, that you have already had a dance."

Mr. Arendell opened his mouth as if to speak but changed his mind. He unfastened his fingers from Abigail's hand before turning on his heel.

"Miss Dupree." Mr. Barringer took her left hand, placed his right hand beneath her shoulder blade, and then guided her in the chassé from promenade position.

Abigail's breath solidified before reaching her lungs. Mr. Barringer was light on his feet, his moves precise, polished. He led her in perfect timing, his hand resting gently on her back. Even with her best effort, disguising her discomfort would be impossible with him as a partner. She stretched onto the tips of her toes, trying with all her might to hide her misery, but it

21

wasn't working, not while shifting her weight from her right ankle. She hoped he didn't notice how her muscles coiled with unease.

She had to find a way to survive this pain without bursting into tears. It was only one dance. After all, Mr. Barringer had removed her from the clutches of William Arendell. With a grateful heart, she would suffer through the stinging, throbbing, and tenderness for one more song.

Leading her downline of the dance with his body pointed diagonally toward her, he gave her a layered look. "I'm glad to see you made it to your destination safely." He steadied his focus on her but it was his playful grin that flabbergasted her.

Telling him she never intended to attend was burning the tip of her tongue.

"Although I am curious how you are dancing so well when I am certain your ankle must be sore and the blisters on your feet are most likely enflamed."

Abigail tilted her head. "How did you know that?" Her eyes widened as he turned and led her in the opposite direction. "Is that why you were laughing at me?"

They met each other's questioning look in the middle of the next step. "Laughing at you? No. I would never find humor in someone else's pain." With defined, grace his head lolled to the right. "I thought it would be an obvious outcome taking such a long walk in a pair of shoes not necessarily meant for exercise. And then to have twisted it just as you—" He paused mid-step. "Well, at any rate, please forgive me if I have offended you."

A slow smile budded in the midst of her frown as he presumed with poise as if he hadn't lost a few beats. "So, you had no knowledge that there were indeed blisters on my feet?"

"In truth, when I saw you in town earlier, it seemed as though you were reaching to rub your foot but then the carriage startled you. It was a mere presumption."

"You did warn me about wearing these shoes. But because I

—" She almost blurted that she had snuck out. Not wanting to stain her first impression more than she had already, she changed her course. "Well, that doesn't matter. These shoes shall never have the opportunity to grace my feet again."

Mr. Barringer laughed out loud and brought her to an abrupt halt amid all the other couples. "Miss Dupree, would you care to get some refreshment? This song is rather long."

Abigail surveyed the couples surrounding them. "Can we just leave the floor?"

His eyes sparkled with his smile. "Of course, we can."

As the shock of Mr. Barringer's suggestion of not finishing the dance faded, she took his offered arm. "That would be wonderful."

Most couples remained intent on their own partners as they exited the floor, while only a few tossed a curious glance in their direction.

Never had a gentleman interrupted a dance for her advantage. The notion plowed through the guarded part of her heart, gnawing at years of buried scars. The ache was bitter, yet tender. Other than her family, no one had ever truly shown sincere concern for her.

Garrett led her across the room to a corner table. "Have a seat while I fetch us a drink."

Oh, dear heavens, she could kiss the man. "Thank you so very much, Mr. Barringer."

Ridges scored into the flesh above his eyes. "You remembered my name?"

Her cheeks burned for more than one reason as he tilted his head, leaving her with that crooked smile, and disappearing into the crowd.

Had it been wrong to say his name? Had she given him an indication that he was memorable? Of course, she was mostly thankful she had not blurted his given name, since the name Garrett had been swimming around in her head since their earlier meeting. Abigail wasn't quite sure how she felt about being persuaded to accept Mr. Barringer's thoughtfulness. She was only certain she must broaden the distance between them. There was something intriguing about the man—a charming blend of strength, gentility, and charisma. And even though this was only her second encounter with him, her fascination had already deepened beyond harmless curiosity. A rarity for her, indeed. Then the thought of actually kissing him robbed her of her breath.

Oh, dear heavens, indeed!

Beneath the privacy of the table and unable to bear the tenderness a moment more, she pulled her right ankle onto her lap and unbuckled her shoe. The freedom from the hard leather almost made her cry out with relief. Gently, she slid her foot back beneath the table and brought the left one to her lap.

She had just finished unbuckling the second shoe when Garrett returned. He carefully positioned the saucer and cup on the table in front of her. She dared a quick glance at him, but immediately her insides performed their own version of the waltz.

Zeroing in on her task at hand, she intentionally blocked her line of sight of the man. "Thank you for the refreshment, though it is not necessary to remain in my company. But I am sincerely grateful for your kindness and for your assistance earlier this evening."

"I did not assist you, Miss Dupree."

Her gaze darted up at him. Maybe she had heard him incorrectly over the combination of deafening music and animated voices. "I beg your pardon?"

He considered her with wide, vigilant eyes. "I allowed you to stay in town alone against my better judgment."

"And let me guess, if something dire had happened to me, you would never forgive yourself." She teased, presuming she was just overly tired from her trek earlier.

"Precisely." His frown deepened, even though he still maintained a look of kindness. Compassion.

Abigail tilted her head toward him. "I am only jesting you, Mr. Barringer."

"And I have never been more serious."

She snickered as she lowered her attention to the refreshment set before her. "Your concern for my safety is truly appreciated, but I assure you I was fine. And furthermore, I was not your responsibility, Mr. Barringer, so you are free to let yourself off that hook." She glowered as she lifted her teacup to her lips. Why did he have to be so incredibly nice to look at?

"I disagree completely. I saw you and therefore it became my duty to see you to safety, as a lady should never wander the streets after dark unaccompanied."

She sighed as she replaced her cup on the saucer. "You sound like my mother."

His brows rose. "A young woman should heed her parents' advice."

Her father's advice, definitely. Her mother's, rarely, she wanted to say but held her tongue. The man before her was stubborn, indeed. Her focus drifted across the room to where her father stood speaking to her mother. Though his attire resembled every other gentlemans', no other man in the room compared to her father. He had remained diligent in his devotion to her mother. A deed that warmed Abigail's heart. And his loyalty to her and her mother had secured her trust.

She knew nothing of Mr. Barringer, and it would accomplish little to share her heart with a complete stranger. "Yes, that is what the Bible teaches."

He chuckled. "I can only hope that you—"

"Hope what, Mr. Barringer?"

His unexpected reply and that same sarcastic laugh leveled the cutting truth right at her. He believed her to be disagreeable.

She went on. "Because you're a lawyer, you consider yourself capable of judging people of whom you know nothing?"

He nodded, as if undermining her words.

"If you remember correctly, my gratitude was offered, sir." Too agitated to think rationally, she fumed, "At what point did you decide I needed your help? Did I look as though I was being threatened?"

"Actually, you would have twisted your ankle or worse had I not been there to catch you. And only moments ago on the dancefloor, you seemed to be seeking an escape."

Every inch of her wanted to criticize him, to insult him, but something stopped her—the wise words of one of the proverbs. *Gracious words are a honeycomb, soothing to the soul and healing to the bones.*

"Are you implying I should thank you for saving me from my suitor?" Apparently, she hadn't given her brain enough time to let the entire verse sink through.

"Your suitor?" A spark of rejection flickered in his eyes. He blinked, looked at her, then blinked again before his focus shifted across the room.

Abigail remained silent, though her tongue wrestled to tell the gentleman the whole truth. To apologize for the blatant lie used only to prove a ridiculous point. "What I mean is..." She stood as she started to explain, unsure of what exactly, but stopped, before blurting more untamed words.

Abigail suspected more than heard Garrett's sharp exhale as he turned from her. Well, he could huff all he wanted. She did not need the distraction of such a man. Only one man could right her wrongs and somehow, she had to convince her father to allow her to return to Asheville.

Garrett turned and then reeled back toward her, thrusting his broad chest with subtle determination. "You must accept my apology."

Then he moved closer.

A gasp slipped from deep in her throat at his sudden nearness. She took a deep breath, inhaling the clean, fresh scent of his stiff white shirt mixed with the minty aftershave clinging to his neck.

"I would never have monopolized your time if I had known that you and William Arendell...Well, at any rate, I should have known, for you suit each other well." He cleared his throat. "It has been a pleasure making your acquaintance this evening, Miss Dupree." He ambushed her with a sledgehammer of a smile. He then coiled his fingers around hers, brought her hand to his lips, and held them there while holding her gaze for several seconds longer as if inhaling her. She sucked in a shaky breath. "It seems as if our song has come to an end."

He walked away before she could respond.

"But I—"

Without another glance in her direction, he slipped through the crowd, leaving her reply dangling in midair.

Abigail felt a hand on her arm and whirled around to see Marguerite. Her friend took a seat across from her. Her childlike expression was a sight for sore eyes.

"Were you just dancing with Garrett Barringer? And talking to him casually as if you two are—"

"You..." Abigail narrowed her eyes. "You are acquainted with him?"

Marguerite glanced over her shoulder as if she hoped to catch another glimpse of the man. "No, I haven't had the pleasure."

Abigail grabbed her hand. "How did you know of his name? I have never seen him until this evening."

Marguerite faced her and leaned forward. "I shall reveal that information once you confess. What were you speaking about?"

Abigail suppressed a laugh. "I assure you, it is nothing worth repeating."

Marguerite puckered her lips. "You cannot keep secrets from me. It is unethical."

"Ha. And you are my overdramatic friend, indeed. I am sorry

to disappoint you, but my conversation with the man bored me to tears."

"Bored?" Marguerite's eyes widened. "Being twirled and doted on by the most handsome man in the room is boring to you?"

Doted on? She could hardly call it that. Recalling how his touch seemed to rouse uncharted feelings, her hand trembled as she pushed in a loosened pin. "I hope to never lay eyes on him again."

"But why ever not?" Marguerite's neck swiveled again in the direction in which he had departed.

"He's arrogant and rude." And much too attractive.

Marguerite gave her that squinty-eyed look. The one that always said she believed none of it. "I have been watching the two of you for some time. And that was not even close to my interpretation." She pasted on a knowing grin. "In fact, he seemed like a true gentleman."

Abigail had thought so too. "False sincerity. The very thing a man processes to bring out the folly in a woman." Yet, even now, Abigail wrestled with the idea that she had fabricated most of his insincere traits for her own heart's benefit.

"My dear friend, we need to get you out more."

Abigail gave a wry smile. "If only I *could* leave."

Marguerite's grin promptly transformed into a grimace. "You cannot leave me. What would I do without you?"

Abigail bit back the real truth. "My admission was only in jest. My future is out of my hands. For I am destined to be married against my will or to be a lonely, old maid stuck with my mother for the rest of my life."

Her deliberation faltered as it landed on the very man in question. Mr. William Arendell leaned against the wall, his eyes zeroing in on her. Of course, he watched her. He was always watching her.

The second choice was sounding better all the time.

Chapter Four

G arrett had performed his good deed for the night and intended to make the most of the evening. When he had found out from Mr. Denison that Abigail Dupree was unmarried, it had surprised him.

Now he understood.

Elizabeth Madden stepped out in front of him, and he faltered in his steps.

He bowed. "Miss Madden, we meet again. May I interest you in the next waltz cotillion?"

Her smile faltered, and he imagined what she was thinking. The dance comprised of changing partners throughout the song, but it would be safer—more reserved.

She curtsied and offered an over exaggerated bat of her lashes. "It would be an honor."

He tipped his head. "If you'll please excuse me for now, I see someone with whom I must speak."

They parted with an agreement to meet before the next cotillion, scheduled in one hour. He walked through the room, intent on his purpose, to learn more about his business acquaintances, including Mr. Arendell. *You suit each other well.* Suit. The word stung. He shouldn't care that Mr. Arendell was Abigail Dupree's suitor.

But he did.

One of the gentlemen slapped him on the back. "Mr. Barringer, you must tell me your secret."

Alarm crashed in his stomach and exited through his throat. "My secret?" His words were solid and full of confidence. The opposite of his reality.

The man's smile narrowed into a thin line. "Yes, your gift for gaining the ladies' attention."

He exhaled, releasing a booming fit of laughter. "I have no gift, sir."

A cluster of business men joined in the laughter and then sobered as the conversation navigated toward the Galveston hurricane last year, that had taken over eight thousand lives.

In the next breath, Miss Dupree's suitor, William Arendell, commented on the invention of the gasoline powered Oldsmobile Model R Runabout and how he planned to order one of the first ones.

Garrett stood back, wondering what kind of man switched from a horrific tragedy to purchasing a vehicle, showing no emotion of the lives lost.

"Mr. Barringer, what brings you to the Queen City?" Arendell asked as he regarded him.

Garrett eyed the man, considering the best way to answer without offering too much information. "Business, of course."

His lids lowered. "What exactly is it that you do for a living?"

"Law," Garrett admitted, even though that was not entirely true, for Mr. Dupree had only invited him as an understudy. A fact that still remained a mystery to him, since he had no college education. In truth, he had been nothing more than a newspaper reporter over the last few years, which allowed him to travel.

Though he would rather the man know nothing of his personal or business affairs, and left the statement at that for him to ponder.

"Is that so?" The man raised a quizzical brow. "You seem mighty young for a lawyer. You must have started studying in elementary school." He snickered. The man's attempt at a humorous statement fell flat. When no one joined him in laughter, Arendell continued, "Though, that is splendid to hear. I, in fact, may be in need of a solicitor's services soon."

Feeling like an impostor, Garrett said nothing in response but allowed the man to prolong his disastrous charade.

"I should have a prenuptial agreement arranged." Arendell's attention bounced to the other men in their group. "Do you agree, gentlemen?"

Though Garrett dreaded hearing Arendell's reply, he had to ask. "Oh? And who is the lucky lady?"

"Miss Abigail Dupree," he sneered. "Of course, I thought she may have mentioned our forthcoming nuptials when you cut into our dance earlier."

So, it had not been merely a scheme to rile Garrett's feathers as he had hoped. "No, she made no remark about an upcoming wedding that I can recall," he claimed, though that was not the full truth either. But he refused to give this man any satisfaction in his offensive discussion concerning the young woman. For, he doubted Arendell's idea of a marriage bore any resemblance to his own concept of it.

"Some women can be so shy about such things. But fortunately, not the least bit timid about others." Arendell elbowed the man beside him and laughed once again, though none of the others joined him. "With her questionable reputation, it's imperative that I protect what belongs to me."

Her questionable reputation? Cold sweat against the hot blood firing through his veins dampened his body as Garrett heard the intended insult against the young woman. Even if

Garrett were a practicing lawyer, there would never be enough money to convince him to offer any sort of legal advice to the likes of a man of Arendell's character. A notion that spoke volumes.

Arendell arched his brows. "Or are you one of those defense attorneys that folks hire when they're facing prison?"

Garrett had never seriously considered law at all. And couldn't envision how any man could willingly take that route. Spending their life defending men who were doers of heinous acts. Men who did not deserve freedom. Of course, there were the exceptions of false blame. But freeing a guilty man only to harm another was a deed for which he would never forgive himself. "I prefer to lean toward the boring side of law."

Ignoring Garrett's reply, Arendell continued. "You know, I hear scores of women attend those courts for the sole purpose of drinking and indulging the lustful passion of corrupt men." Arendell leaned into the man next to him with a shoulder bump that matched his distasteful banter.

"My oldest boy considered the field, but decided to go into law enforcement," one of the others added, veering the conversation into a different direction, and avoiding Arendell's brash comments as if he had not spoken.

Arendell's parted jaw expunged his arrogant demeanor.

It afforded Garrett the much-needed time required to settle down before snatching William Arendell by the collar and dragging him outside.

Garrett offered an occasional nod in agreement as one man recalled a long-standing feud that had started with a legal dispute but ended in a cowhide-whipping that ultimately propelled the two men into a violent and deadly exchange.

Then others spoke of current events, all while Garrett's blood continued to boil. Thankfully no one asked him any other questions concerning law, or Miss Abigail Dupree.

Within the hour, he'd made some new acquaintances and his

temper had finally quieted down. Then one of the men motioned toward the dance floor. Garrett had almost forgotten his promise to Miss Madden. He searched the room and found her just before the music started.

The color in her cheeks deepened. "I thought you had forgotten."

Unsure how to respond without giving false hope, he simply said, "No, ma'am. Shall we?"

It wasn't until they were settled in place that he noticed Miss Dupree and Arendell standing across from each other, two couples down. The young lady looked in every direction but his, and then she whispered something to Arendell. He shook his head in the negative.

She wanted to bow out of the dance. It was clear in her expression. But the man would not oblige. And Garrett had to stiffen his arms by his sides to keep his feet planted in place.

The melody started, and Elizabeth took his hand, nudging his awareness away from Miss Dupree.

"Are you ready?" Elizabeth whispered.

Garrett cleared his throat, and without speaking, spun her around, stunning her into silence. Three partners later, he came face to face with the young woman who'd captured his attention.

"Miss Dupree." He took her hand, not wasting one moment of his time. He held her gaze, determined not to relent under the authority of those captivating eyes.

She lifted her chin, a full smile filling her lips as though she no longer had any pain. Then all at once he realized the woman had shrunk a whole two inches. "Mr. Barringer."

It took every ounce of his determination not to laugh out loud. She was certainly clever and that additional insight of the woman only stimulated his desire to know more of her.

Seconds later, Garrett spun and released her and confidently took the next woman in line, though the flustered tone of Miss

Dupree's voice and the sensation of her hand in his had produced a fretful storm within him.

❧

Abigail's heart continued to flutter long after Mr. Barringer's hand released hers. She had to find a way off this dance floor.

"Mr. Arendell, thank you for the pleasure of dancing, but I must have a rest. My feet are simply worn out."

"Yes, by all means." With a long glance, he swept the area above her head. "Let us step outside."

She gulped down a steadying breath. "Outside, sir?"

His stare folded in on her, his brows lifting. "Yes, I thought we could get some much-needed fresh air."

"Mr. Arendell, that would be inappropriate." She rushed to emphasize her thoughts on the matter, but kept the frustration out of her voice. It would do no good to antagonize him. In her limited experience, she was certain men only tried harder when forced into a corner. "I must find Mother and make sure she's enjoying herself."

His cheeks pinched as he cleared his throat. "Yes, well, I assure you, I meant no harm, Miss Dupree. Of course, you should check on your mother."

Abigail slipped away from him before he had a chance to ask permission to see her again. She walked past her mother and, with a slight glance over her shoulder, headed straight for the lighted garden, praying William Arendell did not follow.

Her anger burned. It was her mother's fault she was in this predicament. She'd hoped to find Marguerite already sitting at the small table as they had planned. The grounds looked empty, but just in case, she chose a corner table and slipped her bare feet, of which none had been the wiser, under the table. She admired the little piece of heaven, bursting with an assortment of every imaginable flower. Burning candles, prearranged throughout the gazebo, bathed the garden with a soft glow.

"Miss Dupree."

Abigail sucked in her breath, her heart dropping to her stomach. "Good heavens, Mr. Barringer, you startled me."

"I beg your pardon. That was not my intention."

At his sudden nearness, a rush of adrenaline raced through her limbs, and her cheeks heated under his steady gaze.

He eyed her with a particular brute manner. "What are you doing out here alone?"

There had been a tiny ounce of hope that they'd meet again before the close of the evening. But his imprudent approach had not been a part of the equation. "I had hoped to escape the room unnoticed. Of course, I did not succeed since, you apparently sought me out and then followed me."

"Sought you out?" Mr. Barringer laughed and then stared at her as if she had offended his honor. "Why, I did no such thing."

"Then, how is it that you knew of my whereabouts?"

His eyes tightened at the corners. "I just so happened to catch a glimpse of you leaving the room and had no choice but to follow."

Abigail tried in vain to suppress a smile at his protectiveness. It was almost charming. Definitely appealing. "Ah, so you, once again, took it upon yourself to make sure no harm would come to me?" She could get used to the gentleman's attention.

"I felt it was my duty to warn you since you seem to have no common sense."

At his reply, the door slammed on that thought. "No common sense?" She stood with bare feet onto the pebble-coated floor as her breath snagged at the back of her throat. "I have never met anyone so rude. So arrogant."

His eyes rotated with an almost undetectable roll. Though, she did not miss the insensitive act. "I do not mean to be rude, Miss Dupree."

"Well, what exactly do you intend to be? Because I find it difficult to glean any other impression from your boorish statements. And from the telling expression on your face that clearly states I am getting on your nerves." Garrett's demeanor was shifting toward remorse, but before he could speak, she pressed on, both hands fastened to her hips. "I know nothing of you and where I go or what I do should be of no concern to you."

"I assure you my intentions have only been for your safety and not to criticize. I do apologize if I have come across as impolite. For I did not mean to hurt your feelings." Garrett Barringer's words were rich with sincerity. His eyes pursued her with gentleness.

"You did not hurt my feelings." Abigail rolled her own eyes. "Well, perhaps just a little."

"It's just…well, you are a very beautiful woman and seem to have a habit of putting yourself in danger. In my opinion, you should not be in this garden alone, unescorted."

The heat of her temper weakened into a puddle of mush. The deep rumble of his voice kindled a fiery warmth within her and it spread through the core of her body as the meaning of his words registered.

Beautiful? She had finally met a man who thought her beautiful but still looked at her in a respectful manner. Spoke to her as if her intelligence took precedence over her appearance. Well, maybe not entirely, since he had mentioned her lack of common sense. Of course, if he knew the details of her scarred past, it would most certainly run him off. Still, she should grant Mr. Barringer the same regard she longed to receive from others and stop condemning the man. "I do appreciate your concern."

"Will you please step back inside, then?"

His protective interest in her safety boosted her appeal of the man. Made her feel valued. Treasured. She avoided his penetrating eyes and instead focused on a section of buttercups. "I would, but you see, I do not wish to return to…" *Mr. Arendell.*

36

He would surely seek her out and demand her attention. The very reason for her presence here.

"To?"

"That does not matter," Abigail said with a tad of defiance. "Besides, there is no danger here, Mr. Barringer. In fact, there's a tangible difference between being here at a ball and being on a street corner downtown after dark. Which, I am willing to admit was not the most sensible decision I have ever made. But here... well, there are people everyone, most of whom I have known for many years."

"Miss Dupree, I cannot hold my tongue even if it offends you. I do wish you would heed my advice and step back inside. For it is not appropriate even for you and I to be here unaccompanied."

"Mr. Barringer, you were not invited to join me and are free to leave." Elevating herself onto her toes, she leaned toward him. "As I told you before, I am perfectly capable of taking care of myself."

His hand lifted slowly toward her face, but then stopped midair as a mask of confusion swept across his features.

Her heart tripped.

She lost her footing and fell back onto the soles of her feet. "If you are so worried about my wellbeing, how can you expect me to take advice from a complete stranger who has mostly insulted me from the moment we met?"

Tiny wrinkles creased his forehead. "It truly was not my intention to insult you. I am only concerned for your wellbeing. You are..." He cleared his throat and focused somewhere above her head, before meeting her gaze once more. His eyes softened as he took her hand and kissed the top of her fingers. "Miss Dupree, if I may acknowledge once again, it has been a pleasure making your acquaintance this evening. But I must leave you now. I can only hope you heed my warning and step back inside."

Abigail followed Mr. Barringer's retreating figure, scrambling for something coherent to say.

But again, she was too late. He had returned to the ballroom. Her vision clouded as his image grew distant with each skip of her heartbeat.

Chapter Five

T he morning lacked the relief of a late summer breeze but
saturated the air with a generous dose of humidity as
Garrett hastened to the side street where Dupree's driver was
already waiting.

"Good morning, sir. Did you care to make a stop along the
way?"

With no time to stop at the local grocer upon his arrival
yesterday, he'd had no choice but to skip breakfast. A cup of
coffee would most likely settle the nerves spinning through his
middle, but there was no time for that. Arriving late would not
do for his first appointment with the gentleman. "Thank you, but
no. If you could head straight to the Duprees', please."

"Yes, sir," the man said as he closed the carriage door.

After a brief travel along the bumpy terrain, the buggy
arrived at the Victorian manor five minutes later. An open court-
yard surrounded by a dark canopy of shade trees, permeated with
birdsong, led him through a flower garden sprinkled with a
variety of shapes and colors. The sweet scent of honeysuckle
enveloped him from a trellis of yellow and white blooms.
Bumblebees flitted from flower-to-flower, humming with a quiet

buzz. For a more suitable man, a man who carried less guilt, its charm may have prevailed.

A tall gentleman opened the front door, allowing Garrett to enter, and he took in the sights around him. Colorful art filled the entry way, and from the high vaulted ceiling, hung a grand chandelier, its crystal rocks radiating a splash of riveting lines across the walls. The grandeur was the exact opposite of his humble cabin located in the woods of the North Carolina mountains.

"Mr. Barringer, it is so good to see you again."

Garrett entered and Mr. Dupree closed the office door behind them.

Mr. Dupree pointed toward a corner chair. "I want to thank you for responding to my offer so promptly."

Garrett took the suggested seat. "It was a great honor to be awarded your trust. I look forward to working with you."

"I do hope you enjoyed your time at the gala."

"It was memorable," he admitted, thinking of his encounters with Miss Dupree.

Mr. Dupree cleared his throat. "I happened to notice you sharing a dance with my Abigail."

"Yes." Garrett straightened. "I did have the privilege to share at least one song with your daughter."

The man stared off through the window. "She cares so little for things of that nature, it truly surprised me that she made any new acquaintances."

"Is that so?" At that moment, he wanted nothing more than to ask for more details about her, but held his tongue, not wanting to seem overly eager about the young woman's affairs.

"It is a wonder she did not find an escape by hiding out in the lighted garden for the entire evening as she has done on numerous occasions."

"The lighted garden?" Garrett's eyes blurred in their long-distance focus. Suddenly, Abigail Dupree's actions were finally starting to make sense.

"Yes. Peaceful serenity suits her much more than loud music and dancing with strangers she hardly knows. Which, is most likely the reason I did not see her dancing with anyone other than you and William Arendell."

Garrett wasn't sure if it was his place to mention such personal matters, but found he could not help himself. "It surprised me when Arendell mentioned something about being her suitor."

"Ah, so you have met the gentleman, then?" He asked, giving Garrett no definitive answer.

"Yes, we had the opportunity to speak briefly the other night." Or rather, he had the displeasure of listening to the man ramble on about things that should never be discussed in private. Let alone in public.

"Mr. Barringer, I do hope you will forgive my bluntness and the mysterious reason I invited you to be my understudy, knowing you have no education or even a desire to be a lawyer."

"I must admit, I had wondered about that."

"I figured as much." The man shot him a narrow look. "Did anyone happen to enquire as to the reason for your presence?"

"The topic did come up. But I gave them only enough information to satisfy their curiosity."

"Very well." Mr. Dupree conceded a smile." I am glad to hear it."

Out of respect, Garrett waited half a beat, before asking the feared question. "If you do not mind my asking? Why all the secrecy?"

Mr. Dupree sighed and his countenance shifted toward anguish. "It was for my daughter's sake."

Abigail? "Is that so?" Shame should accompany his reasons for wanting to know more. Determination did instead.

"Yes." Mr. Dupree clasped his hands and a sneer spread across his lips. "She is the primary reason I am in need of your expertise."

"Oh?" Garrett prayed that his curiosity was not as noticeable in his expression as the effect of Mr. Dupree's answer was having on his lungs. Breathing was getting more difficult all the time. "And why is that?"

"The matter is of great urgency." Mr. Dupree's nostrils flared. "I won't delay in filling you in on the details. But first things first. As you well know, none of what is said today is to leave this room."

"Of course, sir." Garrett could sense that the man was struggling against whatever had brought him to this place. And Garrett was getting a full view of it.

"Under no circumstances."

His lungs tightened even more. "You have my word."

"Because of dishonorable actions executed against my family, we moved to this area five years ago." Mr. Dupree paced the room. His compassion rolled over by fist-balling exasperation. "I'm in over my head with some delicate details that must not be brought to light. My family is being threatened on the matter, and my hands are tied. I have been at a loss as to how to fight against them, until recently. But unfortunately, in my haste to resolve this problem, I have given the hand of my Abigail to a Mr. Arendell of Wilkeshire."

The thought of Miss Dupree married to William Arendell made Garrett feel physically ill.

"Under this agreement, Arendell shall not disclose the information and has promised to take it to his grave." He heaved a deep sigh. "But the matter involves my daughter."

Garrett's brows crumpled. The man made it seem as if it were something dire.

"Our family has a buried secret that must not be found out, or we will indeed lose our last hope of my daughter's reputation. If only I could find a way to dissuade Mr. Arendell from his interest in a union with Abigail, our problem would be solved once and for all. But unfortunately, it's not that simple."

Garrett would gladly find a brute way to discourage William Arendell's affections. But that would not be of help with a buried secret? "How can I be of help?"

Mr. Dupree grasped the table with both hands. "On the one matter, I cannot disclose as of yet. I still have some, let's say, research left to discover. As for the other, my daughter knows nothing of the arrangement made with Mr. Arendell, only that her mother wishes her to spend time with the man. And might I add, against her will. As well as mine."

So, Miss Dupree had been fabricating the truth, after all. A breath faltered in its exit, betraying his delight. It *had* indeed been for his benefit.

Garrett would be honored to do whatever was asked of him concerning Abigail Dupree. But he still had no idea how, or what that could possibly mean.

A hidden strength lay tucked beneath the man's words. But as Garrett delved through the multitude of layers, he witnessed the desperation that fueled Mr. Dupree's formal tone. "I see."

"No, sir. You cannot see. My Abigail is very special. She is something extraordinary, that one. And she deserves so much more than the misfortunes she has been dealt."

Misfortunes? There had been nothing in Abigail Dupree's demeanor that would suggest any thing of the sort. "Mr. Dupree, do you have more than one daughter?"

A full-length, undiluted smile filled the man's face. "No, sir. My Abigail is all I could handle. She is quite the ambitious one."

Garrett smiled, knowing full well what he'd meant by ambitious, and he couldn't help the intrigue swelling in him from the other description. "What is it then that you require of me?"

"My daughter's wellbeing is of prime importance, and I will do everything in my power to ensure it. So, as you can see, Mr. Barringer, this mission is not merely business, but personal and will require much caution on your part."

Caution was not the exact word Garrett had been expecting.

Confidentiality. Or perhaps, discretion. But caution? What did he mean? He could not ascertain anything from the man's speech of which to be cautious.

Mr. Dupree moved in front of the floor-to-ceiling window on the far side of the room. "After I fill you in, I only wish that you will not reconsider our agreement."

Abigail woke later than usual after the long, exasperating night of pretending to be something she would never be.

Rose, her lady's maid, entered and her ready smile instantly brightened Abigail's mood. "Miss Abigail, let me help you into your day dress. And your mother already has a beautiful one picked out for you for dinner tonight."

Abigail rose from the bedchamber and summoned Rose with her hand. "I wish to pick out my own wardrobe today, Rose."

The young maid's brow puckered. "Yes, Miss Abigail. Whatever you wish."

"I know my mother wants a report on everything I say, but in private, can we please be less formal? Did she mention anything about last night?"

"No, miss. She has said nothing. Should I inquire for you something specific?"

"No, but thank you." Abigail stood, her arms stretched out in a full yawn as she walked toward the window. "Rose, the sun is shining and I wish to take Jack for a ride."

"Yes, miss. I shall fetch your riding suit."

"Rose, will you also grab my bathing suit. I shall go for a dip if the weather maintains its conditions." Abigail pulled a few locks of hair framing her face into a pin at the base of her neck, but left the long layers hanging down the middle of her back. No one would see her.

"Here are both suits, miss." Rose handed her the bulk. "Where will you change?"

Abigail took them gratefully, and locking eyes with Rose, she spoke freely. "I shall wear it beneath my riding suit."

Rose threw her hands out to the sides, then rested them on her thin hips. "It shall be too tight."

With a skittering glance at Rose, Abigail clutched the bathing suit to her chest. "Indeed, but worth it."

"This is not a good idea, Miss Abigail." Rose grimaced. "What if your mother—"

"Quit worrying. Just do not breathe a word about this to anyone. Please, Rose. I need a day to myself. I do not want to be interrupted."

"Of course."

"And Rose." Abigail started to wrap an arm around the girl's shoulder, but stopped. How many times had her mother scolded her for being too friendly with the paid help? So many her mind echoed her exact dissatisfied tone. It would be better to refrain from too much affection lest she slip in front of her mother. "Thank you."

How she wished to return to Asheville. To be free of constant expectations.

Muttering about stubborn charges and exhausting mothers, Rose retreated from Abigail's bedchamber.

Now she only had to convince her father's stable hand, Lucas.

As soon as Abigail had managed to squeeze her jodhpurs over her bathing suit, she stuffed her book into her handbag and moved through the house, hoping to bypass any curious eyes until she was safely outside. She trekked the expanse of a tenth of a mile and headed directly toward the stables.

Lucas waved from where he stood by the entrance. "Ms. Abigail, what brings you all the way out here?"

Abigail offered him her most gracious smile. "I figured it

was too beautiful for Jack to have to stay inside a stuffy old barn all day." The mare tossed back his brown mane and nickered at the sound of her voice. "And see, it seems as though Jack agrees. I promise to not keep him out too long."

Laughter rumbled from the depths of Lucas's chest. "Little lady, it has never been easy saying no to you."

Abigail offered a face-splitting grin. "Does that mean I have your permission?"

Lucas side-eyed her and she folded her lips shut.

"My consent isn't the approval you should be concerned about. Does your—"

"I do believe sir, that you have full authority to make these kinds of decisions." She gave him a compelling smile. "My father trusts you immensely."

His mouth pressed into a straight white line. "That's the exact reason I worry about telling you yes."

"But there is no need for you to worry, Mr. Lucas. All is well and my horse needs his exercise, and I assure you Jack will be in a better mood for it."

"I suppose you're right."

Abigail was already saddling Jack, hoping Lucas wouldn't think better of his yes, or even worse, change his mind.

Moments later, Abigail fled across the countryside, leaning into her horse. Her hair flew through the wind. The heat of the day was almost more than she could bear. Especially while wearing a bathing suit beneath her jodhpurs. At least she wore no stockings. If only she could remove the pants so that the breeze could shift up her calves. But traipsing about in nothing but a swimming outfit would be scandalous. Especially if one of Father's workers were to catch her half-dressed.

When she had reached the safety of the trees, she climbed from her mare. The spring was only a short walk from where she stood, and after Jack got a fill of water from his own thirst, she tied her horse to one of the shade trees.

Abigail stroked his forehead. "Jack, I won't be long. You stay put. I'll be back once I've cooled off a bit."

His ears wiggled in reply, and she laughed out loud.

She turned into the shade of a large oak and relished the breeze sifting through the trees. After slipping from the bulky jodhpurs and dress coat, she removed her hat and hung the three items on a thick limb.

Abigail grabbed her book from her handbag and sat along the edge of the bank and stretched her legs, the cool water splashing against her calves. The water tickled her bare feet and she wrapped her arms around her waist. Nervous tension wriggled through her subconscious, something she had always ignored.

Resting against a moss-covered weeping willow, she stared up into the blue sky and inhaled the various scents coming off the water. She opened up to the last read page of her book and was immediately transported to another place.

Sometime later, her gaze met the sun's blinding rays before allowing her eyes to drift to a close for a moment.

Sharp memories of the evening before trickled into her mind as the breeze loosened her braid.

The crinkling of leaves reached her ears and startled her awake. She sat up quickly, her feet now warm at the water's edge. The crunch of footfalls ceased and her heart raced in her chest. She had left Jack a quarter of a mile down the trail.

Then a mumble followed the brief silence.

Chapter Six

Abigail whipped around quickly to get a better view of her intruder. Garrett Barringer was standing less than a yard from her and she scrambled onto her feet.

He reached out to steady her but she secured her hands behind her back.

"Mr. Barringer, what on earth are you doing out here?" Finding her bearings, she took a step forward. Abigail's voice cracked, but she didn't care. "You look as if you have seen a ghost."

Concern swelled in his unwavering gawk, while she struggled to find her composure. It took every ounce of restraint to not lash out at him for sneaking up on her. If it weren't for the fact that a swarm of butterflies invaded her belly at his presence, she would do exactly that. Her brow narrowed as she waited for his explanation.

"I—" His eyes flickered with skepticism as his eyes roamed the length of her. And suddenly she remembered what she wasn't wearing.

"Never would I have imagined a day that I would leave you speechless." The uneasiness in his demeanor was seeping onto her. "Could you please hand me my riding suit? It's on the branch right behind you."

He blinked and reached for her jodhpurs, dress coat, and hat. His long arm broke the distance between them as he offered her belongings. But after she retrieved two of her more modest items, he made no motion to leave.

"May I have some privacy, please?" she asked, her gaze wandering their surroundings to confirm he had approached alone. But still the question remained. Why was he here?

He blinked before turning. Only then did she allow a small smile. Maybe he wasn't as self-assured as she had once thought. Satisfied with herself, she intended to win this unfortunate series of events.

Slipping her breeches on as quickly as possible, she kept her eyes on his dark brown hair resting perfectly against the collar of his jacket.

Feeling as though she were bound in an hourglass with the sand shifting faster than her brain could function, she blurted the first thing that came to mind. "It seems you have stumbled upon me at a most inopportune time." At least it was this stranger who'd found her, instead of her father. She chose the rest of her words more carefully to ensure he would not continue to believe her ungrateful. "I do thank you for your assistance, Mr. Barringer, but you are now free to leave."

Mr. Barringer once again faced her and stood over her in too stern a stance. His shoulders stiff as if they carried the weight of the world. His troubled eyes searching hers for answers. Then his brows narrowed. "Have you lost your mind?"

She straightened her coat and walked toward him with her chin held high. "I beg your pardon?"

"What were you thinking?"

Now, he was being deliberately domineering. Much like that first night. "I'm not sure I understand what you mean, Mr. Barringer."

Still holding to her hat, he waved his arms in the air, his attention zeroed in on the water. "You should not be out here."

"Since you are new to the area, you may not be aware, but this is our land. So, I have every right to be here and this seems to be the only spot on the entire property where I can be alone." She softened her tone. He *had* been trying to save her. Though from what, she couldn't be sure. "So, please forgive me, but I was not expecting company."

"That is obvious."

Heavens. His tactless words made it hard to remain cordial. She trudged forward, anxious to be free of his bossy attitude. With a swift look over her shoulder, she found that Mr. Barringer's long legs had already caught him up to her.

She met his narrowing eyes. "How did you know I was back here anyway? Do you make it a habit to intrude on another's property?"

Garrett looked up sharply, and the concern in his eyes faded. "My habits are not the ones in question here."

Her anger swelled at the audacity of this stranger to conclude that he had permission to show up on her property and to roam wherever he pleased. "I am free to do here as I choose." She snarled and walked ahead. It was much easier to keep moving than to look directly at the man. "We aren't at one of your silly balls where everyone is forced to maintain propriety."

"So, you believe propriety fashions a person's character only in public."

Abigail stopped and spun to face him. "Are you questioning my character?"

"You expect me to believe your father allows his daughter to run around dressed unsuitably?"

"Unsuitably? There is nothing wrong with my riding suit, and it was not meant for anyone to see my…other suit."

He eyed her in a flustered, boyish way. She had uncovered his embarrassment. "That is the reason you felt you needed to hide back here where you could get hurt or worse. I wonder how your father would feel if he knew—"

"You do not know my father." She jerked back at his audacity. "He trusts me completely. And furthermore, it is none of your business what I do on my own property." She straightened her coat, their close vicinity distracting her senseless. "Speaking of how my father would feel, how do you think he would react to a strange man sneaking up on me and—"

"Sneaking up on you? I did no such thing." His furrowed brow spoke more of a man disputing his own conscience rather than one allocating accusation. "Your stable man, Lucas, said you had taken your horse almost three hours ago. Immediately, I took off with one of the other horses. If I had known there was water—"

"Three hours?" Abigail released her breath in a forced rush as she moved out of the shade and into the full sun. "Oh no!"

Abigail hurried to her horse and quickly straddled Jack, not bothering to see if Mr. Barringer had followed.

"Miss Dupree, please wait," the man shouted after her.

She instantly glanced over her shoulder but said nothing as she gently kicked Jack forward.

Jack galloped through the open field as Abigail's eyes swamped with unshed tears. "I am so sorry, Jack. How could I have let this happen?" Falling asleep and staying out so long would surely have her mother in an uproar. The audacity of Mr. Barringer's tone of disapproval replayed through her mind. But even his repeated warning that she should behave was no longer an impertinence. It was the guilt of leaving her horse alone for all that time and now having to return him to his stable since, she could not afford any more time away. She had all but forfeited her every intention of spending the day with Jack.

"Miss Dupree, please."

He was gaining on her. Determined not to let Mr. Barringer

see her crying over her own foolish decision, she pulled at Jack's reins, urging more zest in his steps.

Garrett pulled his horse in front of hers, causing her horse to come to an abrupt stop. She spun toward him, prepared to object, but the exposed agony carved in Mr. Barringer's features splashed cold water over her embarrassment. Her animosity.

"You forgot this." He reached across and handed her the round hat she'd brought. "Now will you please slow down and allow me to see you to the corral safely."

He turned his thoroughbred toward the barn, not waiting for her reply.

Abigail resumed their trail across the grassy meadow, tugging on Jack's reins, granting him full permission to slacken the speed of his steps. She still had to face her mother. Unless she was able to sneak in just as easily as she had snuck out the evening of the ball. If only there was a way to gain Rose's attention before arriving at the house.

The wind whipped at her hair, tossing loosened strands across her warm cheeks. Her eyes still refused proper focus with the glaze of fresh, frustrated tears as they neared the wooden fence enclosing the stalls.

Swiping at the errant moisture streaming down her face, she brought Jack to a halt behind Garrett's mare and within seconds Garrett was there waiting to help her down.

Her eyes skipped to his but she held her tongue while dragging her left leg over the side. He grasped her around the waist as she slid down in front of him. She shut her eyes against the deep pounding of her heart, praying he couldn't feel the movement of her chest.

Garrett led both horses to the stable while she worried what Lucas must be thinking of her staying away for so long. When Lucas poked his head around the corner, she ran toward him.

"Lucas, I am so sorry for keeping him out so long. I simply

lost track of time and please, if you could just forgive me for my tardiness."

Lucas frowned. "Don't you be sorry, Miss Abigail, I am only thankful no harm came to you."

"I shouldn't have stayed away so long. It was not my intention to cause you worry."

He offered a charming grin. "I wasn't too concerned, since I know you enjoy getting off to yourself every now and then. But that Mr. Barringer sure was worried. As soon as he heard how long you'd been gone, he took one of his horses so he could look for you."

"How did he know how to find me?"

"Of that, I'm not sure. After hitching up that horse, I started to explain that you like to go to the water, but he skedaddled out of here before I could finish what I was saying."

Abigail glanced toward the stables. "He did?"

He leaned closer, and his eyes widened. "You should a seen the look on his face when I told him how long you been gone."

Trying to prevent a grin from curving, Abigail changed the subject. "I was so enjoying my book by the water that I must have dozed off."

Lucas slanted his head. "Sounds like a lovely afternoon."

"I'm so thankful you're not angry." Perhaps this was her lucky afternoon and her mother would be none the wiser. Or at the very least would not be angry.

Lucas shook his head. "No, miss. I'm just glad that Mr. Barringer came along."

"I am grateful he found me when he did." Though, the reason for his presence still made no sense.

Lucas's eyes drifted beyond her to the barn. "That one is quite different, if you want my humble opinion."

Abigail's eyes narrowed. "Different?"

Lucas regarded her for a moment before he took a deep breath. "Not standoffish. And when I told him how long you had been away, he didn't miss a beat." The laugh he offered was likely meant to show how much it had surprised him. "That man took off like he was on fire."

It surprised her too. "He did?"

"I never seen a gentleman act like that. One would almost think…" He stopped.

"Think what?"

"I don't want to say something out of turn but you didn't see the look on that man's face."

"What sort of look was it?"

"One would almost think that the two of you was a couple," Lucas whispered.

Abigail's face heated as she glanced over her shoulder at the man still standing by the barn. But the only look she found on Garrett Barringer's face was one of discontent. "You know, Lucas, I believe you are exactly right about one thing. He is a perfect gentleman." Though she still found that hard to admit aloud, especially with the frown spoiling his handsome features. "Thank you again for understanding."

"You don't have to thank me, Miss Abigail. It is always my pleasure to be at your service."

Abigail offered Lucas a warm smile as Mr. Barringer walked toward them.

"Thank you, mister, for finding our girl and bringing her back safe."

Garrett acknowledged his appreciation with a nod. And Abigail could only imagine what he must think of her as he walked past without even looking in her direction.

She followed him and reached for his arm and affectionately squeezed it. "Mr. Barringer, please wait."

His steps slowed at the connection, and he turned to face her fully but kept his focus averted. Then, of a sudden, he swept his arms behind his back, breaking their connection, but still said nothing.

Abigail defeated the lump forming in her throat. "I too wanted to thank you for your assistance."

When his face finally rose, she searched for the look that Lucas had described but found nothing similar. His usual calming smile had faded. Was he angry, then? Disappointed?

"It has been my pleasure, Miss Dupree." With those few words, he turned and walked away leaving her dumbfounded in her stance. He hadn't even bothered to scold her as was his usual tactic of late. And the very idea that he had nothing more to say troubled her. Immensely.

The request to have him stop, to explain his sudden urge to leave budded on her tongue, but at the remembrance of how it had made her feel to be held in his arms, she clipped it off.

What little breath he hadn't stolen from her, she used for the trek back to the house.

Her mind still in a fog from her unexpected meeting with Garrett Barringer, from the lingering feel of his hands on her waist, she walked into the front door, forgetting her desire to stay out of sight.

Chapter Seven

M other met Abigail in the foyer, her eyes creased in narrow lines. "Where have you been, young lady?"

"I—"

"Oh, my heavens." Mother drew in an over-exaggerated breath. "What have you done? Your skin looks like a pot-bellied pig." She lifted her head toward the balcony. "Rose, get down here now!"

"Mother, what is wrong with you?" Abigail put her hands on her hips. "It isn't lady like to scream out."

A cold, hard hand slapped her across the cheek. "What has gotten into you? You are not to speak to me in such a manner."

Stunned, Abigail stared at her mother through the tears blinding her vision. "I hate it here. I want to go home."

Mother nodded her head listlessly. "Please, Abigail. You are a grown woman acting like a child."

Holding her heated cheek in her palm, Abigail turned to find Rose already standing behind them. Abigail wasn't sure how much her lady's maid had witnessed.

"Rose, take Abigail upstairs this moment and do not let her out of your sight until she comes down for dinner this evening, dressed in the costume that I have chosen. But prior to that, powder her face the best you can to hide that horrendous sunburn."

Insecurities welled up and Abigail mentally recollected her unexpected encounter with Garrett Barringer and how hideous she must have looked in his presence. She once again touched her cheeks, the warmth soaking into her palms.

"Rose, under no circumstances are you to let her out of your sight." Mother started to walk away but turned, her jaw squared. "And Abigail Dupree, we have a dinner guest joining us tonight. I am depending on this attitude you have developed to stay clear of my dining table."

Abigail took off in a full run up the stairs, ignoring the sound of Rose's plea for her to slow down, lest she hurt herself. Abigail fell across the bed, allowing all the pent-up emotions she'd held in today to explode into a fit of loud, unapologetic wails.

"Miss Abigail, you mustn't cry. You will have puffy eyes at dinner."

The determination in Rose's voice almost gave Abigail pause for her childish behavior. Almost.

"My mother hates me. Besides, it doesn't matter. Mr. William Arendell is most likely the dinner guest, and I wish to never see him again. Maybe if I appear swollen and burnt to a crisp, he will change his mind about me."

Rose leaned forward and patted her leg. "Miss Abigail, your mother does not hate you. She loves you very much. And I don't think trying to change his mind is the answer. You should tell him how you feel."

Abigail rolled over and faced her well-meaning friend. "Do you not see? I'm not allowed to feel. Mother has been in control of everything since we moved to this dreadful city."

"She only wants what's best for you. At least you had a nice quiet afternoon alone. And I see you managed to fit your riding habit over your bathing suit." Rose's eyes widened. "Oh, dear."

57

"What is it?" Abigail searched the waist of her dress. "Did I soil it?"

"No, but the lace on your jodhpurs has unraveled."

"Good heavens. If Mother had seen that, she…" Tears burned the backs of Abigail's lids, recalling the hard slap. "She must have been too focused on my sunburn to notice."

Rose frowned. "As soon as we get you out of this, I will fetch my sewing basket and have it fixed in no time."

Abigail stood and unhooked the laces of her boots and then proceeded to loosen the ribbon from her waist before pulling the jodhpurs off.

Rose took the pants from her. "Allow me."

Abigail faced the window, for a long moment while trying to recall how or when the lace had been loosened. Had the material snagged a branch in her haste to dress while Garrett Barringer waited? Or had it been when the man helped her down from the horse? A flutter skipped across her chest, as she evoked the feel of being held in his arms. Then in her next breath, her curiosity overshadowed the moment. Why had he been on their property in the first place?

Abigail lifted her arms out and the air stirred as Rose pulled the dress coat away from Abigail's shoulder's leaving her undressed with nothing but her bathing suit.

"At least your mother did not see this attire."

"Yes, thank heavens for that." Or discovering that a gentleman had stumbled upon her. Abigail fixed her focus on her mirror, her face heating as she recalled Garrett's shock at her appearance. She grabbed her silk robe, and looped the few buttons.

Rose held the riding habit out as she surveyed the loosened lace.

Abigail reached for *The Scarlett Letter* on her nightstand. "I am going to read after I give myself a sponge bath. Thank you for preparing my hot water." Abigail touched Rose's shoulder.

"You have been working all morning, Rose. Take a much-needed break and leave the sewing for later. Besides, I don't know when I'll find another chance to wear it."

"Sewing is relaxing to me. Besides, it would be best to not put it off."

"If you must sew, then I will not object, but I insist on gathering my own materials for my bath. Now, go. I shall call you when I am ready to dress for dinner."

Rose stiffened. "Are you sure, miss. It is no trouble to—"

"Rose."

The young woman glanced toward the door. "But what if Mrs. Dupree happens upon you?"

"It is highly unlikely my mother will traipse upstairs." Not wanting to concern the young woman with possible repercussions from her mother, Abigail added, "As soon as I am finished with my sponge bath, I promise to stay here and do nothing more than read my book."

"If you are certain, miss?" Her frown deepened.

"I am."

Rose's brows lifted. "If you need anything, I'll be right next door. Enjoy the bath and your book."

"It is so good." Abigail felt such a strong connection to the main character, Hester. "You should read it when I finish."

"I would love to."

"And so you shall." Abigail took her hand. "Thank you, Rose."

Twenty minutes later, after settling onto her bench by an open window, Abigail turned to the last page read of the book, her heart heavy. Randall Thorne had appeared at her doorstep when she was only a girl of fourteen. She thought she'd never seen a more beautiful man. Deep brown eyes, tall, dark, and handsome just as all princes were described in her books. She had so often fantasized about marrying her handsome prince and living happily-ever-after. But the happily-ever-after never came.

As she started another chapter, her attention drifted. It was no use. She could not concentrate on the characters with her thoughts whirling between Randall Thorne, William Arendell, and Garrett Barringer, the mysterious stranger who kept appearing out of nowhere.

The thought of having to marry William Arendell left her breath weak and unsteady.

What was she doing? Giving in was not her nature. Why would she surrender to something so ludicrous? She had to do something. But what?

She stood and moved to sit at her vanity and brushed an extra stroke of powder across her reddened cheeks and forehead, then pulled a comb through her tangled hair.

Rose entered her bedchamber carrying a bowl of fresh fruit. "I thought you could use a snack."

"How sweet of you. But that is not what I meant by taking a break, Rose."

"I know, but it's hard to relax when I know you are feeling anxious. Did you not enjoy your book?"

"Unfortunately, I had a difficult time focusing on the story."

"Oh?" Rose frowned.

Rose's saddened expression gave Abigail a sudden thought.

"Yes. And now that I'm thinking on it…" Abigail pivoted on her stool as she secured the last bobby pin. "I must speak to Father. Would you mind helping me into my day dress?"

"Of course not, miss."

As Rose transitioned her from the robe and into her dress, Abigail ran over possible scenarios of how best to approach her father with her idea.

As Rose fastened the last hoop, Abigail gave Rose a brief hug and moved toward the door. "Thank you, Rose. Now wait here, but do not let Mother see you."

Rose hurried to her side. "But I should accompany you."

"I need to speak with him in private." Abigail recognized

Rose's discomfort but there was no time to reassure the young woman, so she offered an encouraging smile. "I won't be long."

Rose cast her a troubled look. "Yes, miss. But—"

Abigail made her exit before Rose could challenge her further.

Determination filled each step as Abigail took the back hall, careful to stay out of Mother's view. She entered her father's office, and he was just as she'd expected him to be, slumped back in his leather chair deep in thought. He stood abruptly when he met her gaze. "Abigail, what is it, dear? Are you ill?"

"What?" Abigail questioned, but then remembered how her skin must appear. "No, Father, I was outside and the sun..." She placed both hands across her cheeks, the heat bleeding into her palms. "I must have stayed out there too long."

A glint touched his eyes. "Yes, well, it certainly gave you some color."

Abigail smiled. He always knew just what to say to make her feel better. Perhaps he could give her a much-needed solution to her predicament. "Father, what shall I do? Mother is angry with me, and I am unable to do anything that pleases her. Couldn't I go stay with your sister and Uncle Henry for a while?"

His eyes closed for a lengthy blink. "My darling, your mother means well, but she is dealing with her own hardships."

"What do you mean? Is there something wrong with Mother? Is she unwell?" Steeling herself against alarming news, she locked her focus on her father.

Something dire hung about his eyes. "She hasn't quite been herself lately, but she is going to be fine. There is no need for concern, just yet." He placed a hand on her arm. "I do, however, need you to be strong for me. These things have a way of working themselves out. You trust me, don't you, dear?"

Just yet? Whatever was that supposed to mean? She wanted to question him, but feared his response more. "Yes, Father. Of course. I wish not to be a burden to you or Mother."

He squeezed her arm gently. "You have never or will ever be a burden to us. I love you my dear, and your mother loves you so very much. She only wants happiness for you."

If only she could believe that. If only she could forgive herself. And how could her mother believe that Abigail would find happiness if she was forced into a marriage with William Arendell?

"I know this is hard, but I need you to appease your mother." The ache in her chest grew, for she had no choice but to obey him. "You can do that for me, can't you sweetheart?"

This man with his warm heart and accomplished skills was the embodiment of a father others would envy. And he was hers. She would do most anything to make him happy. "Of course, Father."

"It will make my job a lot easier. And things will get better. I promise." He regarded her with a smile. A smile that projected a quiet confidence that made her feel safe. Better. "I like the color in your cheeks. It enhances your other beautiful features."

"Thank you, Father." Abigail kissed him on the cheek, her determination crumbling to the wooden floor as she walked through his office door.

She had never been able to say no to him.

Chapter Eight

G arrett studied the dark circles under his eyes as he prepared for his evening out. He needed to concentrate on his job and let his past stay in the past. He had no control over how things had ended, but had to find a way to keep it from consuming his nightmares, his every thought. *Who of you can add even a day to his life by worrying about tomorrow?* The verse soothed a microscopic layer of his soul as he wiped the remaining shaving balm from his chin.

It will take time to heal. Each day will get easier, others had assured him. But what about Sylvia? The accident would haunt her for the rest of her life.

Fifteen months, three weeks, and four days later, and still, the pain of Sylvia's loss gripped and twisted his gut with the sharpness of a double-edged sword.

Leaving behind daily reminders with his move to the city had given him slight relief over the last few days and the distraction of Abigail Dupree had diverted his attention more than once. But his sister was never far from his thoughts.

His new job would require more time and more importantly, keep him away. He wiped at the swollen base of his right eye. He needed to get more rest if he was going to be a productive asset to Mr. Dupree.

After securing his tie in place, he headed downstairs to the foyer.

Alexander sat in the reading room alone, and Garrett entered to wish him a good night.

"You have a date tonight with one of the ladies from the ball?"

Garrett chuckled. "No. It is nothing more than a business dinner invitation."

"Ah. The joys of law. Well, I hope all goes well." Alexander stood and walked along beside him toward the front door. "Shall I keep the light burning for you?"

"Yes, I shouldn't be long. Goodnight, my friend. Enjoy your evening."

Garrett climbed into his buggy, which was waiting on the cobblestone drive. He stared through the window as shadows splayed across the large fields adjacent to the Chatham Boarding House, his temporary home.

Thoughts of Abigail riding her horse through the pasture filled his mind, then thoughts of her secure in his arms for the briefest of seconds when he helped her from her horse. And then they slipped unwillingly to the memories of seeing her by the spring—her shapely calves shimmering against the sunlight.

He shook the memory free.

What was it about that woman that drove him nuts? And how on earth would he stand being no more than civil to her during his duty to Mr. Dupree?

Ten minutes later, he rang the bell and was welcomed in by their butler.

"Good evening, Mr. Barringer. Everyone is already waiting in the dining room."

"Thank you."

When Garrett rounded the corner, his gaze collided with

Abigail's. The deep pink in her cheeks, from too many hours in the sun, gave her an appealing glow, making her even more beautiful. She stood quickly knocking an empty tea cup from its saucer. After grabbing it with trembling fingers, she placed it back in position. Confusion dominated the sharp glance she sent in his direction. She quickly turned her focus to the table setting arranged before her.

Mr. Dupree stood. "Please forgive me for not forewarning you of our additional guest this evening. Mr. Barringer, I'm thrilled you could join us tonight."

Everyone followed suit and stood as Mr. Dupree made all the introductions and then led him to the table. Though Arendell seemed to eye him with curiosity.

Garrett took a step forward. "Please, forgive me for my tardiness."

Mr. Dupree's brows lifted. "You are not late, sir, we only arrived early."

"Mr. Barringer, I've saved you a seat next to my Abigail," Mrs. Dupree said.

Abigail's attention shifted to her mother, but instead of complaining, she averted her expression and smiled as everyone took their seats.

Mr. Arendell sat directly across from Abigail and there was a look of pure panic in the man's expression. Was it Garrett's unannounced presence that had confounded William? Or could it be something more?

Garrett shifted in his own seat while he traded a glance with Abigail. For a brief instant, he felt sorry for her, but it vanished just as quickly when she opened her mouth. "Mr. Barringer, my father didn't mention that you and he were acquainted."

Mrs. Dupree leaned back. "Abigail, do you know the gentleman?"

Abigail's lashes flew wide. "I... um..." Her jumbled words fell awkwardly from her lips.

Garrett observed Abigail's reaction to the question with amusement. As he watched her, darkened freckles, of which he hadn't noticed before, danced across her high cheek bones as she moved her mouth like a fish out of water. He enjoyed the moment much more than he should have.

"Yes, ma'am." Garrett cleared his throat. "We have actually had the honor of meeting on several occasions."

Mrs. Dupree pursed her lips after his simple offering. Then Garrett glanced at the young woman. Abigail's brows arched higher as if she wasn't sure whether he intended to inform her parents of their unlikely encounter earlier today.

"Is that so?" Mr. Dupree inquired.

Garrett's focus bounced between the mother, father, and daughter. Seeing the raw fear in Abigail's eyes, he redirected his response. "She's a lovely girl and quite the dancer."

A sparkle of confused interest filled Abigail's expression and for one brief moment, his gaze dropped to her full lips, which glistened with a clear glossy finish instead of the bold red color many ladies were choosing to wear as of late.

"Ah, yes, I remember you mentioning that you shared one dance. I was so busy entertaining my clients, I unfortunately missed an opportunity to enjoy a twirl with my own wife." Mr. Dupree's eyes wrinkled with a smile. "Please forgive me for that, dear."

Mrs. Dupree waved her hand at him as if the statement was quite silly. Though, her eyes seemed to brighten considerably at her husband's comment.

Mr. Dupree clasped his hands. "Shall we pray, then?"

Garrett had mentally armed himself for Abigail's disapproval of his invitation to dine with her family this evening. Had been prepared for a firestorm. So, when she closed the space between them with a soft whisper of appreciation, he pondered his own judgment of the woman.

He leaned closer and whispered his own response. "It is my pleasure, Miss Dupree.

"Mr. Barringer, are you uncomfortable in your seat?" Mrs. Dupree asked him.

He straightened. "No, ma'am, but I do thank you for your concern."

Closing his eyes, he expected to hear Mr. Dupree's strong voice come through, but instead Mrs. Dupree's high-pitched voice summoned, "Mr. Barringer, please take my daughter's hand while we bless the food. It is a tradition at our table, sir."

"Oh, why, yes, of course."

Abigail slipped her bare hand beneath his. She wore no gloves, and her delicate, warm skin trembled beneath his palm. He grasped her fingers in a slightly tighter grip and enjoying the sensation of their brief connection, heard nothing of Mr. Dupree's thanks to the Lord, until the conclusion of the prayer.

Garrett glanced up to find Arendell staring at their adjoined hands.

Noting the awkwardness of the moment, Garrett released her hand and spoke aloud before thinking his thought through. "Miss Dupree, is your foot feeling better today?"

Whether the unusual question troubled Abigail, he could not discern. Her full smile blossomed, brightening the already pink hues of her face. "It is much better. Thank you for asking."

From the corner of his eye, he could see that Mr. Arendell had leaned forward. "Did I miss something?"

"No, of course not, Mr. Arendell. I simply should not have worn a brand-new pair of shoes for a night of dancing," Abigail answered as she reached forward to retrieve her cup. "And Mr. Barringer was kind enough to notice."

"But you barely finished three dances," Mr. Arendell was quick to point out.

"The leather of those particular shoes was unforgiving." Abigail snickered as she lifted the cup to her lips but immediately flattened out the folds of clamoring laughter by taking a sip of hot tea.

"Yes, especially when one walks for miles in particular shoes," Mrs. Dupree scolded.

Mr. Dupree cleared his throat. "Yes, well, we should not allow unfamiliar quarrels to ruin a lovely evening. And we are grateful you gentlemen were able to join us for dinner this fine evening."

Garrett settled back against his seat. "Thank you for the invitation."

Though he wasn't at all certain he should be here. The longer he sat next to Mr. Dupree's daughter, the more he longed to converse with the young woman. Alone. But this was neither the time nor the place. Not with her suitor sitting across from them —a logic that still didn't ring true.

Especially after having the opportunity to speak to her on several occasions.

Sitting here now, Abigail Dupree was a distinguished lady. All neat and prim. Except for the enticing coloring enflaming her cheeks and nose.

Arendell's eyes slammed into his. "Mr. Barringer, if I had known *you* were Mr. Dupree's lawyer, I would have never inquired about securing your services. Since now it would be a conflict of interest. Wouldn't you agree?"

The bold statement exhibited absolute arrogance and utter disrespect against the entire Dupree family. Especially the youngest of the Duprees'. "I agree that it is for the best. For, I am certain, we would not have been a good fit, Mr. Arendell."

A vibration that sounded suspiciously like muffled laughter reverberated in the space to his left as he buttered a roll.

"Oh, and why is that?" Arendell leaned back in his chair and crossed his arms, his brows arched in a challenge. "Are you in a position to choose your clients?"

Garrett should have opted against Mr. Dupree's dinner invitation this evening. Abigail's father wanted Garrett fully aware of William Arendell's character on a personal basis as well as in a business setting. Losing his internal debate earlier against Mr. Dupree's intelligence in the matter had been a mistake. For Abigail's visible sudden unease overshadowed his desire to put William Arendell in his place.

"If I may be so bold as to request, Mr. Arendell, that perhaps it would be best to leave business matters outside of family meals. After all, we are merely guests and we would not want to dishonor our lovely hostesses with the boring details of our professional lives."

In his unspoken response, Mr. Arendell narrowed his eyes.

"Thank you, Mr. Barringer. That is a splendid idea." Mr. Dupree cleared his throat once again as he set his fork on the table. "Shall we leave the business talk for a more opportune time then, Mr. Arendell?"

"As you wish," Mr. Arendell agreed.

However, during the rest of dinner, Mr. Arendell monopolized the entire conversation. Garrett was exhausted from hearing the countless details of Mr. Arendell's success with the railroad. A blatant impertinence to Mr. Dupree's request. To the entire family. Abigail's mouth remained puckered in disapproval and she ate very little, while Mrs. Dupree seemed intrigued by every word the man said.

Garrett tried to maintain a stoic face through Arendell's long, drawn-out descriptions of Hell on Wheels. Ignoring the distraction of having Abigail at his side proved more difficult than enduring Arendell's animated acceptance of gambling houses, saloons, and brothels.

"If you'll excuse me." Abigail started to stand and Garrett stood to make room for her, but Arendell remained seated, unaware of Abigail's request or state. Garrett pulled the chair out and allowed her to pass through.

Arendell seemed to notice the commotion and decided the

time had finally come to bid them all good night. "Miss Dupree, may I have the pleasure of having you escort me to the door?"

When Abigail hesitated, her mother answered.

"Why, yes, Mr. Arendell. Abigail would be honored to see you out, won't you, dear?"

"Yes, of course," Abigail responded as she twisted her hands together and pressed them against her waist.

Abigail's fake smile was one that had become very familiar. Arendell's shady smile gave Garrett the creeps, and he considered following them to the porch.

"Mr. Barringer, can I interest you in a game of checkers?" Mr. Dupree's voice took Garrett's attention away from the couple preparing to exit the dining room.

With nothing to return home to, Garrett agreed. Besides, until William Arendell had taken his leave and Abigail Dupree returned inside, he would be unable to relax. "It would be a pleasure, sir."

Abigail met Garrett's eyes, and her displeasure intrigued him. After a distraught glance at her mother, she played her affection for all of her worth. "Shall we, Mr. Arendell?"

Ah, she didn't use his first name nor had he, so they couldn't be but so close. But how did she really feel about the man? Was Mr. Dupree correct in his thinking that this arrangement would be against her will?

And, furthermore, why was it of any importance to him?

Chapter Nine

Long after Mr. Arendell left, Abigail lingered on the porch. No one would know that the man had left shortly after she had not given into his forceful attempt at a forbidden kiss. Thankfully, he believed her complaint of a headache and did not try a second attempt for she would have had no choice but to slap the man. A deed, of which, she thought best to steer clear. Knowing the man's character, she would not be surprised if he struck her back.

Unsure of her exact motives for lingering outside, she thought it wouldn't hurt to allow Mr. Barringer to believe that the two of them were spending a few moments alone. Or perhaps it was her mother she had hoped to appease. Though, even to her, it didn't make sense to do such a thing.

Mr. Arendell had made it obvious tonight that he was no prize. And the thought of spending any time alone with him made her physically ill. The feel of the man's hands on her still sent painful quivers down her spine.

She walked toward the gazebo, her mind whirling with questions. Why had Mr. Barringer joined them for dinner? And why did he have to have such an effect on her?

Leaning against the railing, she centered her attention on the stars filling the black sky. She couldn't hide out here forever, but she had no desire to run into the man again. Or did she?

Ten minutes later, Abigail entered the front room and voiced an audible sigh. It was loud enough for anyone within hearing range, but no one seemed to notice. Not even that Mr. Barringer, who seemed to be engrossed in his game of checkers.

If only he would leave, so she could throw a proper tantrum.

Surely her own parents could not expect her to marry that distasteful man. Insulting her and her mother by talking about establishments that catered to men by padding it with half-naked women, with not even an ounce of remorse of such talk in the presence of ladies.

If her father had known how he had attempted to put his unwanted hands on her, he would be appalled, and William Arendell would have left with a blackened eye.

Perhaps she deserved that kind of man.

After storming up the stairs, disappointed she couldn't even bid her father a goodnight, she shut the door behind her harder than necessary.

Rose was laying out Abigail's night dress and side-eyed Abigail with a startled glance. "Miss Abigail, if I were you, I'd stop slamming things. Mrs. Dupree will never slack up on you until you do."

Abigail plopped onto her bed, her face in her hands. "You're absolutely right, Rose. Why do I allow everything to bother me?"

Rose sat on the corner of the bed. "Did your mother say something to upset you?"

Abigail laughed out loud. "Actually, she didn't do anything this time. Except maybe to fall over every despicable word William Arendell spoke at the dinner table. But I do not understand why my father allows it?" Perhaps her father also believed there was no other option for his corrupted daughter. That no other man in his right mind would have her. The thought pierced her gut.

Rose placed a hand on her arm. "Surely, it could not have been that bad."

Abigail blew out a deep breath. "Actually, it was worse. Though, I should be used to it by now."

"I don't know." Rose's eyes glinted with curiosity, yet her smile was compassionate. "Something seems different about you."

"What do you mean?"

"Even though you say it was terrible, your facial expression does not match," Rose said, her eyes emerging with an unfamiliar hope.

"Hmmm." Perhaps, it was the presence of Mr. Barringer that had her feathers ruffled. But the more she thought on the idea, the faster she came to realize that Mr. Barringer's presence had overshadowed that of Mr. Arendell, and the evening was more pleasant than she'd expected it to be. Even amidst the untasteful subject over dinner. If that were possible, given the circumstances. And then a new realization dawned on her.

This wasn't the first time Mr. Barringer had come to her rescue.

Abigail clasped her hands. "I have to do better, Rose. I cannot marry that William Arendell. I just cannot. He is despicable. The things he chose to discuss at dinner in front of me and Mother ... well, they are things I would never repeat. And if my father knew what he tried—" She stopped. It was unfair to drag Rose into such horrid details. Even though Rose was her own personal lady's maid, she was also her best friend. And very protective.

"Tried?" Rose straightened. "Did he do something to hurt you?"

"No. However, he does believe we are a couple and therefore tries to take liberties that are not acceptable. Especially with the stories he tells."

Rose stood and thrust air through her narrowed lips. "I will tell him to carry his affections and his narratives to someone more willing. That you are unavailable and you wish to never see him again."

The declaration brought a smile to Abigail's lips. "As much as I would love that, you cannot." She released a burst of air through her lips as she moved to her vanity. "Though, I do wish my mother would see it in that way."

Rose worked to unlatch the back row of buttons on Abigail's dress. "Surely your mother would never allow such a man to take the hand of her only daughter?"

"Oddly enough, his topics of choice did not seem to bother my mother. I almost wonder if she had any clue what he spoke about because she seemed more interested in drooling over his every word."

If only Abigail could go back and erase the one mistake that had changed everything. The one mistake that had influenced the last five years of her life. The one mistake that would determine her future.

Abigail stood and lifted her arms.

Rose removed the dress from Abigail and placed it onto its hanger. "Who was the young man playing checkers with your father?"

"Mr. Garrett Barringer." The sound of speaking his full name hatched a cluster of caterpillars through her entrails. "Apparently, he's working with my father," she said as she removed her stockings. "Though, I'm not certain why he would need to hire such a man."

After helping Abigail into her nightdress, Rose removed pins from Abigail's hair. "What does Mr. Barringer do for a living?"

"A lawyer or something of the sort. He's very good with words." And very nice to look at.

"Ah?" Rose paused. "There could be all sorts of reasons for hiring a lawyer."

"Yes, I just wish *I* knew the explanation." Abigail went on smoothly as though she wasn't perfectly aware of her attraction to the man.

Mr. Barringer's presence had indeed been a distraction and not in an opposing way. His company had actually been agreeable. Like a breath of fresh air in a room thickened with smog.

What bothered her though, was the fact that Mr. Barringer had knowledge of things about her that could fracture her relationship with her father, yet he had said nothing.

Why, after the rude way she had treated him, would he not bring her disgraceful actions to light? Abigail wallowed in memories of how she had done nothing since the day she'd met the man to deserve his kindness.

"He seemed to be a very pleasant gentleman," Rose said as she ambled to her side and met her gaze in the mirror. "Nice to look at too."

"You noticed that?" Abigail couldn't help but smile. "Indeed, he is." She had never met a more confident, yet humble man. Concerned, but bossy.

A dreamy look clouded Rose's eyes as she grabbed a brush and combed through Abigail's long layers. "What if Mr. Barringer is the one who will capture your heart?"

"Do not be ridiculous," Abigail rushed to say, before silly notions could take root.

More than likely, Mr. Barringer thought of her as a spoiled woman and would eventually tell her father everything to gain his trust. But just in case, she would behave and treat him with kindness and never again allow him to catch her in a compromising position.

And that meant only one thing.

She had to become the woman her mother desired her to be.

Abigail spun around on her stool. "You know what, Rose? I'm going to stop my childish ways and grow up."

Rose ambled backward but gave Abigail a delighted smile.

Abigail never spoke the words aloud, but day after day and

every single night, the allegations she charged against herself rose with the moon and the stars. And she prayed and asked for God's forgiveness for the punishment she had brought upon her family, for her short temper, and the many other mistakes she had made. It was time to devote her attention to becoming the woman God desired her to be.

"Rose, I'm going to run downstairs for some milk and cookies. Do you want me to bring you something?"

"Miss Abigail, you just said, I mean..." Rose shook her head, her smile wilting with her growing concern. "Well, what would your mother say if she finds you in the kitchen? I should go and fetch it for you."

Abigail pushed stray tresses away from her face. "You're right. Why don't we walk downstairs together?"

Rose reached for her arm, preventing her from leaving the room. "I could go for you, and you could relax with your book."

Good heavens. The woman was paranoid. "Rose, please? I have made a vow with myself to become what my mother and God expect of me, but for one last time, I'd like to go to the kitchen. Will you walk with me in case Mother is roaming around downstairs? We can make up an excuse if we're caught."

Rose released her and stepped back. "But I've already let your hair down. And you are in your nightdress and have removed your stockings."

"It's okay. The chance that we'll see anyone is rather slim. Mother will have retired to her room by now. And Father has surely returned to his office." Abigail pulled Rose by the arm and led her out of the room and down the back hallway.

They walked through the scullery, instead of the dining room. Not expecting to see the older downstairs maid still lingering in the kitchen, Abigail scurried toward her.

"Good evening, Mabel." Abigail offered her warmest smile, hoping the older woman wouldn't be too put off by their presence. "I am truly sorry to bother you at this late hour."

"What on earth are you two doing down here?" Wariness flickered in Mabel's eyes. "You both should be in your rooms."

"Abigail wanted some refreshment," Rose said, her voice trembling.

Mabel's eyes narrowed. "What if Mrs. Dupree was to happen upon you dressed for bed?"

"It was my idea." Abigail said, glancing toward Rose. "We promise to only be a minute."

Mabel brushed a dishcloth across the countertop. "You best hurry then, before I change my mind and send you both away empty-handed."

Abigail gave the woman a side hug. "Thank you, Mabel."

Two minutes later, Abigail had her dress stuffed with cream-filled cookies, and her hand gripped to a tall glass of milk. "Rose, I'll meet you upstairs. Don't forget the fudge squares."

"Miss Abigail, maybe you should wait for me," Rose argued.

"I'm sorry, but I can't. I'm about to the drop these. And thank you, Mabel," Abigail said as she walked from the kitchen with a quick glance over her shoulder toward Mabel as she took a step into the hall.

Abigail's glass of milk flew from her hand as she slammed into Mr. Barringer. The white liquid sprayed the walls, the floors, and splattered droplets onto her nightdress as well as his dark suit.

"I'm so sorry, miss—"

"Oh, Mr. Barringer. I am so terribly sorry." Her pulse drummed through her fingertips. "Look at what I have done."

"It's quite all right." With a quick swipe against the wet spots dotting his jacket, he glanced at her. "It's only a little spilled milk."

Abigail frantically searched the area. "What are you doing all the way back here?"

He glanced somewhere above her head. "I must have lost my way in my search for the washroom."

Abigail wiped at her own dress, forgetting the cookies, and they tumbled to the floor around her feet. She bent quickly to retrieve the crumbs, unable to meet his gaze. "You must think me a childish woman stealing milk and cookies from the kitchen."

He bent and retrieved a few pieces scattered between them. "As a matter of fact, I would've liked to have joined you had I been invited."

She glanced up at him.

He leaned in, speaking in private tones. "Who doesn't love milk and cookies?"

"Oh, Miss Abigail?" Rose's shrill voice echoed through the passageway interrupting the intimate moment. "What happened?"

Mr. Barringer stood and cleared his throat. "I must take full responsibility. Miss Dupree was simply walking by when I so rudely slammed into her."

Mabel joined them with towels and a bucket of water.

Still bent, Abigail reached for a white cloth. Mabel snatched it from her grasp, sending Abigail nearly onto her bottom. Garrett scooped Abigail's right arm in his and held to her until she was balanced onto her feet.

"Miss Abigail," Mabel said, "you wouldn't want Mrs. Dupree to catch you on your hands and knees scrubbing the scullery."

"No, ma'am." Abigail retreated from her spot, so that Mabel could clean up the spilt milk and crumbled cookies. "I am so terribly sorry, Mabel, for causing you additional work."

Mabel glanced up at her with a sharp glare. "Nonsense, Miss Abigail, you shan't apologize. Rose, if you'll see to Miss Dupree's gown, I'll take care of the gentleman and this mess."

"Yes, ma'am," Rose answered.

Rose took Abigail by the arm and led her a few steps down the hall, but Abigail stopped.

"Mr. Barringer, to get to the washroom, take a right at the

end of the hall and it's the first door to your left. If you could, please forget that you have seen me this evening. And if there's any way possible that I could convince you, I beg you not to mention to my father about our meeting earlier today." Abigail waited for his response, but when he didn't answer, she had no choice but to return to her room.

Being a proper lady was going to be harder than she anticipated.

Chapter Ten

G arrett laughed at himself for his sudden craving of some milk and cookies. He asked his driver to pull the carriage to a stop at a local grocer on the way back to the boarding house. As Garrett walked leisurely toward the store, he saw Mr. Arendell huddled with several other gentlemen near the entrance to the library. An establishment with which he was fairly certain had long closed for the evening.

Garrett couldn't resist lurking behind a nearby tree.

Their whispered conversation grew louder with each moment as the drinks they had no doubt consumed from the pool room across the street settled in. And that fact alone spoke volumes of the man's character.

"I had the privilege of spending the evening with Miss Abigail Dupree. It won't be long now, fellows. She is practically eating out of my hands and can hardly keep her hands off me. Why, I had to literally pry her away, so that I could join you fellows."

The men's boisterous laughter hung in the air.

It sickened Garrett.

Garrett took a step forward, but stopped himself. Abigail Dupree had done no such thing. She had stayed outside an awful long time, but he'd heard Mr. Arendell's buggy leaving within minutes after they departed from the house. A fact that had given him unpredicted comfort.

Abigail was a hard-headed, egotistical woman, but he couldn't imagine her behaving the way Mr. Arendell described. In fact, he was more than certain that it was a bold-faced lie.

Milk and cookies forgotten, Garrett climbed into his buggy, and the driver started once again for the house. His anger swelled with each mile that separated him from what he should've done. His mind was unable to expunge the image of long, wavy tresses falling about Abigail's shoulders, framing her flawless, glowing face and those eyes staring up at him full of doubt.

When he arrived at The Chantom House, he stopped in the entryway, reeling in more memories of Miss Dupree. Abby—the nickname tickled his awareness. It suited her well.

Garrett made his way inside to his bedchamber, intent on writing some notes in his journal from his last few days in Charlotte. There wasn't much in news to report, so he wouldn't get a fair price for any of its content, but Mr. Dupree was paying him well for the position, of which, Garrett was still not quite sure all that it entailed.

Thinking through the few details Mr. Dupree had mentioned, he found no obvious issues with his mention of travel, since exploring different places was something Garrett did often. Still, he was uncertain how that could be of any help.

Something drew Garrett to the young lady. Perhaps it was the way she fumbled when he arrived, the way her hand fit perfectly in his during prayer, or the way she tried to help the maids as if she had always done so. All of those things made his determination to keep his distance from her cloudy. But he had no regret in his decision to take on Mr. Dupree's quest to save his daughter from a lifetime of misery with Mr. Arendell.

Above all else, Abigail Dupree deserved better than a cad like him.

❧

Abigail had managed to stay out of trouble the entire week and was beginning to feel her new role wouldn't be so hard after all, until Garrett showed up on her doorstep Saturday morning. She descended the stairs, trying to ignore the way her pulse kicked when she saw him standing in the foyer speaking with her father.

What business could he possibly have with her father that would bring him to the house on a Saturday morning? She considered turning and trudging back up the stairs, but it was too late. He had already seen her.

Her belly tightened when he met her gaze and held it for several long seconds before looking away. Nibbling on her lower lip, she took the stairs carefully. Her foolishness bloomed like a morning glory in his presence. She would have to remember to use her manners, no matter what. And it would be best to stay silent.

Garrett returned his attention to her when she reached the bottom stair. "Miss Dupree."

She glued on her best smile. "Mr. Barringer, it's so nice to see you again."

If she could have reached through her throat and removed the words she'd just spoken, she would. They sounded rehearsed, but nothing could be done about that now. He made no further comment, and she stepped forward to kiss Father on the cheek.

"Good morning, my dear. I hope you slept well."

"Yes, Father. Please excuse me, gentlemen."

She padded through the foyer to the dining room. The table was already brimming with an assortment of food and glasses of orange juice. "Good morning, Mother. I hope you had a pleasant night."

Mother never looked up, intent on her list. "Abigail, I feel it's pertinent that I apologize for slapping you. But you must understand that it is for your own good. I cannot allow you to speak to me in that manner. And we shall never speak of it again. It will be as if it never happened." She cleared her throat. "Now, sit and have your breakfast."

Abigail studied her mother's trembling fingers. What had her in such a state this morning? It had nothing to do with the way she'd spoken to her. Mother never let something so minor bother her for more than a few minutes. What could have happened? Perhaps, it would be better to pretend she hadn't noticed.

She placed a napkin in her lap, hoping she wouldn't have to have breakfast in Garrett's presence. "Has Father taken his breakfast already?"

"Yes. You were late and your father blames me for your tardiness."

Abigail willed herself to stay silent lest she say something in haste and make matters worse.

"Well, what do you have to say for yourself?"

"Please forgive me, Mother. I wish not to be a burden to you."

"Make sure when you venture outside, that you always wear your hat. Your porcelain skin is a priceless quality that would be a pity to taint." Mother stood. Her heavy breath was her last affront as she turned and walked away.

Initially, Abigail remained motionless. She may be ignorant to much of the world around her, but certain injustices were universally comprehended. Her mother was the only woman she knew who could spoil a compliment with reproach.

It was no secret the problem that Abigail had caused for her entire family. Even she had been unable to come to peace with her past—to survive through the pieces of her broken heart. A clear picture of Randall clouded her vision. She felt the heavy burden of her pain daily, yet with a subtleness she had grown to ignore. Why was that suddenly taking precedence in her mind?

Rose stepped from the kitchen only moments after Mother

disappeared around the corner. "Miss Abigail, do you wish to have your breakfast here or sent to your room?"

The idea of sitting alone in her room depressed her further. "I shall eat here." Abigail lowered her voice so her words wouldn't reach beyond the dining room. "Please give my apologies to Mabel for my tardiness. I do not have an excuse."

Rose's eyes widened as they flickered in one fleeting second toward the doorway and Abigail drew in a sharp breath. Had Mother been listening? She would never approve of her apologizing to the hired help. Rose dipped in a curtsy and turned to leave the room.

Then the sound of a throat cleared.

A male throat.

Frazzled, Abigail turned to scan her surroundings and there at the entrance stood Garrett, staring at her from across the room.

Cautiously, Mr. Barringer took a step forward. "Do you mind if I join you?"

The multitude of caterpillars returned, tickling every inch of her. She held her tongue, but pushed her lips into an unnatural curve and knotted her trembling hands into her lap.

Before Garrett could take the seat across from her, Mabel entered and handed him a cup of coffee. "Thank you, ma'am."

As soon as Mabel retreated from the dining room, Garrett reached for the cup in front of him. "I'll take that as an affirmative."

How was she supposed to appear proper and elegant with him watching her eat? The first words that came to mind flew out of her mouth before she could stop them. "I wasn't expecting to see you again. Why *are* you here?"

His full smile fell into a slanted, questionable smirk and he straightened. "I'm working directly for your father. He had another meeting, so I was asked to wander the grounds until he finished."

"Oh?" Alarm gushed through her chest and bottomed out of

her stomach. Why would her father need a lawyer? It would do no good to voice her questions. He wouldn't be able to answer, so she tucked them to the back of her mind. It was hard to remain unruffled with the man sitting across from her. "I must admit, I'm having a hard time picturing you as a lawyer."

The tiny lines surrounding his mouth relaxed and his freshly shaven chin glistened in the morning sunlight. "Oh? And why is that?"

"I pay attention to conversations going on around me. And it doesn't seem that your verbiage nor mannerisms depicts the traits of an attorney. Not to mention your age." The tug to look into his eyes was fierce, but instead she focused on his cheekbones, determined not to look him directly in the eyes.

He crossed his arms. "Then I should pay attention lest I speak to another in your presence."

She blinked and zeroed in on the cleft dimple that gave him that roguish smart look. "I do not mean to imply that I eavesdrop. I simply pay attention to things of importance."

"So, I can assume then that I am important to you?"

It was his reply that made her succumb. He considered her with amiable, observant eyes. Heat blazed her neck, slowly rising to her cheeks. And she laughed.

He exposed a mischievous grin that had most likely melted the hearts of at least a dozen young ladies. "I'm only teasing. You've made it very clear in our brief encounters that I am of no importance to you."

The man emanated confidence and grit and she detected a trace of warmth.

Abigail reached for a piece of toast. "I apologize if I came across as rude. That was never my intention." She lathered her words with sincerity all while lathering her bread with apricot jam. "I am certain, though, that you are of great importance to someone."

"What makes you say that?"

"I would hope that we all have someone in our life who thinks that of us." A little thrill trickled through Abigail's middle. What this man thought of her was suddenly important.

A muscle twitched under his eye. "Yes, I suppose you are right."

She tipped her head slightly toward him and offered a smile. "It would be a horrible thing indeed, to be of no importance to anyone."

Mr. Barringer's attention shifted though his eyes never moved. "What was your intention, if I may be so bold?" he asked in a voice that held more curiosity than accusation.

Abigail shrank back a little into her seat as if she had said something untoward. "My intention?"

"Yes, you stated it was never your intention to come across as rude and I simply wondered what was your intention, then?"

Her brows narrowed. Not wanting to add more gas to his fire, she simply said, "I have no intention where you are concerned." Why had she said that? That wasn't what she meant to say. The truth was the lawyer had been too smart for her, coercing her into a conversation, manipulating her with those irresistible eyes. "What I mean is, I am happy you are acquainted with my father, for whatever reason. I should only hope that you will keep the other day…" She stopped, the blood in her veins thrusting violently.

Ridges scored into the flesh above his eyes. "I'm not sure I know to what you're referring."

A tornado of torment ripped through her stomach, scattering the fuzzy creatures. "When you happened upon me near the water. At the time, I didn't realize that you were working directly with my father." She rambled on not considering how childish it must sound. Yet, she couldn't stop. "And if he were to find out that I was traipsing about…without Rose, he would, well, it would upset him."

"Oh. I see." The landscape of his face brightened. "I would never wish to cause you distress, Miss Dupree."

A harsh breath exited her lungs, betraying her relief. "So, I have your word that you will not tell him?"

He scrutinized her, his expression far too adamant. "If you wish me not to mention our meeting, I would consider it under one condition."

Abigail drove her head back. "What condition?"

"That you would stop putting yourself in dangerous situations," he said with such boldness, that she could do nothing but stare at the man closely for a long, few seconds at the conclusion of his explanation.

Dangerous situations? The subject made her habitually irritable. Her temper flared and her breathing intensified.

Mabel entered the dining room and curtsied toward Garrett. "Sir, would you care for more coffee?"

"Yes, please."

Abigail was thankful for the distraction for she could do nothing more than stare at the man. While Garrett answered Mabel, Abigail refocused her thoughts. Every encounter with him had led to his opinion of her inability to keep herself out of harm's way. She had to calm down before she ruined any virtue the lawyer potentially observed in her.

Every argument he brought against her, she disputed. But now, she had no choice but to agree with him. If Mr. Barringer told her father about finding her by the water, and her state of dress, it would disappoint him. Abigail could make no more mistakes in front of Garrett, especially now that she knew he worked for her father.

"Can I get you anything else, Miss Abigail?"

Abigail adjusted the scowl on her lips, transforming them into a grateful smile. "No, thank you, Mabel. That will do."

Mabel bowed in a formal curtsy and left the room, and Abigail was once again alone with Mr. Barringer.

Abigail made no motion to reach for more of the appetizing course spread out in front of her, and it didn't go unnoticed. She hoped the man would take the hint and leave. Resuming an untainted conversation would be impossible. Especially now that he had made it clear that he would not keep their secret if she did not behave.

"You have no intention where I'm concerned?" He took a measured sip of his coffee. "Not sure whether to take that as an insult or a compliment."

She gritted her teeth into a smile. "Please, take it as a compliment. Surely my intentions are of no use to anyone."

He returned his coffee to the table and then tucked his fingers under his chin in a brooding pose. "I am certain that is untrue, though you do have a terrible habit of recklessly entering into precarious situations."

She could no longer hold the vicious wield of her tongue. "That I would intentionally put myself in harms way is not a reasonable judgment. There are times I simply wish to be alone."

"Solitude." His smile was sympathetic, deflating her defensive attitude. "A rare commodity."

"Yes. Rare indeed." Especially in this house. If she could, she would be traveling to another city, another state, exploring every nook and cranny to her heart's desire.

He stood. "Excuse me, Miss Dupree. I will allow you to enjoy your meal in peace."

"You do not have to leave." Yes, he does. *What is wrong with me?*

Abigail wanted to apologize, but her mouth wouldn't cooperate with her brain. Why did she keep allowing him to bring out the worst in her?

"Actually, I do. I hear your father calling my name. But it has been a pleasure Miss Ab—Miss Dupree. I look forward to seeing you again."

His stride was confident, and she was getting a full view of his broad-shouldered stature from where she sat. Shame should divert her gaze, yet fascination with the man commanded her focus. With his departure, the dining room was suddenly too quiet. The silence rebuked her. Considering on how to prove the young lawyer wrong, she reached for her toast, forced a small bite, and leaned back in her chair.

If she hadn't known it before, she did now. The man was a gentleman. And she was a spoiled brat, something she vowed to never become. The very thing she detested.

Even though she had berated him for calling her careless, his distress over her safety overshadowed her argument. His sincere concern amused her, though she didn't quite understand why Garrett Barringer, a perfect stranger, would waste time worrying over her.

Her effortless laugh flowed freely. The man was actually worried about her. Things suddenly looked brighter than they had in months. And then there was that one part of their conversation that brought her laugh to a halt and replaced it with longing.

The part where he almost called her by her first name.

Chapter Eleven

G arrett was led to a study down the hall from Mr. Dupree's office. The man already sat with outstretched legs on a mini sofa covered with gold stripes. Garrett took a matching chair directly across from him.

"So, Mr. Barringer, how are you getting along with my daughter?"

A deep churning settled in Garrett's stomach. "Fine. She's a lovely young lady."

"Lovely indeed." Mr. Dupree's bellow echoed off the high ceiling. "Though I'm surprised she hasn't made things difficult for you."

Garrett held the smile vying to escape. She'd done more than make things difficult, but he couldn't stop thinking about last night. He'd stayed awake for hours replaying the scene over and over again trying to make sense of her reaction to their paid help. How her dark blue eyes had aligned with his. How he'd found it difficult to look away.

"I think it would be in Abigail's best interest to send her to stay with my sister for the remainder of the summer."

Lead plummeted into Garrett's stomach, the dead weight taking his breath. Though he could not ascertain the reason. Then just as quickly he agreed it would be best to remove her from the threat of William Arendell's intentions toward her. "Oh?"

Mr. Dupree leaned forward. "The timing and way we departed from Asheville never sat well with my Abigail. She has always been quite the explorer and would be much happier in the country. It may do her some good to be separated from her mother as well."

"Separated from her mother?" That statement went against all of his logic. In his experience, mothers and daughters were always close and usually inseparable.

"Let's just say they have not been seeing eye to eye lately. And Abigail is longing for a visit."

Garrett studied the man's torn expression. It was clear by the break in his voice, he didn't want to send his only daughter away.

Though it wasn't his place to ask, he could not contain his question. "How will you explain your decision to Mr. Arendell?"

Crossing his legs, Mr. Dupree leaned back against the sofa. "This—" He waved his hands in the air. "—all of this is an illusion. None of it belongs to me or my family. A dear friend invited us to care for his property for the duration of five years while he traveled across America for business. Our time is nearly up."

"So, will you and your family be returning to Asheville?"

"That is the plan, but there are some things that need to be… well…manipulated, before I permanently put my daughter back in the very position that forced her away."

Instead of asking the question begging for clarity, Garrett chose a different route. "I do not understand what that has to do with the gentleman."

"Arendell knows nothing of our history, only what he thinks to be true. And he is under the assumption that when Abigail marries him, he will be the hero by solving all of our problems. But that is not his only reason. And I know a union with the man would only lead to more problems—problems we will never be able to reverse."

Garrett cleared his throat as he stood, knowing he also agreed that if Abigail were to marry that man, he would destroy her. Yet still, he pressed on, with the question at hand. "Why is that?"

Mr. Dupree glanced toward the closed door and lowered his voice. "Mr. Arendell is hoping that by marrying my daughter, he will inherit a grand portion of wealth."

Garrett's brow lowered with understanding. "But there is none?"

Mr. Dupree nodded his head in agreement. "There's only enough to get us back home, where we will live humbly, yet comfortably. When Arendell finds out the truth, I'm hoping it will be too late. I'm hoping to be long gone. And enough time will have passed that it will no longer matter about Abigail's past."

Her past? All of the secrecy had something to do with Abigail's past, but what? That was a question he could not respectfully ask, so instead he reveled in the news that thankfully it was not Mr. Dupree's desire to have his daughter marry Arendell. And knowing a small portion of important information would have to be enough for now.

Mr. Dupree stood and moved toward the window, his shadow spreading across the thick red carpet through the filtering sunlight. "I have to find a way to prove Arendell's disloyalty, or find someone else to take his attention away from my girl while she's away." With a steely stare, Mr. Dupree met Garrett's eyes. "Only then will I have even a small effort of saving my daughter's reputation."

"I don't understand. Why would Miss Dupree's reputation be in question?" Garrett asked before he could think it all the way through.

"I haven't said anything before, because I didn't want to taint your impression of my Abigail. But I fear, I have no choice. For I see now that I cannot do this alone. Especially with a man blinded by his hunger and his knowledge of her past sins. Not to mention his belief that they will magically evaporate into the arms of a man who is willing to do whatever it takes to marry her."

"And you do not trust Arendell's intentions?"

"Not in the least. Nor will I ever." Mr. Dupree's words held challenge, and his lifted shoulders said that he meant every word. "I have seen the man in action and the only thing he cares about is an opportunity for his own reward. It has brought me physical pain to watch this fiasco for months now."

Even with what little Garrett knew of Abigail, it twisted something deep in his very core to imagine any harm coming to her. He would do what he could to help. "What would you have me do? What role shall I play in all of this?"

"That is the very thing I wished to speak to you about." Mr. Dupree took his seat. "I need you to accompany Abigail to Asheville and to not leave her side until I can settle things here."

"Accompany her?" To Asheville? *I can't return.* "But sir—"

Mr. Dupree released a deep breath. "I know I am asking much of you, but you are my daughter's only hope of a future away from the secret that could potentially destroy her life."

❧

Once again, Abigail had allowed her tongue to lead the flow of the conversation instead of her brain. What was it about that Mr. Barringer that caused her to speak in such an erratic way? Why, she couldn't remember the last time conversing with a man, any man for that matter, had been difficult. Of course, most of the men, of which, she had been acquainted were either too old, too young, or married. Except for one man. And unfortunately, William Arendell had too many other unfavorable qualities. And not one of them brought about any favorable feelings of any sort.

But when Garrett Barringer entered a room, for some reason, it always took her breath. There was something about his generous smile. Or his occasional day-old stubble that left a dark shadow from his chin to his side-burns. Or maybe it was the unmistakable attraction that always colored his cheeks in her presence.

Of course, the last one was more than likely wishful thinking. And the longer she sat at the breakfast table, the more her mind wandered to precarious thoughts.

"Can I get you anything else, Miss Abigail?"

With a skittering glance at Mabel, Abigail stood. "No, thank you so very much, Mabel. Everything was just delicious."

Before Abigail moved toward the door, Rose rushed to her side. "Miss Abigail, your father has requested your presence in his study."

"Me? Now?"

Had Garrett said something about seeing her by the spring? What reason would he have to betray her? She hadn't been overly obnoxious earlier. Nor had she had a chance to put herself in another of Mr. Barringer's idea of a perilous situation.

Then a different thought occurred. One even worse than the other. What if her father had given in to Mother and insisted that she marry Mr. Arendell?

"Did he say why?"

"No, miss." Rose led her into the foyer. "Only that he needed to see you immediately."

The daunting questions hummed around Abigail's head like angry bees as she approached his study. She opened the door to find him settled comfortably behind his desk, and some of the worrisome weight lifted from her shoulders. "Good morning, Father. I was told you asked to see me."

Her father sat forward, enthusiasm budding in his eyes. "Yes, my darling, come in please and have a seat."

He never asked her to sit, and her shoulders braced for the

blow. "Is something wrong?" Her reserved laugh surely betrayed her nerves.

"No, in fact, I have good news."

Instantaneous relief flooded through her veins, but the bobbing effect of her uncertainty produced a tidal wave through her head as she fully entered the room.

While taking her seat, the distinct sound of shuffling feet in the corner caught her ear. Heart lurching, she tilted her head with the slightest of motions to find Garrett Barringer standing in the far corner by the window. Though utterly thwarted, her awareness sparked to life, kindling the flame within her that he had ignited earlier.

Why was he still here?

Surely her father didn't wish to speak to her in confidence while in Mr. Barringer's presence. Then she reasoned. It would not be something that should be kept secret. She waited for an explanation of his presence but when her father offered none, she turned to Garrett. He met her gaze and she noted a look of vulnerability. Of uncertainty. He said nothing but continued to stand there shifting his weight from one leg to the other.

Abigail considered him only a second more before returning her full attention to her father. "Good news?"

"Yes, I have spoken to my sister. Louisa and Henry have requested your company this summer."

"They invited me to come for a visit?" In her excitement, Abigail stood and barely registered Mr. Barringer's presence suddenly there next to her.

"Yes. It seems as though your uncle has acquired a position with George Vanderbilt, and he thought Louisa could use the company."

"You will allow me to leave?"

When her father's gaze collided with hers, his enthusiasm faded as brokenness etched deep within his eyes, though he appeared to be trying to hide it. "Yes, it seems I have no choice

with your persistent appeal for a visit." His face softened. "You
will be greatly missed."

"Oh, thank you, Father. How long will I stay?" The rest of
her questions dissolved on her tongue. There would be plenty of
time to gain answers to those when additional parties outside of
her family were not present.

"We did not discuss dates in detail, but perhaps through the
remainder of the summer."

"Really?" Abigail stood there, her heart skittering all over the
place. Clinging to the long-lost hope with so much might, she no
longer cared that her father was speaking openly in front of a
complete stranger.

"When?" She toned her excitement down several notches.
"What day am I to leave?" She dared not ask for more. The last
thing she wanted was for her father to be hurt over her happiness. And she most certainly did not want to look like a foolish
child in front of Mr. Barringer.

He leaned forward then. "The matter of your mother
remains."

Her hope vanished into the thin air. Mother would never
agree to this. "You haven't told her?"

"Not in so many words. It will be much easier to gain her
approval with your help."

Distraught, Abigail gave no reply. She'd thought it impossible to lose more hope than the bit that had just been snatched
from her. But as she stood, her heart became a quavering mess.
And dark splotches flashed before her eyes.

Before she could find her tongue, her father continued. "I
have entrusted Mr. Barringer in our full confidence and he—"

❧

Fear burned a trail to Garrett's heart as the young woman
collapsed toward him in one quick motion. Scrambling to keep

her from hitting her head, he kicked the chair out of the way all while gathering her into his arms.

"Abb—? Miss Dupree?"

Her father grabbed her hand. "Abigail?"

"Please, wake up." Garret didn't understand his own reaction to the woman, but one thing he knew for sure though he didn't know why—he would do anything to protect the woman lying in his arms.

The moment he caught Abigail from falling to the floor, her long, blond tresses fell loose down her back. Her cheeks, usually a darker shade of pink, were now pale. And it scared him.

It scared her father too. He had nearly flipped his chair over in his haste to get to his daughter. "Abigail, my darling."

It wasn't until her father used the endearment that Garrett realized she had woken. Still, she didn't move from her position in his arms. The rhythm of her racing heart alarmed him. "Are you all right?"

"Oh my…" Her eyes widened as if she had been caught doing something horrendous. "Mr. Barringer, I…" The statement dwindled as she tried pushing her body up with both hands, but then just as quickly she limped back against him.

Sensitive to her circumstance, Garrett lifted her gently, helping her into a sitting position. Her dress flared across the floor, covering the span of space beyond her.

"What happened my dear?"

She stared at her father with a look of uncertainty.

"I do not know. I must have fainted."

Mr. Dupree exited the room immediately, his voice still coherent. "Rose, let's get Abigail some water. She isn't feeling well."

Before Mr. Dupree could return, Abigail started to stand but didn't get very far before the force of her weight thrust her back against Garrett. She unleashed a deep sigh, turning slightly into him. "I am so terribly sorry. I do not know what has come over me."

"Please, do not apologize. Are you still feeling unwell?"

"The dizziness has eased, though I am still weak. But I must get up."

It took every ounce of restraint not to settle her into the safety of his arms and argue that there was no hurry. Instead, he complied. "Here, let me help you into the chair."

As he took her trembling hand and, placed his other arm around her slim waist, he leaned closer. He could still feel the erratic pounding of her heart. When she was settled in the chair, he bent so that their eyes had no choice but to connect. Hers were wild with embarrassment and instinctively, he took her hand.

"Is there anything I can do to make you more comfortable?"

Insecurity guarding her eyes, she jostled a grateful smile into place. Then her focus darted to the doorway as her father reentered.

"Here darling. Drink this. It should make you feel better."

"I will be fine if Rose could just help me to my room so that I may lie down awhile." Her lids drifted down, almost closing. "Perhaps, I am just tired."

"Maybe it will be better if I escorted her up the stairs." Garrett would rather see to her being tucked into her bed, than to take a chance of her falling again.

Abigail gaped at him with widened eyes.

"Yes, I think that should be wise," Mr. Dupree agreed.

"But Father." Abigail's tone and eyes pleaded with her father. "He cannot possibly escort me to my bed chamber. What if Mother sees him approaching my room?"

"I will handle your mother. Besides, she is out this morning. Mabel has taken her into town. I trust Mr. Barringer fully where you are concerned."

Her father's message to him had been clear. Guard Abigail

with his life, but he had also warned Garrett to guard his own heart. Abigail had the ability to strip all reason from the most practical of men. To give in to her antics to be set free would lead to dire consequences and he could avoid all disaster by simply not looking too deeply into her eyes. Most importantly, Garrett was to keep her safe until her father could join them in the foothills of North Carolina.

Abigail didn't say a word in response to her father, but she followed his movements with erratic eyes. Then she inhaled deeply, moistened her lips, and rose to leave the room. When Garrett approached her side, she fastened to her stiffened lips a stubborn, detached frown and walked from the room.

Brimming with compassion, Garrett followed, being careful to stay close enough in case she needed him, but at enough distance to give her the desired space she craved in that moment. Even he had not come to terms in his own head, his own heart, that he would accompany this beautiful woman on a trip to the mountains of North Carolina for an extended length of time.

And he was beyond certain, he was already in trouble.

Chapter Twelve

Several days had passed since Garrett had been invited into the Dupree home. Several days since he had seen Abigail Dupree. Several days of rethinking his promise to accompany the young woman to Asheville.

Since his arrival, there had been no sign of her presence. He could only wonder if she had pulled another one of her stunts to seek mere moments of solitude.

They were leaving in the morning and he had not spoken to her since his last visit. He understood Mr. Dupree's reasons for choosing to send his daughter away, but he wasn't certain it was the best option. If Abigail learned the truth, that Mr. Dupree had entrusted Garrett in his confidence, Abigail would surely never speak to Garrett again.

Now as he left Mr. Dupree's office, he chanced one more glance toward the top of the stairs. As he took a left and headed to the front entrance, soft footfalls echoed against the wooden floor behind him. Garrett turned to find Abigail advancing toward him.

His gaze traced the outline of the young woman's face. "Miss Dupree."

Abigail settled her hands on her hips. "Mr. Barringer, I did not expect to see you this afternoon."

"Nor I you. Though, I am glad for the opportunity," Garrett said, with no small dose of sarcasm. For he had actually anticipated seeing the young woman standing before him.

A tentative smile graced her lips. "I am surprised to see you again so soon. I hope my father isn't overloading you with work."

"On the contrary, I have enjoyed working for your father."

Abigail pulled her hands behind her back, the material of her dress tightening across her chest. Reprimanding his thoughts, he forced his focus on the dark blue eyes seized with confused interest.

A diminutive frown wavered on her lips. "You make it sound as if you will not be working with him much longer."

"I'm uncertain of the length of time he will require my services." Part of him wished she were correct. Noting how he already had difficulty extracting the woman from his mind, this trip would only complicate matters. The woman had most certainly put a stamp on his heart that would not easily be removed. "I hope you are feeling better."

A touch of color tinted her cheeks as she glanced toward Rose, who was waiting in the shadows. "Yes, I am much better, thank you."

"Have you been able to pinpoint what caused you to—"

"I have not." As if noting his awkwardness, she cut him off. "Though, my mother is hoping to seek another physician's opinion on the matter." Abigail cleared her throat and spawned a breathtaking smile. "Speaking of which, I missed the opportunity to offer my gratitude for your assistance the other d-day," she stuttered. "Or last week."

It had been three days and four hours to be exact. "It was my pleasure."

"I was so worried my mother would not allow me to travel.

Especially after that episode. But much to my surprise, it did not dissuade her decision."

"For your sake, I am happy to hear it."

"Thank you." The tip of her tongue ran between her lips. "I will leave you now, I have taken up too much of your time already."

"I actually wondered if I may have a moment of your time." Garrett closed the small gap that remained between them. "I was hoping to speak with you in private."

Glancing over her shoulder, she turned back toward him. "I hardly think that will be appropriate."

What was he thinking? Garrett shook his head. "Of course, you're absolutely right. Where were you headed?"

Abigail's eyes widened, the skin stretching away the tiny lines surrounding her eyes. "I beg your pardon. Are you asking me to disclose my whereabouts to a complete stranger? That would be unwise and dangerous. Do you not agree?"

The words he wanted to say, jumbled into a mixture of stupid questions being in the same vicinity with this woman. He deserved that. "I hardly think we're complete strangers. After all, I...well, I think we've spent enough time together for you to know I only have your best interests at heart."

She dropped her arms by her sides as her gaze lowered to the floor. Then she looked up at him. Her dark blue eyes were pools of charisma that contained a magnetism that had arrested his heart and had yet to release. "I'm only teasing you, Mr. Barringer. But after your obvious tactic to prove your point the other morning, I believe it was well deserved."

It was at that.

"Abigail, why are you walking around the house undressed when we have a guest?" The harsh tone of Mrs. Dupree echoed off the hardwood floors.

At the sound of her mother's voice, the color in Abigail's

cheeks deepened as she glanced down at her own waist. "Mother, this is a perfectly good dress."

The long, gray gown made from cotton, wasn't the usual attire he had become accustomed to seeing her adorn, but the color highlighted the gray specks in her dark eyes. Emphasized her natural beauty. Accentuated her soft curves. With a jolt of awareness, he quickly turned his attention to Abigail's mother.

Mrs. Dupree's eyes narrowed into thin slits as she glanced again at her daughter. "Where is Rose? I told her not to let you out of her sight."

Rose stepped out of the shadows. "I'm here, Mrs. Dupree"

"Oh, good heavens, girl. How could you have allowed her to come downstairs wearing…this." Mrs. Dupree narrowed her eyes at Rose. "Well, don't just stand there. Go now and find her something decent for company."

"Yes, Mrs. Dupree."

Mrs. Dupree shook her head as Rose hurried up the stairs. "If she continues to disobey me, I will have to—"

"Mother, she has done nothing wrong. I am not a three-year-old child roaming freely without supervision. Rose is my best friend and you should not speak to her in such a way."

Mrs. Dupree harrumphed, but Abigail ignored it.

"And if she is punished for my desire to have a few moments to myself, or to pick out my own wardrobe, I shall never speak to you again. Please excuse me, Mr. Barringer." Abigail brushed past him and ran up the stairs.

Mrs. Dupree expelled a sharp gasp. "I am truly sorry. I cannot believe that my daughter would act in such a shameful manner. And in front of a guest."

The stricken look on Mrs. Dupree's face only twisted the knife even deeper of having been responsible for the upheaval. "It's entirely my fault."

"That's nonsense. You did not force those preposterous words from my daughter's mouth. What is that girl thinking

103

calling the hired help her best friend?" She said more to herself than to him. "Now, if you will please excuse me, Mr. Barringer, isn't it?" she asked, though not seeming too concerned whether that was truly his name or not. "I really must see to her before she embarrasses me further."

Best friend? "Of course." His reply was weakened with the two words still echoing through his mind.

Mr. Dupree hadn't been stretching the truth. Those two barely tolerated each other. He hated to leave now without speaking to Abigail first. But he had no choice. It would have to wait until the morning.

He was moving toward the front door, when the echo of footsteps resounded from the stairs behind him. He turned to find Abigail rushing with each step. Wanting to stop her from moving fast out of fear that she'd slip and fall, he took several steps toward the stair railing.

"Mr. Barringer," she called out his name, with labored breaths.

"Please, call me Garrett."

She blinked, her damp lashes brushing the tops of her eyelids when she opened them. "Please forgive my unruly behavior and for not being dressed appropriately. For guests." She hesitated. "If you would give me a few moments to change into something more fitting, I would very much like to meet you in the parlor for that private conversation." Just as quickly as she had appeared, she hurried up the stairs and disappeared around the corner.

This was a mistake. He shouldn't be here, wanting to talk to her, wanting to take her in his arms, wanting to remove the deep pain settled in every move of her mouth.

He paced the foyer for several minutes, challenging himself. The woman was a chain of inconsistencies. Her stubborn desire to put herself in needless danger was done unintentionally, yet she begrudged his intervening protective nature. She saw no fault in dishonoring a high-society elite with smirks and chuckles when warranted. However, her devotion to their hired help was unmatched by any woman he had ever the occasion to witness. Though her style was elegant and she bestowed grace, her hair constantly loosened from their pins and she persistently attempted to tame the fallen strands. A most desirable trait, indeed.

His opinion had altered wholly, compared to his perception of the young woman in their first encounter. He should approach Mr. Dupree and beg his forgiveness. For he could not accompany his daughter to Asheville for one simple reason...he did not trust himself. He did not trust his heart.

"Mr. Barringer?" Abigail's panicked voice stopped him from taking the first step toward her father's study. At the sound of her advance, Garrett turned to find Abigail standing right behind him. "I worried you would leave. Rose would not allow me to step out of the room until every single button was looped into place."

That she had tried to escape before Rose could finish, brought a smile to his lips.

"Thank you for waiting."

In his experience, she had changed quickly.

The gown she now wore had more embellishments than the other, but it paled in comparison to Abigail's natural beauty. Her gentle character. The way the color in her eyes deepened with no forewarning. Flustered, he tore his focus from hers.

Finding no other escape, he offered his arm. "Shall we?" He gave a confident smile, though he felt none of it. Still chiding himself for getting into this mess, he led her to the parlor. He had been wrong in assuming she was like every other girl he'd met on his life's journey.

"If you would please allow me to apologize. I should never speak to my mother in that tone, but to do so in front of guests is...well, it was cruel. And dishonoring to my mother. Unfortunately, my tongue tends to function ahead of my brain too much of the time. As well as my actions."

Indeed. Although, she had not mentioned any of her flattering attributes. The kind that made Abigail Dupree a woman any man would be fortunate to possess.

When they were standing face to face in the privacy of the parlor, unease stabbed at him the way she held his gaze.

"And here I am blabbering and monopolizing all of your time when you were the one who requested a private meeting. And now, I promise to silence my tongue."

Unblinking, she scrutinized him, her essence far too affectionate.

When he said nothing, a slight frown tipped her lips downward. "Was there something you wished to speak to me about, Mr. Barringer?"

He ached for her as he drank in the smoothness of her jaw line, the curve of her lips. "I wanted to apologize as well."

She took a step closer, her black boots brushing against the wood floor, the scent of lilacs enticing him even closer. Her deep blue eyes glistened with retained moisture. "Please, Mr. Barringer, do not apologize. For, I am the one who is entirely at fault."

A sudden rush of emotion splayed across his chest, tightening through his middle. How was he to defend himself against those eyes? The very thing her father had warned him against. Not allowing another moment to pass, he took her hand in his. Meeting her gaze, he pulled her small fingers to his lips. "I think...maybe it is better if I take my leave. Good day, Miss Dupree."

"But..."

With one last glance in Abigail's direction, he hastened to the foyer and slipped out the front door.

Chapter Thirteen

F<i>oolish woman.</i> Abigail remained by the fireplace in the parlor, eyes slid closed in humiliation for the hundredth time since Garrett Barringer's departure. She had stood on the threshold of spending time alone with the man. On the day before her departure, no less. An opportunity she never believed would have occurred.

Why then had she ruined her chances by blurting out most of her faults within the span of not even a full minute's time? Faults he may not have even realized. Speaking liberally as if she were eager for his forgiveness. His approval.

Why had she not stayed upstairs instead of running back down, desperate to see him? Because she was eager to be near the man. More eager than even she had realized.

Only days ago, in the presence of Mr. Barringer, her father had announced that she would return to Asheville. When she had thought the worst, that her father had told Garrett everything, Abigail had proceeded to make a fool of herself by fainting in front of the man.

Literally falling at his feet.

It wasn't until she had been removed from her father's office, that she'd sobered from the initial shock. Father would never trust a living soul with her secret.

And now once again, she had made a fool of herself and ruined her last chance of a shameless goodbye.

At the sound of voices in the foyer, Abigail's stomach fluttered and she rushed from the parlor. Garrett had changed his mind and returned. But it wasn't Garrett Barringer standing in the foyer looking at her. It was William Arendell.

"Abigail. I had to come as soon as I heard."

"As soon as you heard?" she asked, not having a clue what the man meant.

"That you will be leaving for a few days."

A few weeks. But what she had planned was none of his business. So, why then had Father told him? "How did you know?"

He reached for her hand. "I make it my business to know everything concerning you."

Abigail snatched her hand away. "Mr. Arendell, you are—"

"I am tired of this proper act," he whispered, impatiently. His unexpected admission directed the cutting truth right at her. He believed them to be a couple.

With each step he took forward, her feet fell backward until obstructed by the wall.

Abigail's instinct was to lash out against his assertiveness. But she was convinced there was nothing she could say to satisfy the man, who was apparently blind to the fact that she wanted nothing to do with him. So, she kept quiet.

Hands clasped at the small of his back, he leaned in closer. From one breath to the next he'd gone from guest in her parents' home to dominating admirer, and her independent disposition objected. Not caring what her mother thought, she pushed her way through to the opposite side of him. "I must ask you to leave."

His relaxed posture stiffened. "Leave? But I have only just arrived."

"And you have already overstayed your welcome."

"Is that so?" he muttered brusquely under his breath as he grabbed her arm and pulled her closer. "If you wish me to keep certain things in confidence, I would suggest you start playing your role better."

Her role? Unease crept in about her stomach and coiled up her spine. What did he know?

The vice on her arm tightened. "I am a very eligible bachelor who could have any woman I wish."

"Mr. Arendell?"

At the sound of her father's voice, William released her arm.

Abigail exhaled. Her shoulders loosened at her father's approach.

"Mr. Dupree." William took a giant step backward and extended a hand.

A look of offense cloaked her father's expression. He hesitated before accepting the man's offering. "I wasn't expecting a visit?"

"I was in the neighborhood and thought to drop by but was just on my way out." He lubricated his voice with deceptive charm.

"Excellent," her father said, dryly. "Please, allow me to see you to the door, then."

"Of course." William's eyes wrinkled with a strained smile. "Miss Dupree, as always, it has been a pleasure."

Giving a silent warning, her father raised his eyes to the upper story. With a grateful heart, she excused herself and scurried upstairs to her room, and closed the door quietly behind her.

The entire afternoon, Abigail hoped to find Garrett Barringer sitting at the dinner table that very night, joining her family for dinner. Giving her one more chance to redeem herself. But instead, her mother, with a scowl filling her face, sat in silence the entire half hour...the most miserable thirty minutes of Abigail's life.

"Mother, I wanted to apologize for my disruptive display this morning."

Her father chimed in, "Did I miss something?"

Her mother finally looked at her and then at her husband. "Nothing of importance. In fact, I can't seem to remember to what she is referring."

Father's brow lifted. "Abigail, perhaps you should plan to turn in early. You have a big day tomorrow."

"Yes, sir."

"Goodnight, Mother. Thank you for allowing me—"

Her father cleared his throat. "That will be all, dear. We will see you bright and early."

Although unsure why her father would be rushing her out of the room, Abigail complied. When she reached her room, Rose was already there waiting with her night dress.

"I lifted a window." Rose cast a glance in Abigail's direction. "I thought you would enjoy some fresh air."

"That was nice."

"Why do you look so gloomy?" Rose walked toward her. "I presumed you would be anxious with such a big day ahead of you tomorrow."

"Never more so. And everything is fine." There was no reason to cause Rose worry on their last evening together.

"Would you like for me to undo your hair first?"

"Oh, yes, please." Abigail sat at her vanity. She watched in the mirror as disobedient strands of long hair had already managed to collapse from their pins. Maybe she should give up on trying to be a proper lady and simply cut it shorter. It would certainly be easier to manage. "I wonder how I would look with shorter hair."

After a sharp intake of air, Rose argued, "Your hair is beautiful as it is."

Abigail pulled a few loosened locks through her fingers. "It isn't as thick as I wish it to be."

Concern tightened Rose's brow. "But your natural waves and shine are a perfect look for you."

"You only say that to make me feel better as you always do and for that I am grateful. But truly, there's no need to worry. I wouldn't dare chop it off. My mother would never forgive me for such an offense."

Pricked by past sins her mother had not forgiven and which Abigail had brought to light by her own admission, she sank deeper onto the stool. That was an offense that would never be forgiven. Or forgotten.

"I only thought it would help in enticing Mr. Arendell to attach to another of his long list of eligible women he seems to have in his back pocket."

Rose frowned. "It would be such a waste to do anything to appease that man. Whether it helped your fate or not."

"Of that, you are absolutely correct."

The young woman's brow gradually softened.

And then with Abigail's next breath, the thought of Garrett Barringer and their earlier conversation invaded her thoughts. A conversation that had significantly slackened her excitement over leaving tomorrow.

"I have made a complete fool of myself."

Abigail hadn't realized she'd spoken the thought aloud until Rose's fingers paused midway in her search of another pin. "Surely not, miss?"

"It's true." Abigail blew out a frustrated breath. "I am indeed a foolish woman."

"Why would you say such a thing?"

"Mr. Barringer asked to speak to me." Abigail moaned. "In private."

A treasured gift granted but just as quickly forfeited.

"What did Mr. Barringer have to say?" Rose hesitated. "That is, if you wish to share the information."

"That's just it. He never said anything."

It could have been the perfect last moment. A moment she would have cherished. A moment that could have made returning home easier. Instead, it only created another pang of disappointment.

"I monopolized the entire conversation babbling about my own need of his forgiveness."

Rose placed a cluster of pins on the vanity table. "I'm sure it isn't as bad as you believe it to be."

Abigail tried to recall Garrett's expression while she spoke. Nothing critical had settled in his features nor had he seemed annoyed. He almost appeared flustered. Intimidated. Two things she was certain did not correspond with what little she knew of the man. He must have felt embarrassment. For her. And being a gentleman, he had removed himself from her presence before she could humiliate herself further.

"How was dinner?" Rose shuffled to the right. "Were there any unexpected guests this evening?"

"Fortunately, no, and unfortunately, no. If that were possible." Abigail rubbed her temples. "I can't stop thinking how I all but groveled in the man's presence earlier today."

Rose removed the remaining pins and set them in a glass jar. "I'm sure Mr. Barringer did not see it that way."

"But what if he did? I will not have a chance to redeem myself."

Rose took a brush and combed through Abigail's hair, leaving the long layers to drape over her shoulders. "You are too hard on yourself, miss."

"And you are too easy on me," Abigail said, thinking aloud. "I do wish you were accompanying me on this trip."

"So, do I, Miss Abigail."

She had no choice but to put that Garrett Barringer out of her mind. "I am leaving tomorrow and there are more important concerns to consider. Randall Thorne for one."

Rose's brows furrowed. "What do you mean?"

"I can see it so clearly now."

Rose's head tilted to the side.

"I would have been a far happier woman in fighting for him than I have been in letting him go. Once I convince him to marry me, I will be able to restore my good name." At least in her mother's eyes.

Rose gasped. "Miss Abigail, you cannot ask the man to marry you."

Abigail inhaled a revitalizing breath, pressed her hands against the stool, and lifted her chin. "No, but I plan to do everything I can to convince him to fall in love with me."

Unfastening the last button loop from Abigail's dress, Rose took a deep breath. "I should stay here in case things do not work out as you have planned."

Abigail met her gaze in the mirror. "You believe I do not have what it takes to convince Randall Thorne to fall in love with me?"

Rose shook her head. "No, miss. That is not what I meant."

Abigail stood. "I'm only teasing you."

In all truth, Abigail was uncertain in her ability as well. For she had failed the first time.

Rose tilted her head in a questioning manner. "But you can't be serious?"

"I most certainly am." Abigail stood and regarded her maid with a prolonged look as she lifted her arms. "Do you not believe I deserve my turn at love?"

"At love, yes." Rose lifted the gown over her head. "But didn't this particular man leave you for another woman?"

"Yes, with Lydia, one of my closest friends."

Rose swapped Abigail's dinner gown for her nightdress. "She never explained?"

"No. There's a part of me that believes she wanted to, but did not want to hurt me more than she already had. Though, I know in my heart our friendship would never be the same." Abigail positioned her silk nightdress into place. "I never saw that they had married."

Rose blinked owlishly. "But what if—"

"Do not worry yourself, Rose. I am well aware that it may not work out. He could very well be married. Although, I have not heard of any marriage announcements. No news at all to indicate he has been attached to another. So, there is still hope."

Rose shrank back from Abigail's stare. "I do not want you to get hurt."

"Me? Hurt? Nonsense." Abigail coughed out a laugh. "No man will ever have the privilege of breaking my heart again."

"What if you are unable to gain what you are looking for?"

"If nothing else, I can find closure and put him out of my mind, once and for all." At least that was what Abigail hoped. "I do wish though, that you were accompanying me on this trip."

Tears welled up in Rose's eyes as she once again brushed through the fine layers of Abigail's hair.

Abigail focused in on the young woman's trembling lips. "What on earth could be wrong? Surely you are not so concerned over the matters of my heart that it would bring tears to your eyes?"

Rose swiped at an errant tear, streaming down her cheek. "I am so sorry, miss, for not keeping my emotions in check. It's just that, I will truly miss you."

"But why are you crying? Surely, I will be back before you even have time to miss me." She stared at Rose for a long moment. An unwelcome heaviness settled in the pit of her stomach. Rose was keeping something from her. "What did you mean by you should stay in case things do not work out? You will be here when I return, will you not?"

Rose shook her head. "No, Miss Abigail. I am leaving you."

"What?" A shiver crept down Abigail's spine as she stared at the woman's reflection. "Whatever do you mean? Are you leaving for a trip of some sort while I'm away?"

With a deep sniff, Rose continued. "I have been offered a position at the Biltmore."

Abigail swiveled on her stool, her mind spinning as she tried to unravel the woman's meaning. "The Biltmore Mansion in Asheville?"

"Yes, miss."

"When?" Abigail managed to squeak, though her throat swelled with unbridled emotion.

"Most likely before you return from your trip."

Abigail cleared her throat. "You have been offered a position serving the Vanderbilts?"

Rose nodded and Abigail inhaled, shirking the piercing sting of despair.

"This is wonderful news, indeed. Why then, do you look so disheartened?" Affixing a smile, Abigail did her best to hide the sorrow that nearly took her breath. "This will be a great opportunity for you."

"I do not wish to leave you, miss."

Abigail placed a hand on the young woman's arm. "It isn't as if I will remain in this house forever."

Rose sniffled. "I had always hoped I would accompany you when you left."

Abigail had anticipated that as well. Of course, stating that detail now would only cause more needless heartache. For them both. "Are you implying that this was not your idea?"

"No. Of course, not. Your parents arranged everything. The request, the contract. All of it."

Abigail's breath caught and she stood. *That means...* "Oh no!"

"What is it, miss?"

"Perhaps you not accompanying me is for my own preparation in that I will no longer require a lady's maid." She reached over and gripped Rose's arms. "Your departure can only suggest one thing. My parents expect my marriage to William Arendell as soon as I return."

A trace of alarm stirred in Rose's eyes. "Surely not, miss. I will tell your parents I simply cannot leave you."

"But you must go." Pushing away her own anguish, Abigail smiled, recalling their many years of friendship.

Oh, how she needed this time away. For many reasons.

Though now, she second-guessed her urgency to leave. She would miss Rose deeply. But she had no choice. Abigail had to make Randall Thorne fall in love with her. Quickly. She bit back a groan of despair.

"We must look on the bright side," Abigail blurted, needing to shift the course of her thoughts before she could consider them too carefully. This would possibly be their last evening together. They should make the most of it.

With a stunned flutter of lashes, Rose looked at her. "You believe there is a bright side in all of this?"

"Of course, I do." Abigail's nod was instant and confident. "You are on the brink of embarking on an incredible journey." She smiled as though every muscle in her heart was not writhing in torment. "Consider all the new friends you shall make. If you remain here, you will never have any opportunity."

Rose frowned, her brow crumpled with defeat. "I will be working. Here, I am a lady's maid. There I will be no more than an under-house maid or scullery maid."

"Yes, but you will be working among countless others. And you shall advance quickly. Of that, I have no doubt." Suddenly, Abigail regretted coercing Rose, at times, to treat her as a friend instead of an employer. What if she had sabotaged Rose's chances? Had her mother been preparing Rose for this position all along? "Just think of it. Here there is only Mabel and our butler. There…why there will be men as well. And plenty of them. Useful men. Footmen. Perhaps a younger butler. And the valet." Abigail took the young woman's hands. The Lord had blessed Rosalind Whitmore with lovely features, both inside and out. Any man would be fortunate to call her his own. "In your new position, you may meet the man God has intended for you. This is wonderful news, indeed."

Rose fashioned a sheepish half-grin. "It would be pure foolishness to consider such a thing. You know as well as I that relationships between employees would be prohibited."

Abigail's role in cheering the woman up weighed more heavily than her own need to be comforted and she responded accordingly. "I never was one for following the rules."

Rose leaned back in laughter. "What am I going to do without you?"

Abigail released Rose's hands and wiped her tearstained cheeks. "Whatever will I do without you?"

Chapter Fourteen

A fter a restless night of little sleep from the excitement of having a break from Mr. Arendell for a long while and the despair of leaving Rose behind, Abigail had woken with swollen eyes and puffy cheeks.

Now as she took one look around the room, she heard Rose enter behind her. "The carriage is outside waiting for you, miss."

"It's time, Abigail." Her father's affectionate voice reverberated from the floor below.

Sweeping Rose into a crushing hug, Abigail clung to the woman as if her life depended on it. There would be no other opportunity for a heartfelt parting in the presence of her mother.

"This is not goodbye for I will see you again. Somehow. But until then, I wanted to thank you, my dear friend, for all you have ever done for me. I will miss you terribly. And I wish you all the best of luck on your new adventure."

Through a muffled cry, Rose managed to say, "And you as well."

Abigail descended the stairs, her bags already placed in the overhead luggage transporter in the carriage. With slow, careful steps she scanned the area, hoping for one last glimpse of the very thing she never expected to see. Garrett Barringer.

He was there and her heart jolted in response at his presence.

Standing by the carriage, his focus didn't rest on her, but drifted just past her.

His being here certainly wasn't for her benefit, but most likely for business affairs. Father must have a meeting right after her departure, and Mr. Barringer had no choice but to wait. Straightening, Abigail tried to mimic his relaxed posture. But it was unbearable. She yearned to explain herself, to not leave him believing her to be a spoiled, rich girl not caring for anyone but herself.

It was not to be. Not here. Not now. Instead, she needed to say her goodbyes.

Perhaps when she returned, she'd have the opportunity to prove to him that she was a strong, independent, compassionate woman. Of course, then it would be too late.

Abigail approached her mother first. Better to get over with the argument sure to stem from a moment like this. A moment she would have never believed possible.

"I will miss you, Mother."

Her mother said nothing at first, only scrutinized her travel wardrobe. "I suppose this will do for a trip of this length." Her frown loosened a bit as a solemn light glazed over her eyes. "God has blessed you with a beautiful, porcelain complexion. Be sure when you venture outside that you wear your hat. You mustn't scorch your skin."

"I promise, Mother."

"And ignore any gossip you may overhear. We do not want to encourage the sin of a wicked tongue." Her mother's eyes glowed with compassion. "We certainly know the suffering it can cause," she added, lowering her voice.

Instead of voicing another apology, Abigail wrapped her mother into the strongest hug she could muster.

Mother sniffled and pulled back. "The hour is getting late. We must stop this blubbering so you can be on your way."

Abigail stole a peek at her mother's retreating form.

Next, she moved to her father and allowed him to sweep her into his arms as he had in her younger days. He held her for several long moments all the while giving fatherly instructions. Instructions that chimed out like a broken record. Instructions she had strived to obey, though there were certain rules with which she struggled.

Then he added one last request. A request that stopped her cold. "Anytime you must leave the homestead, stay within sight of your aunt or Mr. Barringer."

Confusion struck her to the core and Abigail held to her father's arm as unsteadiness gripped her. The question sprouted on her tongue, but she spoke softly as he did, so that no one would overhear. "Mr. Barringer?"

"Yes, I have invited him to accompany you for the duration of your trip."

"What?" Disbelief ripped through her mind. "Good heavens, Father. You do not mean to have Mr. Barringer accompany me to Asheville?"

"I do. I need to know you'll be safe, and I'll feel better having him there with you." Her father considered her with vigilant eyes. "Surely, you did not expect I would allow you to travel alone?"

"I honestly had not even considered the travel part of this trip." Abigail glanced over her shoulder at the man still standing in solitude, yet his focus was now zeroed in on her. "But Mr. Barringer? He is no more than a perfect stranger."

"Only to you. I have known the young man his entire life. And I am well versed with everything there is to know about him. You must trust me, my love."

"Does Mother know?"

"I told her this morning. That was my reason for not telling you both sooner. She worries you will fall in love with the man and will ruin your chances with William Arendell."

Fall in love with him. Abigail swallowed the lump forming in her throat, but she was sure she failed at hiding her flaming cheeks.

"There's no time to go into all the details, but this trip will be unconventional, though necessary. So, perhaps it will be best to keep the details to yourself." Father's calming smile wavered. "I will miss you, my darling. Have a wonderful time and try not to worry about your mother. I will take care of her. In time, she will come to realize we are doing the right thing."

Not trusting her own voice, she didn't respond, but pondered her father's words. Unconventional? Whatever had he meant by that? And why the sudden rush to send her away? It was as if he believed something terrible would happen if she did not leave.

With a hefty measure of uncertainty, she turned, not sure what to expect, but found Garrett still watching her. His expression carried none of the regret she'd expected, but instead it held warmth. And it only deepened with his lingering gaze.

Maybe he wasn't as disappointed to be her guide as she had feared. Not having even a moment to get used to the idea of traveling with the handsome man standing by the carriage, she did the only reasonable thing she could...pretend she had known all along.

The morning was cool, the air pure. If only Abigail could inhale enough to cleanse away all her dark, ugly sin.

Garrett led her around to the front to assist her into the carriage.

"Where is the driver?"

"I will be driving."

Abigail glanced toward her father. She supposed there was no need to worry since she had witnessed Garrett's proficiency with a horse.

"Then I should wish to accompany you in the front." With Garrett's assistance, she stepped up and settled into the passenger seat for the bumpy ride. "That is if you do not mind."

His brows lifted. "Not in the least."

Garrett walked around and climbed in on his side and leaned forward to take the reins. "I should have told you."

Abigail pulled her shawl tight about her shoulders. "Told me that you would be driving?"

"I should've told you I would be accompanying you."

She scanned the fields stretching out ahead of them for miles. "Oh, that."

The brim of his hat lifted, enabling her to see his grimace. "Yes, well, it came as a bit of a shock to me as well."

"Was that the reason you asked to speak to me yesterday?" she asked, even though she already knew his answer. Though something deep within had hoped for something more.

"Yes, indeed it was."

Foolish as it was, Abigail winced.

She should apologize for monopolizing the entire conversation. For her behavior. She cleared her throat. "Mr. Barringer, I —"

"Please..." He turned his head toward her. "Call me Garrett."

Her cynical laugh pierced the air. It was a wonder she hadn't already slipped and called him by his given name. As often as she mumbled the name in her silent thoughts. Something she never did with any other male in her circle of acquaintances. "We barely know each other."

He granted her a chirp of a laugh. "I believe that shall soon be a thing of the past, Abigail."

Hearing her Christian name spoken with admiration from this particular man triggered a deep longing, occupying a corner of her heart she hadn't known existed. Unable to resist, she smiled, releasing a deep breath. "If that is what you wish, I would be most honored to call you Garrett."

He returned her smile. "Good. Shall we?" he asked as the carriage rolled forward at his nudging of the horses.

Detaining a sigh, peace cloaked her apprehension. If she

could have chosen anyone to travel with, it was most definitely the man sitting next to her.

They rode in silence for several moments before she stole a long peek at him. Donning a casual suit, Garrett, sat tall accentuating his striking features. His strong legs were bent at the perfect angle and with relaxed arms, he held the reins loosely.

Something about the man made her self-conscious, so Abigail sat with her elbows tucked securely at her waist, careful not to sway with each bump and turn. Only after several minutes did she suffer the effects of undertaking such a posture. If she continued sitting in such a position, she would be sore and unable to move by the time they arrived. Giving up, she loosened her shoulders, stretched out her legs, and took a deep breath. The relief was instant.

"I'm surprised my father, and especially my mother, are allowing me to come on this trip unaccompanied."

"Unaccompanied?" His lips expanded, and for an instant she thought he would smile, but his lips never actually arched. "I am accompanying you."

"Precisely. All the more reason to be wary. I hardly know you." His Adam's apple fell and rose as if in slow motion. Why was she focusing on his neck?

Then before she could shift her attention away from him, he cleared his throat and met her gaze. "Are you usually very familiar with your chaperones?"

Heat traveled from her head to her toes, lingering in unsuspecting places, raising her awareness of emotions she had been certain died long ago. Garrett's eyes moved over her in a neutral manner, as if anticipating her reply. His probing look snapped her from her musings. "There aren't many occasions where a chaperone has been needed."

"Oh? And why *is* that?"

"Mother prefers to keep me within her view. At all times." Squinting against the sun, Abigail scanned the landscape beyond them. "Speaking of which, I was advised to stay in the presence of you or my Aunt Louisa should I venture out." Abigail laughed at such a suggestion, beyond certain that Garrett Barringer would oppose.

"That should be no issue."

A faint nudging of Abigail's temper flared, although she couldn't decide if she was more upset over her father's instruction or Mr. Barringer's quick approval of such an idea. "I certainly hope you do not plan to enforce that rule."

For a moment, his features hardened, revealing a touch of protectiveness. "Your father entrusted me with your care. And I do not intend to let him down."

If Garrett Barringer or her aunt were to be present at all times, how was she to spend time alone with Randall Thorne? Only one solution would solve this problem. She had to convince Garrett Barringer otherwise, which would also mean ignoring her father's instruction. Impossible.

"I am from the Asheville area," she said. "So, it is highly unlikely I will find myself in danger."

"There are plenty of dangers. No matter how familiar the area or the people may seem."

It would take more than simply stating her thoughts on the matter. She would have to prove to him that she could be trusted. Not intending to tarry on the sore subject of her inability to see dangers all around her, she changed the topic. "How long have you been in Charlotte?"

"Not very long at all." He glanced toward her. "I too am from the Asheville area."

That statement brought her head up. "Is that so?" A short silence stretched between them as additional questions festered in her brain. "You know my father very well then?"

Garrett nodded in disagreement. "Actually, no. He inquired of me over a month ago and offered me the position after we met in person. It was the same day I first ran into you."

"But I thought he had known you for years."

Garrett snickered. "Why would you think that?"

Abigail looked beyond the horizon, her thoughts wandering back to the conversation with her father. "Something he said."

If it were not true, why then had her father articulated such a statement?

Chapter Fifteen

Garrett didn't probe. It didn't matter what Mr. Dupree had told his daughter and how much her father actually knew of him. What mattered was the promise he had made to keep her safe.

As he focused on the road ahead of them, watching for any movement that didn't belong, countless thoughts waged war in his mind, distracting him. The miles they covered were nothing but a blur.

Abigail Dupree wasn't your average female. And the effect she was having on him was inconvenient. Mr. Dupree had chosen him to care for his only daughter. Needed him to think of Abigail as a sister, not an available, beautiful young woman only three years his junior. Impossible. Especially with the way she looked up at him with those dark blue eyes. Sitting next to him with a soft, clean scent and charming smile. His gut tightened with longing. Garrett scowled. Was he really so impressionable, that he would succumb to a woman he hardly knew? But even that wasn't the worst of it.

Mr. Dupree's reasons for sending Abigail on this trip were understandable. But Garrett was sure he disagreed.

Abigail couldn't handle the truth. He would give anything to take this plight from her, but there was nothing physically or emotionally that he could do to ease her burden. He had promised her father that he would remain silent unless the circumstances became dire. Mr. Dupree had entrusted him in his confidence over the last few weeks, and he was certain if Abigail knew the knowledge he now held, she would never speak to him again.

Silence settled between them for a few miles. The sound of birdsong and the rustle of wind against the buggy's canopy created a peaceful hum.

Abigail shifted in her seat, her knees pointing more to the left as she turned slightly. "Well, Garrett Barringer, if we are to be on a first name basis, we should get to know each other better. Don't you agree?"

That would only complicate things further. But that would be a bridge to cross later. "I suppose you're right."

Within his peripheral vision, he could tell she sat taller.

"With all the miles ahead of us, there is no time like the present."

Garrett gripped the reins, forcing his focus to stay trained on the road, even though the urge to see the expressions flitting across her face compelled every impulse within him. He could only envision Abigail's animated features as she spoke unreservedly.

"What would you like to know?" Had he actually just said that? It would only lead to answers he wasn't inclined to give. Today or ever.

"Let me see. There are so many things, of which, I should like to inquire, I'm uncertain where to begin."

As did he. He wanted to learn everything there was to know about Abigail Dupree.

She shifted a bit more, until her leg was softly touching his with each bump and crevice. "I shall start with the basics. Does your family still live in the Asheville area?"

The undesirable direction of questioning squeezed his lungs and he inhaled a deep breath. "They do."

"Oh?" Her whole upper body lifted. "Do you have siblings?"

Emotion clogged his throat as he thought of all his sister had lost. He cleared it with a forced cough. "One sister."

"A sister?" Abigail sighed and leaned back against the bench. "I have always longed for a sibling. I have always imagined a sister would be like gaining an instant best friend, of whom, to share all your secrets. Perhaps that is the reason I have treated Rose more like family than my mother approves."

Instead of responding, Garrett silently absorbed his own decisions. Prompt remorse flushed over him in a sickening wave. He had been blessed to have Sylvia for a sister. The young woman had always been a breath of fresh air, even when the two of them didn't see eye to eye. And he had abandoned her when she needed him most.

Abigail almost bounced forward and clasped her hands. "Do you plan to visit your family while we are in Asheville?"

For once, someone had asked that question out of curiosity and with no trace of judgment. "No, I hadn't planned to."

"Why ever not?"

The power behind her question forced his gaze toward her.

Abigail glared at him beneath a quizzical brow. "They must miss you fiercely."

They most certainly did not. Of that, he was sure. "I did not think there would be time."

Abigail stroked his sleeve, the sensation of her touch radiating up his arm. "You mustn't allow me to hinder you from seeing them. I would never forgive myself."

He couldn't allow Abigail to accept any blame in keeping distance from his family. Perhaps, if Abigail joined him for a brief visit, it would lighten the discomfort of facing his sister after so many months. All while lessening his grief from staying away so long.

"Tell me about your sister." Abigail once again touched his arm, then as if realizing her bluntness, yanked it back and onto her lap. "What is she like?"

"There's a certain glow about her." At least there once was. Before the accident. "As if every evening she visits heaven and is given a new breath on life. Joy seems to radiate from her."

"What a lovely, thoughtful way to describe your sister and with such adoration. You two must be very close."

He glanced at Abigail. Her beautiful spirit inspired him. "You remind me of her."

"Me?" Delight glistened in her widened eyes. "In what way?"

Garrett's eyes circled back over Abigail's face. He noted that a touch of color painted her cheeks with his lingering pass then he paused at the deepness of her eyes. "You display that same glow."

Abigail shook her head, yanking her focus from him. "No, not me. Maybe Rose. She never complains."

This young woman with her big smile had witnessed too many cruelties in her short life and in this moment, he could not resist setting aside his own professional boundaries and reached across to touch her arm. "Perhaps you have rubbed off on the young maid without being any the wiser."

Abigail shifted restlessly, obviously uncomfortable receiving approval. Or could she be experiencing the same electricity hovering between them that had his skin tingling.

"I do not see myself that way, though I am overflowing with gratitude at such a flattering compliment. Especially coming from you."

"Oh? And why exactly would a compliment from me be such

a shock?" he challenged, forcing his thoughts into a safer direction.

"Do you really have to ask that question?" She pressed her hands against her thighs. "Of all people, you have seen me at some of my most undesirable and embarrassing moments."

Of course, he already suspected the exact times she spoke of, and had to physically ward off the unobstructed vision of one particular day as it flashed through his mind. But wanting to see her smile again, he couldn't resist asking, "Are you speaking of our meeting near the water? Or do you mean that very same evening when you flooded my coat with milk?"

She laughed, just as he had expected her to. "Both, as well as others of which I shall not remind you."

"I would have never guessed that those incidents troubled you in the least. You always handle yourself with such grace, it seems that it would be impossible to steal your joy." Except perhaps when Abigail's mother disapproved.

"You, sir, are being overly generous. Yet, if I had to be completely honest, I do somehow feel content in my heart even when it seems impossible."

"Contentment. The very thing of which we could all be more sensible."

"I once heard a wise man say, 'Joy is the flag that is flown from the castle of your heart when the King is in residence.'"

Garrett could only stare at her.

Then she continued. "Even when all else in my world seems to be failing, I have the comforting knowledge that the King of Kings is in residence in my heart."

Heaven help him, this woman would make it extremely difficult to keep his heart in check. "Beautifully said. And it certainly shows."

"Do you travel much, Mr. Barringer?"

He was thankful that the subject had deviated into a direction away from his family. His guilt. His feelings for the woman. And he answered freely. "I have actually had the opportunity to travel quite a bit over the last several years."

"Is that so? What places have you been?"

He repaid her enthusiastic smile with interest. "New York for one."

She sighed. "Oh, how marvelous."

Garrett gently tugged on the reins. "Where is it that you would wish to go?"

"Anywhere. Everywhere. I want to write about all of the things I see and fill a whole book with my adventures. New York is definitely at the top of my list, though."

"What is it about New York that interests you?"

"There are so many things to see in New York. The Statue of Liberty. The Brooklyn Bridge. Central Park."

The woman was a ray of sunshine. Acclimating himself to her was the very last thing he needed. Still, he couldn't resist. "Is that it?"

Abigail ambushed him with a baffled smile. "What do you mean, is that it?"

Knowing very well where his chain of questions was headed, delight stormed through his veins. "You wouldn't be interested in attending a ball at a mansion on Fifth Avenue?"

"A ball? Most certainly not." Abigail laughed with an acidic splutter. "I almost forgot. There's also a zoo in Central Park."

He should most certainly stop the words forming on his tongue, but losing the battle to his own pleasure he continued. "So, you mean to tell me you would rather visit with monkeys than accompany me to a ball where we could dance until blisters form on our feet."

"You are very funny, Garrett Barringer. But you cannot tell me that you would rather dance in some fancy building than see a real lion or tiger. There are probably elephants and giraffes too." She turned toward him and the bulge of his throat wrenched up. "Did you have the opportunity to see them?"

"Unfortunately, I did not visit the zoo."

"How could you not?"

"There was no time," Garrett said, his eyes aligning to hers.

Abigail dropped her lower lip into a pout. "I am ashamed of you, Garrett Barringer."

Garrett sharply pulled in a deep breath of air. "Ashamed of me?"

"Yes. It sounds as if you never take time for yourself. Or do not realize the importance of taking advantage of every single day."

His abdomen pulsed with a hint of laughter. "Perhaps I would prefer to dance, over watching exotic animals being forced to live in a caged atmosphere instead of roaming freely in the wild."

Her eyes glistened as if she agreed with the sentiment.

He continued. "And are you telling me that if we happened to be in New York at the same time, you would not join me for a dance? One that we could finish?"

Abigail's expression smoothed, though he could tell she was fighting against a smile. "I would be honored to accompany you in a dance. But I could not promise that I would willingly attempt to add any sort of blisters to my feet."

His flesh tingled at the thought. "I would not mind you going barefooted."

Abigail gasped before her musical laugh filled the open air. "Garrett Barringer."

He loved the way Abigail voiced his full name in that tone. It was hard directing his attention ahead of them when he knew the color of her cheeks had deepened even more. But direct it he did.

"I do not believe anyone else realized you had abandoned your shoes." With that statement, he glanced her way and when their eyes connected, breathing grew difficult.

Her lips curved away from the O she had formed with her mouth, and her complexion softened into a delicate pink.

"And how was it that you became aware?"

Redirecting his attention once again to the road, he inhaled. "Let's see. For one, you were more than an inch shorter."

Abigail laughed out loud.

"But what gave it away was the fact that you seemed to suddenly move freely as if you were no longer in pain."

"It was just horrible." Abigail's hands fell to her lap. "Though, it was my fault alone. Walking into town. It was not one of my more sensible decisions."

Thinking back on that night, he nodded. "I agree with you there."

"Of course, you do. You've made that clear on more than one occasion. Though I am grateful for your noble intentions."

The topic sobered him instantly. He needed to keep a tighter rein on his feelings for the woman. Changing the subject was long overdue. "Asheville has a grand new home."

"Are you referring to the Vanderbilt's famous Biltmore?"

"You have heard of it?"

"Has not everyone?" She tucked her skirt beneath her leg. "Reading is one of my most favorite past times."

Her answer tugged his thoughts back to the day he'd found her by the river. Garrett chuckled, in an effort to clear the image, but the quizzical spark of her eyes said she hadn't meant it in jest.

He cleared his throat. "So, Asheville must not be all bad."

Her eyes wandered back toward the open fields. "I loved Asheville as my home. More than I have ever cared for Charlotte. Though, I am grateful for the opportunity to have lived in the city."

"You prefer to live in the city, then?"

She shook her head. "No, but it has made me appreciate the peacefulness. Miles of land or hills between each home is my preference." Her gaze seemed to drift somewhere beyond him. "I wish only to visit the places I've read about."

"I see." He took a deep breath and the aroma of fresh air sweetened the back of his throat. "Well, I do hope all of your dreams come true."

And he meant every word.

Chapter Sixteen

A bigail Dupree was a lovely woman both inside and out, and Garrett should tread carefully where she was concerned or he would find himself in serious trouble. When she walked toward him after their third stop of the trip, he could not stop his eyes from drifting to her lips.

As soon as she was settled back into her seat, she turned toward him. "We have only just left and already I miss Rose, my father, and even my mother, more than you can imagine." Abigail said nothing more for a long moment and he forced his attention to remain on the road no matter how he longed to steal another glance.

"Perhaps," she said, "you will allow me to accompany you on your visit to see your family."

How would he ever face them again? His sister? Why was he already being led to return home when he hadn't yet come to terms with his own guilt?

Her brows arched at his pause. Why did her eyes have to swallow him up in warmth like a crackling fire in the hearth at Christmastime?

"Please, forgive me. It was not my intention to invite myself."

"No, I do not mind at all." The solution to his guilt could be finally confronting his family. Maybe it would be easier to face them all having Abigail by his side. "I would love for you to accompany me."

"Really?" She grabbed his arm and did not release him. "Do you mean it?"

In the narrow area of his peripheral vision, he noted the delight that flickered across her face, which only enhanced the affection he felt having her hand connected to him. Certainly, an emotion he hoped to witness again. "Yes, of course."

Then she leaned back, a full smile brightening her complexion even more. "I shall be looking forward to meeting your family, Garrett Barringer."

After a few minutes, Abigail chatted merrily as they rode along the countryside. Twilight was upon them, but the orange and red hues of light cast glows through the deep blue sky.

"I love the country. The wide-open space to roam freely. No traffic, no noise, only the sound of birds, and rushing water from the streams. I miss it."

She spoke as though she'd forgotten he was sitting next to her.

"I must confess I worried you thought of me as self-centered." She looked toward her feet, and so did he, unable to resist the glittering shoes catching his attention.

Shoes that had no place for a trip like this.

So vivid were his memories of their first few encounters, he couldn't help but laugh out loud.

She frowned. "You did, didn't you?"

"You did not fail to mention how your shoes were costly."

"I'll have you know, as soon as those words were out of my mouth, I regretted them."

"If I remember correctly, I witnessed that remorse in your eyes. Still though, you were hard-headed and would not allow me to help you. Though, I certainly cannot condemn you for being overly cautious at my approach. At least on that occasion."

Abigail laughed.

The day had been long and they had covered sixty miles already in a span of ten hours. Garrett slowed the buggy a few minutes later, when he spotted the location already chosen for setting up camp.

"Why are we stopping?"

Garrett climbed from the buggy and jumped to the ground, the leaves crunching beneath his feet. "I have to set up camp for tonight."

"Set up camp?" Her voice trembled. "How much longer could it possibly take to get to Asheville?"

"Another full day."

Abigail looked across the open expanse of the field surrounded by woodlands.

"It is for only one night. We should arrive late tomorrow."

She touched her mouth with her fingers. "This is all my fault."

"What do you mean?"

"If I hadn't requested to stop so often, we would've made more time. We would be closer."

"That's nonsense. I needed to stop as well. It did me good to get out and stretch every few hours."

"What shall we do when you grow tired, again?"

"We will stop."

She was looking at him now. Her eyes glazing over with fear.

"I need to get started on the tents. Why don't you stay here and relax."

"Mr. Barringer, I have never slept in a tent, much less the woods."

The terse statement caught him off guard. "Where did you expect we would sleep?"

"The thought of having the need to stop never occurred to me."

Too tired to contemplate the worrisome look on her face and too relieved to finally have brought the carriage to a stop for the day, he took the most truthful route. "I assure you, it will be fine." He would protect the woman with his life. Her worry was unnecessary. "We will sleep a few hours and start again at dawn. As long as we don't run into any trouble, we should arrive sometime tomorrow afternoon."

"But I brought nothing to prepare for a stay in a tent."

He couldn't imagine Abigail Dupree would have any inclination of what preparations were needed for a stay in the woods. "I have brought everything we will need."

"But the temperature is dropping. Won't we freeze?"

"The weather is actually very nice for this time of year. But I packed plenty of blankets."

"Couldn't we drive a bit more? I promise to not complain."

He couldn't remember her complaining once, even when she needed a bathroom break with no convenient place to stop. He chided himself for not speaking earlier, but hadn't wanted to ruin her trip and had enjoyed her company and their conversation. The small insight she'd allowed him had lightened his mood and had ignited the flame he'd buried when he left. Compassion for his beautiful charge filled him and he stopped and gave her his full attention.

"The sun is already setting and soon it will be too dark for me to navigate uncharted roads." He turned at seeing the fresh sheen of moisture filling her eyes. "Try not to worry. I'll get everything set up and come to get you when it's ready."

"Wait, Garrett. I will come with you."

The hysteria in her voice made him turn. She started to climb from the buggy, but Garrett caught her arm. "No, you should wait here. It will take me a while."

Her eyes met his and the wild fear filling them alarmed him. He stopped himself from reaching out to her.

She shook her head and the look disappeared. Lifting her chin, she cleared her throat. "Certainly, you don't expect me to stay here while you do all the work?"

"I do, indeed. You must be quite tired and this bit of rest without bouncing will do you some good. Besides, I've hired some men to keep watch while we sleep. And they will be able to help me set things up."

"Some men? Where are they?"

He nodded toward the bed of a buggy only a few yards from where they stood. "They came earlier and are probably still sleeping."

She jumped from the buggy as if she'd been stung. Garrett caught her just as her shoe wedged into the step. A soft whine fell from her lips as she fell into his arms. She forced herself free and straightened her dress, wobbling on her heels from the uneven ground beneath their feet.

Abigail leaned closer and whispered, "Why didn't you tell me there would be men waiting here for us?"

"I wasn't keeping it a secret."

"How well do you know them?"

Garrett contemplated her reaction to the full truth. And thought better of telling her that he had not personally met the men, but had found them from a trusted source. "Well enough."

Abigail looked over her shoulder. "Shhh, they'll hear you."

"I need to wake them anyway. I need their help."

She took a step closer. "Oh."

Confusion filled her expression, and he wanted to take her into his arms and make all her doubts disappear. But that wasn't his job. "Please wait here in the buggy until we set up camp. I'll come get you as soon as we're finished."

❦

A fear like Abigail had never experienced wrapped its way around her until she thought she would suffocate. It came not only from the thought of sleeping in the woods, but from the idea that maybe her family could not afford an overnight stay at an inn. Or for her to travel by train. Had that been what her father meant by an unconventional trip? And his warning for her to keep it quiet?

Would their financial stability improve with her acceptance of William's hand in marriage? His fortune was no secret and her union with the man would be advantageous.

Garrett woke the two men, and they emerged from the buggy. The three of them walked toward a small clearing surrounded by woods, and she wrapped her arms tightly around her waist. Garrett turned at the last moment and his eyes met hers. His expression was hidden, but warmth filled her from the compassion he'd shown her earlier.

A chorus of calls, yipping, and howling reached her ears. As well as the fluttering of wings unseen, the crackling of dried leaves beneath her feet. And dark shadows were already emerging from every direction.

This would be the longest night she had ever endured.

She was staring through the starry pathway leading down the hill when Garrett spoke. "Everything's ready. I set your things inside for you and you should have plenty of privacy."

She nodded, unable to voice anything reasonable. Trembling from head to toe, she allowed Garrett to guide her down the hill. Then he stopped abruptly.

"You're shaking."

"I'm just a little cold."

"Here," he said, draping a blanket across her shoulders.

She tugged at the heavy material and tucked her hands beneath it, feeling warmer instantly as she noticed the two cloth coverings placed ten yards apart from each other. Only a few pines separating them.

With each step closer to the tents, her longing to stay near Garrett intensified. "Will you be sleeping there?"

"Yes." He pointed in the direction of the other covering ten yards from hers. He cleared his throat. "You will be within my hearing should you need anything." Garrett took an extra blanket out of his bag. "If you need anything, all you need to do is tell one of my men, this is Andre, and this is Louis."

She turned to face the men for the first time, almost forgetting their presence.

"Gentlemen, this is Miss Dupree. They are at your service for anything you may need."

"It is very nice to meet you both." Did he mean to push her off on his men to take over all her needs? "And if I should need you, Mr. Barringer?" Once again, her mouth beat her good senses.

The look that crossed his face caused a rush of heat to race through her body, and she regretted her hasty decision to say such a scandalous thing.

"I will come immediately."

Though it was only yards, it felt like miles. She didn't want to be separated from him, to be the responsibility of two men she had never met. She turned away from Garrett as her eyes glazed over with fresh tears. Thankful for the first time for the darkened sky, she took a few steps forward. A long moment of uncomfortable silence hung in the air.

"Your things are already inside. We'll leave you to get settled in."

Having no choice, Abigail walked toward her tent without saying goodnight. She didn't trust herself. The thickness clogging her throat would be revealed with even a slight response. Before she could step inside, Garrett grasped her wrist and the sound of his heavy breathing against her neck nearly sent her over the edge.

"If you need anything, just call out for me."

Gazing into his worried eyes, she ached to beg him to move his own tent next to hers. But he had already worked so hard and she couldn't ask him to do such a thing. It would be dishonorable. Besides, starting all over would take more time. And he had to be tired after driving all day.

Abigail straightened. "Thank you so very much for all of your hard work, Garrett. I do hope you sleep well."

"I hope you do as well."

She slipped from his grasp and stepped through the doorway. The cloth fell back into place separating her from Garrett. With a quick sweep of the small area, Abigail found a lantern hanging from a hook in the center of the tent. A cot placed in the corner was neatly made with heavy blankets and a plump pillow at the head. A luggage bag her mother had ordered from Paris was tucked in the corner, and she lifted it from the ground and placed it onto the cot. She unlatched the buttons and opened it to find items she didn't recognize.

She paused when the voices from outside subsided.

Had he already turned in for the evening? But what of his men? Were they lingering near her tent?

Ready to crawl onto her cot and sleep the time away, Abigail pulled out a beautiful, white night dress that had been neatly folded right on top. The design was one she didn't recognize, but was very delicate, very beautiful. The silky material felt odd between her fingers in a place like this. There was no doubt her mother had also ordered this and packed it into her bag.

Perhaps she would be able to wear it tomorrow night when she would have help unlatching all the hard-to-reach loops. She had no choice but to sleep in her day dress. But perhaps it was for the best in the event that something happened and she was given no time to change. Rose had helped her dress for all occasions since Abigail's arrival in Charlotte, and hot tears burned her eyes at the thought of being out here alone. Without her dear friend.

Why were they sending Rose away? Had it been her fault? Had Mother overheard something Abigail had said to her in confidence?

What if she never saw Rose again? What if Rose did not perform well at her new position because of Abigail's own lack of propriety? Instead of wrestling with the buttons, she sat on her cot. Within moments, the tears she had kept pent up for the last hour poured in streams down her face.

"I am so sorry, Rose," Abigail whispered. She should have helped her prepare. Instead, Abigail would be responsible for ruining both of their chances.

Chapter Seventeen

Garrett kept Louis and Andre facing in the opposite direction, up on the hill, as he kept his own eyes locked on Abigail's shadow. He hoped she'd finished changing, so he could stop worrying about the men, but she stopped midway through and sat down.

He led the men to the other side of the wagon, not anticipating being able to see her silhouette. "Stay here and keep your eyes averted until I give you permission."

"Oui, Monsieur." The men said in unison.

He'd taken more time in choosing the appropriate men for this journey than he'd taken in all the other preparations. So far, he'd been pleased with their respect of Miss Dupree. Even at first sight, they showed no hint of surprise at her beauty. Dressed in the satin midnight blue gown, which matched her eyes, every man in the area would have to be dead to have not noticed her.

Making more noise than necessary with the crunching of dried branches beneath his heavy boots, Garrett made his way back down the hill toward the tent. He studied the tall trees, avoiding the direct view of the tent. But she shifted, and he faltered. The thin line of her silhouette drew him in, and he couldn't tear his gaze away. She stood again, in slow motion.

When she turned the outline of other features caused him to break out into a sweat. He scolded himself for his weakness when her gasp reached his ears.

Without thinking, he burst through the canopy separating them and took her arm. "What's wrong?"

Her eyes widened at his appearance. "Nothing. It's just that...well...where can I relieve myself?"

"Oh." With hesitance, he released her arm. "Please, allow me to show you."

Garrett led her down a small trail and toward a private area for her aforementioned need. He forced himself not to lower his head as he followed, but could tell she was still wearing the same dress and had not yet changed.

A few minutes later, they returned to the camp and he stopped her before she stepped back inside. "I apologize for bursting in without first checking to make sure—"

"It is fine. I feel a little better now, knowing I can depend on you."

"I won't let anything happen to you, Abigail." He took a step closer, his eyes falling onto her lips. A sudden rush of longing to love this woman for the rest of his life came over him so strongly it gave him pause.

Without looking back, Garrett retreated from the tent. "You should try to get some sleep. We have a long day tomorrow." With that, he secured the tent's door.

In order to have the strength needed to finish their trip, he had no choice but to try to get some rest. So, he ventured inside his own tent and prepared for a long, torturous night.

Unable to fall asleep, Garrett listened to every word being said between his two men. Though it was difficult to make out what they were saying from so far up the hill and with most of their words being spoken in French.

Could he really trust them with Abigail's welfare?

After a few minutes of tossing back and forth, he gave up on the idea of getting any sleep. After opening his own tent's door, he lifted his cot and bedding and carried it out into the open night.

"Monsieur, Barringer. What are you doing?"

He ignored the shocked look on the men's faces as he placed his bedding directly in front of the doorway of Abigail's tent. "It's too stuffy. I'm used to sleeping under the stars. You are excused to sit by the wagon. I'll stay here."

"Ahhh. Monsieur, Barringer. Amour."

"Amour?"

"Love. You are in love with Mademoiselle Dupree?"

With a grunt, Garrett plopped onto the cot and wrapped himself with the heavy blanket. It was nothing more than concern for her wellbeing.

Or was it?

&

Abigail stayed curled into a ball for most of the night, trying to stay warm. The sound of wind slipping through the trees and snapping branches didn't bother her nearly as bad as the men's voices. Their constant chatter seemed to go on forever until she thought she would never fall asleep. At first it made her feel safe having the men there, but the accent which she had once thought was so beautiful, suddenly wasn't. She couldn't understand half of what they were saying and that made things worse.

Were they talking about her? How well did Garrett know them? How well did Father know Garrett? Who could she trust? She had been suddenly thrust into the wilderness with three men.

In the morning, she stood, her body aching from lying in the same position. She pressed the wrinkles out of her dress, hoping to keep the acknowledgment of being unable to change into her night dress to herself. Garrett may have been willing to assist her if only she had asked, but deep down she knew without a shadow of a doubt, it would have been against his better judgment. And hers.

If she had been traveling with Mr. Arendell instead, she most certainly would not have been able to say the same for his character.

She brushed through her tangled hair and tried to twirl it into the same braid Rose had taught her, but it never turned out the same. After five minutes of trying and just about in tears, she finally settled on a loose braid that fell down one shoulder. The sun had only been up for a few minutes. She had heard no stirring from any of the men and wondered if any of them had woken yet.

Thankful she had made it through the night, she took a deep breath and pulled the cloth door covering separating her from the world outside. All that mattered now was that only a few hours separated her from Asheville.

The cool morning air brushed against her cheeks, and she drew in the welcoming fragrance of sausage sizzling on an open fire.

Garrett noticed her first and stood. "Good morning, Miss Dupree. I hope you slept well."

She gave her most convincing smile. "Good morning. I did, thank you. I hope you did as well." It wasn't until he glanced at her dress that she realized something she hadn't before. Of course, he would notice she was wearing the same one from yesterday.

After breakfast, the men loaded camp and they were on their way, much to Abigail's delight. The sooner they left, the sooner she'd get to Aunt Louisa's.

§.

The rutted trail led them closer to their destination, Asheville, North Carolina. Garrett couldn't help but enjoy the sweet fragrance filling the air surrounding them He could get used to listening to the soft rhythm of her steady breathing.

Abigail gave him a searching look before fiddling with the buttons at her waist.

After several seconds, she blurted, "What does your family do for a living?"

"Farming."

"Oh? That is something that has always fascinated me. You never said why you traveled to New York." Thankfully she had skipped to a safer topic. "Did you attend Columbia University or one of the other law schools?"

"Unfortunately, I did not."

"Oh?"

Garrett hadn't quite caught Abigail's expression. So, he was unable to determine whether or not disquiet resided there.

"Where then *did* you do your studying?"

The barrage of questions pounded against him like stinging bullets, each one digging closer to the truth. Better to be honest than not. Resigned, he freed air from between his stiff lips. "I did not actually go to school for law."

"But I thought…" Abigail's voice trailed off.

"I am considering the idea of law," he interjected before she could think on the subject too long.

Garrett gave her a sidelong glance and he caught a glimpse of the furrowing of Abigail's brows. "I am what you might call an understudy."

A fog of confusion swam in her eyes. "I thought that to be a theatre term."

"It is. And in fact, it is in some ways similar to our agreement."

Abigail sat up a little straighter at his affirmation. "So, you are pretending?"

"No, that is not what I meant. It's rather complicated." He

paused in his struggle to find a simple explanation. "Your father hired me for the position and I accepted it."

"But he is unaware?" Abigail's voice dawdled to nothing as she suddenly looked as if she were sitting next to a complete stranger.

Swallowing a laugh at the look of sheer panic on Abigail's face, Garrett reached over and touched her arm. "He is fully aware."

Abigail caught his eye, maintained a look of hesitation for all of three seconds, then released a full grin. "If you are not a lawyer, what exactly is it that you do?"

"I travel and write about the people and places that I visit."

Abigail crossed her arms. "Don't you dare tease me, Garrett Barringer."

"Me?" Garrett smiled at the return of the trusting glint in her eyes. "Never would I presume to do such a thing."

"Very well, then." After a rather exasperating sigh, she continued. "You must tell me every single detail of the perfect position."

"The perfect position?"

"Indeed." Abigail laughed. "Why didn't you know? Traveling the world and filling a book with all my adventures is one of which I have only dared dream."

Garrett eyed her curiously. How was he to explain that he had all but given up the opportunity presented to him only a few months ago?

Chapter Eighteen

They arrived at Aunt Louisa's late that afternoon. The outstretched arms of her aunt waiting to embrace her caused a fresh wave of tears. They remained in an embrace for several minutes before Aunt Louisa released her. Ignoring the bouncing sensation from the many hours on the wagon trail, Abigail stretched out her hand. "This is—"

"The Mr. Barringer I've heard so much about. It is such a pleasure to finally meet you." She reached for Abigail then and led them both inside.

Aunt Louisa's reaction to Garrett didn't surprise Abigail as much as the familiarity she seemed to have with the man. What had Father told Louisa? *I've known him his entire life.* Rekindling her father's words, curiosity welled within her. How much did Aunt Louisa know of Garrett Barringer? Night would not fall before she asked her aunt that very question.

Garrett Barringer had been working his wiles on her from the moment they met. An effort that was working, indeed. But she could not make the same mistake with Garrett Barringer that she had made with Randall Thorne.

She would not.

So, as soon as Garrett stepped outside to gather their bags, Abigail asked her long-awaited question. "Have you seen him?"

Confusion tightened the bridge of Louisa's forehead. "Seen him? Mr. Barringer?"

"No." Abigail glanced over her shoulder to ensure Garrett had not returned, yet still she whispered. "Randall Thorne?"

Aunt Louisa propped both hands against her slender hips. "And here I thought you came all this way to visit me?"

"Of course, I did." Gradual shame inched over her at her thoughtlessness. "I missed you so much."

"I have missed you as well. How was the big city?" No response was needed. With one glance, her aunt understood. "Your father wrote to me about all that was going on." Aunt Louisa frowned. "I knew you would not be happy about the arrangement."

Heart in her throat, Abigail swallowed hard. Father had told her? That meant that he intended to see it through. How would she ever go through with a marriage to William Arendell? There would no longer be any hope of finding true love. Not that she fully expected to ever find someone willing to overlook her past sins.

Would her penalty ever be paid in full?

She had already lived through the most painful period of her life. All her grief had been self-inflicted, but she'd paid the price, time and time again. And would continue to pay. Her father had comforted her, while her mother only blamed her. Abigail had believed her father would never give in to the idea of his only daughter's marriage to a man she could barely stomach for the benefit of forever concealing her shame.

Apparently, she had been wrong.

Taking a deep harrowing breath, Abigail put on a brave face. "It's the best thing for the family. I have certainly caused enough trouble for my parents to last a lifetime. This will be my way of making it up to them." She had no choice. Not unless her plan worked. A plan that had been spinning a web through her mind, the minute she learned that she would be returning to the foothills of North Carolina. "Unless, I can convince Ran—"

The door closed behind her. Heart in her throat, Abigail swallowed hard.

Mr. Barringer grunted. "I do believe that is everything, then."

"Wonderful." Aunt Louisa stepped forward. "Thank you, Mr. Barringer."

"I do need to see to the horses."

Just when Abigail managed to control her pulse, she glanced his way and his gaze melded into hers.

Then his brows furrowed. "Should I leave the bags here for now?"

"Yes, please."

Garrett complied, although uncertainty lingered in his features.

Aunt Louisa continued. "I will show you to your rooms when you have seen to your horses."

"Very well. I shall return."

Abigail glanced up once more at Garrett as he retreated to the door.

"Your father made a good choice in Mr. Barringer. He's a very pleasant gentleman."

"Yes. He made the awkwardness of the trip…more comfortable."

Abigail glanced toward his retreating form. Not only had he made her more comfortable, he had made the prospect of marrying out of obligation even more daunting. Unbeknownst to the man, Garrett Barringer had rekindled a spark in her heart that had been dead for five years. Which made Abigail wonder if her father's choice had been ill-advised. Or rather ill-timed. Unfortunately, a future with Garrett Barringer was unattainable with her tainted past, but with a marriage to Randall, the prospect of love was at the very least possible.

Of course, if she convinced Randall to fall in love with her, her parents would have no choice but to approve.

Abigail searching longingly at her aunt. "I do, however, need—"

"Let's not worry about things until we need to." Aunt Louisa placed a hand on Abigail's arm. "You are here, now. And if I understand correctly, you will stay for the rest of the summer."

Regulating her disappointment, Abigail smiled. "Yes. And I am so thankful for the opportunity to spend time with you."

"It has been more than a year since I have seen your Mr. Thorne, Abigail." Apprehension tightened the corners of her aunt's mouth. "We will have the best time, though. I have so many things planned."

Had he moved, then? Allowing the disappointing news to settle in her heart, Abigail searched the living space. "I do love your home. Everything is so quaint."

Abigail faced a small sitting room where bright rays of sunlight poured in through the front double windows. The pastel colors of the furniture complemented the dark wood floors. An oil lamp decorated with golden designs sat on the end table next to the rocking chair. A pencil drawing hung in the corner near the fireplace.

"Thank you. It's humble, but ours."

"I think it is absolutely perfect." Abigail moved in front of the drawing of a mountain range as she imagined having her own place someday. The picture faded as that thought quickly turned toward a dark corner as she remembered Rose would not accompany her to a new home. Unable to bear the thought of losing her dear friend a moment more, she shook her head to clear her vision. "You have everything decorated so pretty, but this is my favorite picture."

"That is one of my students' artwork. She's taking an art class and draws almost as much as she reads."

"One of your students? How old is she?"

"Only thirteen."

Abigail's mind spun as she admired the creative genius of a person so young of age. "Wow! It's wonderful. She must have been truly blessed with opportunity."

"Unfortunately, the girl comes from a very poor family, as do most of my students."

"Oh?" Abigail frowned. "I am so sorry to hear that."

"I suppose there wasn't much work for the men in this part of the land." The tight lines on her aunt's face gradually softened. "That is, until Mr. Vanderbilt decided to build here."

"Father mentioned that Uncle Henry is working at the Biltmore Estate?"

"Yes, there has been no shortage of jobs, thanks to George Vanderbilt and the construction of his new home. Now, that the Biltmore is complete, he has added other projects. Keeping your uncle very busy. The work has certainly been hard with long hours, but undoubtedly rewarding."

It had been five years since they had moved to the city, but she recalled that job security had been one of the main reasons for their departure. At least that was her father's reason for leaving the area, even if it had not been her mother's. Though looking back, she had no interest in her parents' reasoning, only that her own heart was being ripped to shreds. Broken and bruised by the very man she had come back to this very place to find.

If it hadn't been for their departure, though, she would never have met Rose.

Abigail swallowed the emotion that thickened in her throat. "Speaking of men," Abigail glanced beyond her. "Where is Uncle Henry?"

"Still working. But he should be home in plenty of time to join us for dinner. He is anxious to see you as well and looking forward to meeting Mr. Barringer."

Aunt Louisa's statement brought Abigail back to the question she had intended to ask. "How is it that you already knew of Mr. Barringer?"

"I didn't, exactly. Only what your father wrote of him."

"My father said that he had known the gentleman his entire life. And he did mention he was from this area. But Mr. Barringer stated that they had only just met."

"I'm not certain, but there is one indisputable detail." Aunt Louisa gave her a pointed look. "Your father would never allow you to travel accompanied by a complete stranger."

"I am well aware of that. So, imagine my surprise when the man showed up on our doorstep and within weeks my father gave him the sole responsibility of becoming my chaperone for this trip." A deed, of which, she still wasn't sure she approved.

"I imagine it was a surprise, but it seems you get along well enough."

"Yes, but it was not so easy in the beginning." Especially with him treating her like a child who couldn't take care of herself.

"Oh?"

"Our first meeting was at a ball." Abigail shook her head. "No, actually I ran into him prior to arriving. Where he thought to save me from myself. Though uninvited."

"This story is sounding more interesting all the time." Aunt Louisa took a seat. "I should love to hear the full account some-time before you leave."

Abigail laughed and took a chair across from her as she thought back on their first conversation. "And I should be happy to oblige." Which, thankfully, led her thoughts in a different direction. "I have heard the Vanderbilts' new home is wonderful. Do you think perhaps we would—"

Garrett stepped back inside, interrupting her thought.

"That should take care of everything, then." Garrett held her gaze for several seconds, then frowned. "Please, forgive me. I did not mean to interrupt."

"Oh, no." Abigail swallowed. "You didn't. I was only complimenting Aunt Louisa on her beautiful home."

He stepped forward. "I should thank you as well for offering me a room in your lovely home."

"You are most certainly welcome," Aunt Louisa said. "And thank you so much, Mr. Barringer, for accompanying my niece. I can't tell you how very happy I am to have you both here."

Garrett clasped his hands behind his back and rocked on the balls of his feet. "It has been my absolute pleasure."

Moved by his sincere courtesy, Abigail felt the room tilt and she wobbled back.

"What is it, Abigail? Is something wrong?" Garrett took her arm, exposing his apprehension of her unstableness. Probably reining in memories of the other day when she fainted in his presence. "Do you feel unwell?"

Garrett Barringer would make a wonderful husband. Attentive. Appreciative. A rare man to find, indeed.

As quickly as the notion materialized, it vanished along with her stamina. Garrett Barringer would never be available to someone like her. And she should never allow such thoughts to enter her mind again.

"It's nothing. I'm most likely overly tired from the trip." She looked across the living room and into the kitchen. "May I lie down awhile before dinner?"

Garrett harrumphed. "Unfortunately, I do not believe she was able to get much rest."

A grimace folded Abigail's lips. She knew she had most likely cost him his fair share of sleep as well.

"Yes, of course. You both must be exhausted and anxious to get settled. There is plenty of time for you both to relax before we take our evening meal."

Garrett's silence had been evidence of his unease, but it was as if all discomfort had vanished. Her heart suffered from loss, from the obligation to her family, from the long, frightening trip.

It had all cost her much. But he had been there for her through it all, and had settled her anxiety whether he was aware of his affect or not.

When she looked at him, he blinked and lifted a warm smile. Affection lurched in her stomach. It was becoming increasingly difficult to keep her heart in check where Garrett Barringer was concerned. And she couldn't afford the luxury of giving in to silly notions.

"What I mean is, we didn't get much rest and I would like to join her."

Abigail's eyes widened.

"At the same time. Not the same place," he verified, springing a laugh from all of them.

"Yes, of course," Aunt Louisa said with residual amusement. "Let me show you to your rooms and you can both relax while I prepare dinner."

After Garrett was settled in his room, Aunt Louisa led Abigail to the next bedroom.

Abigail stopped. "Is this it?"

"Is something wrong with it?"

"No, it's just that…" Abigail lowered her voice to a whisper. "Garrett is right next door."

"Yes, but I have no other options." Aunt Louisa lowered her voice even more. "I do not believe you have anything to worry about. Mr. Barringer is highly respected."

She was fully aware of that. "That is not what I meant. Thank you, this is a wonderful room."

Sluggishly, Garrett settled onto the bed, but at the sound of voices next door, he stilled. Abigail had said something about the room. When he'd first met her, he would've thought she would complain that it wasn't big enough, or nice enough, but now, he knew better. It would have nothing to do with that. And then he heard his name.

She was disappointed to be placed in the room next to him. Surely, she wouldn't think he meant her harm. But what other reason could there be?

Just as he dozed off, soft voices seeped through the thin walls. He inched up with too much force and slammed his arm against the headboard. The voices dissipated, replaced by a distinct sound of rustling of clothing for a full minute before they resumed.

"I have to see him."

Garrett paused. Him? Him who? Could it be the man of who Mr. Dupree had warned him?

"I'm not certain that is the best decision."

"Aunt Louisa, I have no choice."

Tightening his jaw, he leaned closer against the wall as the pleading resumed.

"There's a chance to work things out. Especially if I tell—"

"Abigail, no. It's a mistake. Your father would never allow this."

"You don't understand." Another brief pause. "This could be the answer. Please, Aunt Louisa? I can't marry William Arendell. I would rather die." Abigail's voice broke with exhaustion.

She needed rest, yet she was worried over William Arendell and finding the man who Garrett had hoped would never be brought to light. Yet, now he regretted his decision to hold back information that would put the young woman's heart at rest. But he had hoped to learn for himself of the man's character before turning him loose with Abigail's heart.

A long silence lingered after the door closed. Then Abigail's voice came through even clearer.

"Father God, please get me through this. I want to be in Your will, not mine."

The soft, yet powerful prayer was familiar. The angst of

wanting to stay in God's will, yet desperation to retain some control was a generality that, of which, he assumed most Christians struggled. Especially of things that would seem detrimental in our limited vision.

But God always wanted the best for His children.

It was the letting go of fear and laying it at the Father's feet that personal yearnings most often got in the way.

His chest tightened with affection. The hesitancy of caring for Anthony Dupree's only daughter in her father's absence had taken a sharp turn. As exhausting as Abigail Dupree could be, it was her heart that had captured him fully.

Unable to pinpoint the exact moment the duty to her father transformed into a desire to protect her for himself, of one thing he had no doubt...he had grown attached to the woman.

Chapter Nineteen

A few days had passed since Abigail had returned to Asheville and she was no closer to finding Randall than if she were hundreds of miles away. Hope still lingered that if she could find only one chance to plead her case, she could convince Randall to fulfill the promise of taking her hand.

But with Garrett determined to follow her father's wishes to have her remain within sight of him or her aunt, the deed of finding Randall, let alone making him fall in love with her, proved more difficult with each passing day.

Garrett had taken his leave for a meeting, so Aunt Louisa had brought her along to run a few errands in town. Abigail wanted nothing more than to get out of the house for a few hours. Perhaps to even have an opportunity to ask a neighbor or two of Randall Thorne's whereabouts.

Aunt Louisa parked the carriage and stepped down from it. "I need to grab some staple items for the pantry while we're here. Is there anything specific you or Garrett would enjoy having for a meal?"

"You are a wonderful cook, Aunt Louisa. Anything you prepare will suit us fine." Abigail looked ahead at the familiar shops. "Do you mind if I walk around for a few minutes?"

Aunt Louisa tendered an uncertain smile. "I suppose not. Just don't wander off too far. I promised Mr. Barringer to keep you within my sights."

Abigail gave her aunt an unenthusiastic look. The whole thing was becoming a little ridiculous. What sort of trouble could she get into here? And what was he so worried about anyway?

Abigail allowed a peek of a smile that was buried behind her displeasure of having to explain herself. "I'll stay close."

Still harboring a look of doubt, Aunt Louisa nodded. "Okay, then. I shouldn't be too long."

"Take your time."

The mountains loomed even larger than Abigail remembered, though she had lived in the area most of her life. The white tips matched the gathering clouds, enhancing the blue hue of the sky. A sight she had missed even more desperately than she would have thought.

The merchants and locals hadn't changed much over the last five years, and most greeted her by name. She entered a shop on the corner and scanned items on the first few tables as she inhaled the familiar scents of wood and spice.

"Miss Abigail Dupree? Is that you?"

Abigail turned at the distinctive high-pitched voice of Mrs. Lewiston. One of the ladies her mother had cautioned her to avoid. "Yes, ma'am."

"How lovely to see you. Isn't it just wonderful, Margie?" Mrs. Lewiston asked of her companion. "How is your mother?"

"And your father?" The two questions merged into one as if asked by a lone individual. The two ladies were known for their ability to share information at any given moment about the happenings in the community.

Abigail looked up. Mrs. Lewison's eyes, magnified by the lenses she wore, still waited for a response. Abigail's gaze shifted to Mrs. Taylor who offered a superficial smile.

"They are very well, thank you."

"That's wonderful to hear, dear." The sincerity in Mrs. Lewiston's statement gave Abigail pause.

"I hadn't realized your family had returned to the area." Mrs. Taylor's deeper tone reverberated with more than simple interest. "You must tell us where to find her. It has been too many years since we have seen or heard from her."

A quiver of unease squirmed through Abigail's middle. The women could not have been less obvious in their intentions to gather information. The very thing of which her mother had warned.

A hard lump of apprehension clustered in the back of Abigail's throat. There was only one way to answer truthfully. "Unfortunately, my parents did not accompany me."

Mrs. Lewiston's tongue clicked as if with disapproval. "Is that so?"

"Yes, ma'am," Abigail said, anxious to move away from their questioning eyes and to continue in her search for—

"It's a wonder your mother would trust you to come all this way alone," Mrs. Taylor said, as if allowing a wayward daughter to travel unaccompanied compared to committing a heinous crime.

Abigail would never admit that her parents had in fact allowed her to make the trip across the mountainous excursion with a man only three years her senior. A very handsome gentleman.

If they were to ascertain that additional information, the two women would be horrified.

The insinuation festered old wounds as thoughts of her past and her mother's warnings not to offer too much information collided in her head. No need to leave the women with any negative thoughts pertaining to her parents. "My father sent a chaperone to see to my safety."

"Oh? Well thank goodness for that. Your father has always

been a very level-headed gentleman, so there is no doubt he chose wisely, for you are a very attractive young lady."

"That is so kind of you."

The chaperone her father had chosen was indeed too good to be true. And unfortunately, Garrett Barringer would never think of her more than—

"What brings you all this way, then?" Mrs. Taylor gave her a questionable look.

Although Abigail worried about saying too much, she didn't think the truth could cause much harm, so she answered, "I am here to spend some time with my Aunt Louisa."

"Oh?" Mrs. Lewiston's brows arched. "I had almost forgotten about your father's sweet sister. Louisa must be tickled pink to have her only niece come all this way from the Queen City."

Mrs. Lewiston's knowledge of their whereabouts unnerved her. The critical way she named the township even more so. Had her mother kept in touch with the woman all of these years?

The light dimmed in Mrs. Lewiston's eyes. "But still. It is such a shame your parents were unable to join you, for I would have dearly loved to have visited with your mother."

"Yes, that would have been so nice, dear," Mrs. Taylor declared, her frown matching Mrs. Lewiston's.

"I am certain my mother would have enjoyed that as well," Abigail offered even as the idea of their silent accusations rankled her. "I will be sure to mention that I ran into you ladies."

Mrs. Lewiston took Abigail's hands into her own. "Oh, yes, please do." Her suspicious pause caused Abigail another spasm of discomfort. "And it is absolutely wonderful to see you. You certainly are lovely, Abigail."

"Isn't she though. I always knew she would grow into a beautiful young woman," Mrs. Taylor added.

Abigail blinked away some of her harsh judgments of the two ladies. Had her mother been wrong about their sincerity?

Though cynical, they did not seem quite as critical as her mother had described. "It is so wonderful to see you, both. Perhaps I will have the pleasure of meeting you again, before I return home."

"Yes, dear. We do hope to see you again. But if not, you take good care of yourself."

Mrs. Taylor lifted a gloved hand. "And please do not forget to tell your parents hello and give them our well wishes."

Abigail answered with a generous smile, her cheeks flaming over her previous concern to hide any pertinent information from the ladies.

"Could've had her choice of any man in Buncombe County," one of the ladies continued as if Abigail weren't still within hearing range.

"Shame she had to leave on account of her mother's illness," Mrs. Lewiston said in a softer yet still eligible tone.

Her mother's illness? Abigail pondered the women's words as she left the store. Whatever did that mean? Had her mother forged a story to keep Abigail's reputation untarnished?

Turning to walk in the opposite direction of which she had come, her breath caught in her throat as she nearly ran into Randall Thorne.

Chapter Twenty

"Abigail Dupree? Is it really you?"

He remembered her. Warmth spread through her veins entirely too rapidly. In an effort to hinder her mouth from smiling too widely, she bit her lip.

Randall considered her intently. "You are the last person I ever expected to see when I ventured out this morning."

Abigail watched him closely during his extended look of shock.

He kept his gaze locked with hers. "What on earth are you doing in Asheville?"

She retreated half a step. Had he not remembered this had been her home? A home where some of her family still resided. "I'm visiting...my aunt...for the summer," she said, with false confidence.

"Oh, that's right. I had forgotten you still had relatives living here." Randall glanced about them before realigning his eyes with hers. "Did your husband accompany you?"

Heat raced up her neck as she remembered in detail his own lengthy proposal. "I have not married."

His eyes widened. "You? Unmarried?" The favor she had experienced from the gentleman's leer as a younger woman intensified within the span of a few seconds. Randall closed the distance between them with one deliberate stride. "I cannot believe you are actually here standing before me. And unmarried. Fate must be on my side. You have changed so much."

"Have I?" It had been nearly five years since they had last set eyes on one another. She pulled at a tendril that had fallen loose from her bun. "I could say the same of you." But it wasn't exactly a true statement. Perhaps his hair had thinned out a bit or the receding lines of his hair was deeper. She couldn't be certain. Still, he was a sight to behold.

"I must say, you are as beautiful as ever. Only more so, if that were possible." His words resonated with admiration, leaving little room for her response. She certainly couldn't return the endearment. No matter how handsome she may think him to be.

Now though, in her examination of him, she found herself assessing the differences between him and Garrett Barringer.

Good heavens. Comparing the two men was preposterous. Especially since her only likely marriage options were the man standing before her or the repugnant choice waiting back in Charlotte.

Randall cleared his throat. "How long did you say were you planning to stay?"

"I didn't, since I'm not certain of the length of time. However, I should remain in town a few weeks at the very least."

"Is that so?" He clasped his hands together as if he had just won a grand prize.

His gape roamed the length of her and the simple gesture launched a chill straight through to her bones. Remembering that last night in his arms, once again her neck flamed.

Randall gave her an all-too-innocent look. "I do hope you will be willing to spare some time for me."

Abigail bit her lip to tame her smile. "You wish to spend time with me?"

"Of course, I would. But I am jumping ahead of myself, as

usual. How are you, Abigail? Or should I say, how have you been?"

Of course, she would never tell him the answer to the real question he was seeking. "I am well." It was mostly true. He couldn't possibly know the torture this was causing. Or how she had suffered at his departure. Nor would she ever tell him.

"That is so wonderful to hear," he said imperiously, raking his eyes over her as if he still held possession.

She sketched on a smile. "And, how have you been?"

"Well. There's more work than play, but maybe now that you are here that will change. I have missed you," he admitted in a broken whisper as he took her hands and ran his fingers over her knuckles intimately. "I often thought of writing, but did not want to cause friction with your family since my leaving came at an inopportune time."

An inopportune time? Was that what he believed? They were to be married and after seducing her into a sinful night of intimate passion he'd disappeared without a word, but with another woman.

"I have so wanted to talk to you, to explain my leaving." His frown seemed to beg for release of any pain he may have caused her. "So many things have happened since our last meeting."

He would describe their last night together as a meeting?

All the blood drained from her head and flashes of dots appeared before her eyes. She blinked against the sudden wave of dizziness assaulting her.

Seeing him now put the last five years in a whole new perspective. But perhaps he had changed his ways. Perhaps now he would do the honorable thing. She had allowed this man to affect her for one-half of a decade and would not abandon her motivation over a foolish statement.

Randall would be a far better match for her than Mr. Arendell. And it seemed from the way he looked at her, that it wouldn't be difficult to regain his hand. She only had to convince him to marry her as he had promised all those years ago. Then things could resume to their natural state because her family's honor would be restored. Though nothing would ever cleanse her of the filth that had desecrated her in those reckless moments.

He took a step closer. "I am so very happy to see you, Abigail. I thought after what happened between us…" He paused and glanced around to make sure no one was listening. "I thought I would never have the opportunity…"

She stepped back, putting much-needed distance between them. He stood in his familiar stance. The way he'd always held control of her. She would not allow him that authority. He'd manipulate the situation and within seconds would have her heart reined in. She had to maintain control. She had to retain all the power this time. "Well, as you can see, I am here now."

The quizzical look in his eyes made her wonder if she'd been mistaken all along about his true feelings toward her. If he had really regretted how things ended? Had he? If so, why then had he not come for her?

"Yes, you are. Much to my great delight. And there's much to discuss."

Abigail looked away quickly, worried she would give into him, but when he took her chin in his fingers and forced her to meet his gaze, something stirred within her—something she hadn't expected. Apprehension.

"It seems as though we have something in common." He took her hand. "I too have remained unmarried."

Before she was able to respond to his admission of their similarities, a hand touched her shoulder.

Startled, Abigail turned. "Mr. Barringer?" A rush of awareness at Garrett's sudden presence brought a wave of emotions that nearly took her breath.

He was focused on Randall, but his features, though rigid, remained appealing. How could she think such thoughts at a time

AN UNLIKELY ARRANGEMENT

like this? Comparing Randall to Garrett. There was no comparison. With a rush of logic, she realized suddenly that Randall Thorne wasn't perfect. His irises were set apart a little too far, making him the slightest bit, cock-eyed. A smile played on her lips. She wasn't as hopelessly in love with this man as she'd believed from the time he left.

She drew in a much-needed breath. "Mr. Barringer, what on earth are you doing here? I never expected to run into you."

He said nothing but continued to scrutinize Randall.

"Please forgive me. I would like to introduce you to Randall Thorne." Abigail's face burned, and she watched the slow reaction of Garrett's steady expression. His features never wavered other than his perfect lips creasing thin lines into his tanned cheeks.

"A pleasure to meet you, Mr. Thorne. I am Garrett Barringer. Abigail's guardian."

Her guardian? How dare he use that term when introducing himself to this man of all people! She wanted to turn and storm away from them both, but she held her ground.

What good would that do anyway? She would look like a complete fool. Her brows creased into firm lines even now, and she needed to force them free or she would be caught in her ill state of mind. Taking another deep breath, she relaxed her shoulders.

"Mr. Barringer, the pleasure is mine." Randall gave a slight bow of his head. "And now that you are here, I can offer my request."

Garrett's eyes narrowed. "Your request?"

Randall reclaimed her hand. "Yes, I was hoping to steal Abigail away for a few hours."

A few hours? Randall's request reeled through her mind. For an instant, fear shot through her frame. Of course, she had no say-so over the matter. Garrett would have to give his permission first.

169

And if he did allow her to spend time with Randall, it would be difficult in the presence of Garrett or her aunt, but she didn't have much choice. Unless she found a way to sneak away. Much like the very night she first met Garrett Barringer.

Abigail dismissed the thought. Time wasn't an entity she could afford to waste. She had to see her plan through. And things were going even smoother than she dared dreamed. Although the prickly edges of doubt shooting through her veins were making it all very painful. Though, better to be wary of the man, than to be smitten.

"I'm afraid I cannot let you do that," Garrett replied, his voice flat, but dominant.

Blood quickened through her veins. Garrett's fingers grasped her shoulder, and though the feel of his hand sent a sudden surge of tingles down her arm, anger overrode every other jumbled emotion.

"In fact, I must take Abby home now."

The pet-name loosened a torrent of butterflies in her chest. Abigail sucked in a deep, agonizing breath. Before she could gather her wits, Garrett continued.

"If you wish to visit with her, it must be in the presence of her aunt or myself."

Randall took a step forward. "Excuse me, sir? But you must not know who I am?" He stood straighter with both hands behind his back, relaxed and confident. Too close to her for comfort.

"Of course, I do. Would you believe her father to be so ignorant a man that he would send his beautiful daughter away without giving every detail needed for her wellbeing?"

Her father had told Garrett about Randall? How could he?

"And you presume that I would wish her harm?" Randall challenged.

As a slow thread of humiliation traveled to the forefront of her mind, she stole a peek at Garrett. Not even the slightest hint of his confidence waned under Randall's accusation. And it was only then that she noticed that Randall stood a quarter of a foot shorter than Garrett.

Garrett gave a sarcastic chuckle. But even that did nothing to mar his handsome features. "I presume nothing, sir. I only adhere to the orders I was given by her father. Now, if you'll excuse us, Mr. Thorne, Abby has a prior engagement."

At Garrett's boldness, she stood motionless, his hand still gently attached to her.

"Her name is Abigail and it would be in your best interest to not use pet names for someone so important to me. I will see you soon, Abigail. I will come to your aunt's house, if I must," Randall said, giving Garrett a side-eyed glare, "so that we may finish our discussion. In private."

Abigail nodded at Randall before turning toward the market. "I must find Aunt Louisa."

"I have already spoken with her and told her of my plan to see you back to the house. Now, we must go." Garrett took her arm and led her to a rented carriage a short walking distance from them.

Abigail dared not look at Garrett as she snatched a corner of her dress and took a step up into the carriage. Garrett, who was trailing right behind her, climbed inside and took the adjacent seat.

Abigail stretched her legs out and crossed them together, her focus on the hem of her skirt. Garrett was silent and aloof as the buggy rolled forward. Abigail took a deep breath and lifted her head to look at him. She wanted to ask why he had rented a carriage, but her humiliation dominated her train of thought.

For a mere heartbeat, she resolved to never speak to him again, before blurting, "How dare you embarrass me!"

His eyes locked with hers and never wavered as he concentrated on her with such depth, a torrent of nerves danced through her stomach. "Embarrass you? That's funny. For it was my intention to keep you from doing that exact thing to yourself."

Her fascination with Garrett Barringer blended with searing anger, salvaging her good senses. "What on earth is that supposed to mean?"

Garrett leaned forward, bringing them only inches from each other. "He showed no respect for you, yet you were nearly falling all over the man. Allowing him to touch you in that way. In broad daylight."

In what way? Hot flashes of regret swam through her veins. Had Garrett been sitting there watching through their entire exchange? How much had he witnessed? Her mind spooled backward to her first reaction to seeing Randall?

Garrett leaned back, his focus abandoning hers for the first time since the argument started.

"You were watching me?" She should've known. "Respect, huh? Mr. Barringer, would your version of respect include leering at a woman while she is unaware by the river and not fully dressed?"

"I was not aware of your undress that day as I approached," he said, unruffled. "And furthermore, I was not leering."

"But instead of leaving, you stayed. Even after you saw me in my…" Her eyes darted around the cab. Why had she brought that up?

"Your what?" he said, with an arrogant tip of his chin as if the accusation did nothing to deter him.

Her insides sparked with shades of red. "My state of undress."

He continued to stare through the window. "I was only concerned for your safety and shocked that a woman of your stature would traipse about…" His words stumbled into a pause. "Well, at any rate, if I had known the incident would be thrown into my face, I would have kept my presence unknown but would have still seen to your safe return."

With that, his gaze met hers fully and held hers for several moments. Her heart drummed violently under his steady stare until she was forced to look away.

"I made a promise to your father." He scoffed, tugging her focus back to him. Sadness surfaced in his eyes, not anger. "I intend to keep that promise."

Abigail inclined toward him and spoke for their ears alone. "I was with my aunt."

"Yes. And that was my mistake alone, trusting that you would remain in her presence."

Abigail jetted a hiss through a crack in her lips. "That is absurd."

"Is it, though? Your aunt was nowhere in sight and if she had seen the way you were behaving in the middle of town for all to see…" He flung his hands out, but then quickly brought them back to his lap. "I am beyond thankful that I showed up when I did before you could damage your reputation."

The reprimand whipped her body back, and her mouth widened with shock. "How dare you question my modest behavior. He is a gentleman who also happens to be a former family friend."

"A gentleman?" The grim twist of his lips deepened. "And modest behavior is the uttermost opposite of how you exploited yourself in the man's presence."

Abigail glared at him. "I beg your pardon, but you know not what you say."

He blinked once, clothed entirely with all the confidence that she lacked. "As for a gentleman, I am not certain he is deserving of such a title. Since a gentleman would never encourage such a public display of affection."

An awkward grimace took possession of her. More truth glared in Garrett's discernment than she cared to admit. But what of his perception of her?

A bitter ache moved down her throat. Had she behaved in the way Garrett observed? Had she been so desperate to reunite with

Randall that she gave no regard to her morality? Had she made a fool of herself and lost a possibility to regain her good name and her only chance at reconciliation?

Garrett said nothing further and kept his attention averted, a glower breaching his mouth.

The thump of each crevice in the road reached through her. An overdose of heartache and responsibility for her careless actions had left her desperate to right them.

"You cannot keep me from seeing him."

"No, I cannot." His eyes joined hers in an implacable lock. "But you will see him only under my supervision."

"Is it your intention to treat me like a child?" A mixture of hurt feelings and raw emotion fought their way to the surface. She struggled to keep them in balance. "Or are you attempting to punish me?"

His gaze fell to her neckline, and heat warmed her insides. "You are no child, Abby. You are a beautiful, young woman. And…"

Abby? It wasn't the first time Garrett had shortened her name, nor had it been the only time he had referred to her as beautiful. The pet-name had made Randall angry, but it wreaked havoc on her already quavering nerves. She gathered her legs beneath her, and smoothed down her skirts, needing a moment to calm her racing heart. "And what?"

"Nothing. That is all I meant to say."

He stared through the window, while she took several calming breaths as she listened to the unhurried rush of his breathing. Her remaining anger subsided over the next few moments as she fought through her own uncertainties. A longing to be held in high esteem by the man sitting across from her made things more difficult indeed. Not only did his opinion of her matter for reasons pertaining to her father, it was vital for reasons she couldn't quite fathom.

They had spent several days together and he had treated her

with the highest regard, as though she were the most important woman in the world. As if he enjoyed being in her company.

"Was it necessary to embarrass me?"

He pegged her with a pained look. "I don't know what you mean."

Her posture bled of its tension when she glanced in his direction and found his countenance had softened though he kept his eyes trained through the open window. "Your charge, Garrett? Is that how you think of me? Is that *all* I am to you?"

That got his attention. He pivoted toward her, and the expression that crossed his features grabbed hers.

She wasn't sure when or how, but though the buggy still moved, it was as if they did not. They sat staring at each other and no sound existed, not even the wheels bouncing beneath them.

Her heart dropped and landed in the very pit of her stomach when his hand steadily stroked her brow and departed with a loosened strand of her hair slipped in between his fingers. Electricity danced over her skin as her heart thudded against her chest. He leaned in closer, his lips parted, his focus locked on her mouth.

What was he doing? What was she allowing him to do?

With a stunned flutter of lashes, Abigail shrank back from Garrett's gaze.

In the next moment, it was as if something snapped him back to reality. He straightened and turned from her.

The driver opened the door and Garrett hurried off the stoop before stretching out a hand to assist her. "Let's go."

Her heart still pounding in her chest, she placed her trembling fingers in his hand. With a few steps forward, she gained her feet as she relished the tender moment that had been only a few heartbeats ago.

Garrett led her along the sidewalk and didn't slow until they reached the railing in front of Louisa's house.

She moved to stand in front of him. "You failed to answer me. Do you see me only as your charge and nothing more?"

His eyes remained focused on the house. "I made a promise to your father to keep you safe. And I intend to keep that promise whether or not you deem it beneficial to you. Now, I must take my leave. I have a meeting to attend."

Abigail's humiliation doubled at Garrett's heartless reply after such a warm display of affection. Or had she imagined the entire scenario in the carriage?

No. She most certainly had not.

Uncertain of the exact reason why, she fled past him into the house, hurried to her guest room, and locked herself inside.

Chapter Twenty-One

G arrett wrestled with his inconvenient feelings for Abigail as the driver steered the horses through another acre of deep winding roads.

Finding Abigail standing across from Randall Thorne this morning had brought about an onslaught of protectiveness that exceeded even Mr. Dupree's requirements. For Abigail's father had warned that the young woman wanted nothing more than to reunite with Mr. Thorne. Something, of which, Garrett had trouble envisioning.

Seeing Thorne pursue her on a busy street of Asheville with curious eyes looking on, unchained a fury in Garrett that surpassed his resentment of William Arendell. A pang of regret poked at him as he recalled Abigail's look of utter shock at his intrusion.

Now that he'd had time to think on the matter, Garrett had come to realize that his duty to Abigail had distorted into something way beyond a professional commitment. A forbidden characteristic by his own measure. For, he had almost given into his desire to kiss the woman. "God, you have provided me with work. Have brought me back to my hometown. But why, Lord, have you placed this woman in my path and allowed my heart to soften toward her if I am to hand her over to another man?"

No answers were forthcoming, so he stared through the open window, until, finally, ahead of him, the extravagant structure loomed. A sight for which he had not been mentally prepared.

After he exited his carriage, Garrett walked toward the main entrance. There stood a man already waiting to escort him inside. "You must be Mr. Barringer?"

Garrett nodded. "I am."

"Wonderful."

Garrett followed the man through the front entrance.

"We have been expecting you. Is this your first visit?"

"Yes, it is." Garrett scanned the ornamentation adorning the front room. "Please excuse me for gawking, the place is beyond magnificent."

"That it is."

"It must have taken countless men and construction hours to complete." Garrett admired the arched entrances that encircled a winter garden. "Richard Morris Hunt was the architect?"

"Yes." The man led Garrett deeper inside and stopped. "With Vanderbilt's vision and Hunt's expertise, the two of them have accomplished the unthinkable."

"And Fredrick Law Olmsted designed the gardens and grounds."

"That is correct, and then came the time to add another layer of magnificence to this place."

"The dairy and milk barn." Garrett took out his note pad. "I admit, it caught me a bit by surprise to hear of Mr. Vanderbilt's desire to add a farm to his home nearly two years ago." It must have been an honor to be the one chosen to tell the world.

"With the hundred and twenty-five thousand acres the man owns, the two could be separate entities. And now for the latest report, though it is not to be announced until after the fact."

"Which is?"

"President Roosevelt has been invited to attend a dinner party, and he and his family have accepted the invitation."

Garrett scribbled the man's words on the first page before glancing up. "My word. That will be grand news, indeed. Mr. Dupree did not exaggerate in the least."

"How is my dear friend, Anthony, these days? And his beautiful wife, Catherine?"

"They are well. Though, Mrs. Dupree has some unresolved health issues."

"Health issues?" The man's brow narrowed. "I am so sorry to hear that. I do pray things will work out in her favor."

"As do I." Garrett considered the man. "I did not realize you knew the Duprees' personally."

"Yes, we've been friends for many years. With so many hours spent together analyzing the land development, we were bound to get to know each other beyond a business relationship." The man took a few steps forward. "I have the plans already laid out on the conference table and prearranged to be examined. Then we can visit the grounds so that you can see the entirety of his vision."

"If I may be allowed to speak freely, Mr. Dupree had me come for other reasons as well."

"Yes, and I must admit, Anthony has informed me of the other matter involving William Arendell, so that I would be prepared." The man's jaw slackened. "Is there anything you need to attend to before we get started?"

"No, sir. I am ready." Garrett paused before moving forward. "But I wondered. Are you by any chance familiar with a Mr. Randall Thorne?"

"Randall Thorne. Yes, as a matter of fact..." The man's words dawdled as if he was unsure if he should continue. "Apparently, Mr. Thorne has come unto the knowledge that he is a long-lost relative of George Vanderbilt."

A relative? A sick suspicion churned through Garrett's stomach.

"But if you ask me, I believe your friend Randall favors a young woman in Vanderbilt's circle of acquaintances," the man said in a lowered tone. "Invitations to frequent dinner parties certainly has its advantages."

A sharp pain pierced through his temple. Perhaps the man was mistaken. Since surely Garrett had witnessed admiration for Abigail in Thorne's eyes.

Had he been a gossipmonger, he would have revealed his own limited knowledge of the man. Instead, he bit his tongue and offered a surprised hum.

❦

The moment Abigail awoke from a long nap, she recalled her very first memory of being in Garrett Barringer's company. How he had reprimanded her for wearing such shoes on a cobblestone street. How he had wanted nothing more than to see her to safety. How he had been a gentleman even then, leading her off the dance floor after a song had already begun. And had done it to spare her more pain.

How then could she remain annoyed with the man? Though she did not agree on all of his tactics, they were without a doubt for her benefit. Her safety.

Even now, she recalled how she had snuck a peek from the tent and found Garrett's cot placed directly in front of her entryway. Ensuring his ready availability if she were to need him. Or, even more so, assuring his hired men had no access to her should he drift off to sleep. Though, he had never admitted to it.

And she had never even acknowledged the chivalrous act nor offered her appreciation for such a deed.

Would Randall Thorne have done the same? As hard as she tried, she could not envision that scenario.

Why then, did she continue to sit here? Wallowing. Sulking. Spoiling a perfectly good day. Rose would certainly advise Abigail to reconsider her behavior.

And Rose would be correct. Just as she had been in every other situation where Abigail needed to adjust her attitude. Acting like a child would do more harm to her character. Abigail laughed at herself as she tidied a few tendrils of hair that had fallen loose. That is the exact thing her mother would say to her if she were here.

Garrett must have been wondering what had come over her, and instead of thinking of an excuse to get herself out of this predicament, she had wasted all of this time pouting.

Abigail stood. After opening her door, she exhaled and stepped from the bedroom.

She had been waiting for nearly five years for the choice that was finally before her. Yet, with Garrett Barringer in her presence, choosing to pursue Randall Thorne became cloudier with each passing moment. But none of that mattered. She had no choice but to stick to her plan.

Gaining Garrett's trust would be the tough part. Facing him would be unbearable. How could she have left her heart unaware? Why now, when she was so close to obtaining the very thing for which she had prayed for five years?

She reached the living area and Garrett stood across the room, his attention trained on her. She couldn't look away fast enough. Hot flashes of racing heat burst through her veins. Why did he have such a strong hold on her? It would be impossible to avoid Garrett Barringer when he had made it clear he would always be there to supervise.

Holding her head high, she walked toward him, her focus settled on his white collar. "I'm surprised to see you have returned. It must have been a very brief meeting," she stated, and walked past him, not expecting a reply.

"Abigail?"

Abigail startled at the sound of Randall's voice. With the turn of events and her unsettled emotions, she wasn't sure she could handle conversing with the man right now. Especially with an audience scrutinizing her every word.

Abigail turned slowly to face Randall, keeping her hands folded behind her back. Keeping a safe distance from his reach. "Mr. Thorne, I didn't expect to see you again, so soon."

"I ran into your aunt in town and gained her permission to visit." It seemed to be a direct shot fired at Garrett, whether he meant for it to be or not. Then Randall stepped closer as if victorious in his aim. Perhaps, it had been intentional. "I was hoping we could talk."

Abigail's heart quickened. She needed to talk to Randall as well. How did he perceive their earlier encounter? Did Randall believe her actions to be inappropriate? Or would he even have a reliable opinion on the matter?

And then there was Garrett. A discomforting essence tangled around her heart in his presence. The intensity had multiplied since their earlier conversation, an intensity not easily dismissed. She only knew that if Garrett had to remain present during her visit with Randall, she could not bear that this minute. She needed time to sort through her thoughts. Her feelings. "I wasn't expecting—"

"I apologize for the unannounced visit, but I could not wait." His grin was broad. However, there was something unpredictable in his smile. "Has your aunt not returned from town?"

Abigail traded a brief glance with Garrett. "I have not spoken to her since my arrival."

Randall moved precariously closer. "She gave me her address and said I was welcome to visit, but to wait a few hours. So, I did, and here I am."

"Oh?" With unsteady fingers, she reached for a loose tendril of hair and pushed it behind her ear. "It is so good to see you again, Mr. Thorne, but I am afraid our visit will have to be postponed. I am not feeling well."

A mixture of chagrin and amusement stirred his lips. "Perhaps next week then. When you're feeling better."

A wave of regret swept over her. "Next week?" Why would he wait so long? She should not have let her complicated feelings for Garrett Barringer deter her. "I don't think—"

"Yes, of course." Garrett stepped forward. "There will be plenty of time next week after Abigail has settled in and is feeling better." Garrett opened the door. "We wish you a good day, Mr. Thorne."

Not meeting her eyes, nor Garrett's, Randall turned toward the door. Why had Randall put it off so long? Why had she? Why did Garrett have to interfere again? She didn't need an entire weekend to recover. And now it was too late. Randall had taken his leave immediately as if he had no more desire to be in their presence.

As soon as the departure of Randall's buggy reached Abigail's ears, she stepped outside. Beaming rays of sunlight illuminated the white picket fence which was perpendicular to Louisa's house and the gravel road. Abigail leaned against the porch railing, her thoughts torn between two very different men.

Randall had stolen her heart and ensnared it for five years with wishful ponderings. She had always envisioned Randall Thorne finding her and pleading for her forgiveness. Pleading for her hand in marriage. But that day had not come. Yet, finally her chance for a reconciliation was upon her.

Now though, it was Garrett Barringer who held her musings captive. The man made her heart take flight with his undisputable talent of incarnating every fairy-tale prince she'd ever fallen in love with.

If only Garrett Barringer was the knight-in-shining-armor of her story and had come to her rescue. Delight bubbled up in her as the scene played out as if in a theatre production. But there was no happily-ever-after version in her script. Instead, she was doomed as the author of her own nightmare. Even if Garrett Barringer would accept her, she could not give into her own heart's desire. It was the very thing that had nearly ripped her family apart, and Abigail vowed to sacrifice her own happiness to rectify the pain she had caused her parents. No matter the price.

At the sound of the screen door opening, Abigail straightened, her teeth catching her lower lip.

Then seconds later, Garrett joined her. "I am sorry."

"For what, Mr. Barringer?" Abigail retorted, hoping to prevent the predictable blush from springing to her cheeks. "For once again interfering in my conversation with an old friend? Or for postponing my visit with him until next week?"

"If I am not mistaken, you were the one who delayed it. I only encouraged it. For, I believe you are still in much need of rest after our long trip."

It unnerved her how her heart gained rhythm and bordered on wild in Garrett's presence. "I am perfectly fine. And capable of making my own decisions."

Garrett kicked his boot against the fence post. "Then why did you tell him you didn't feel well?"

Abigail most certainly could not be honest and tell Garrett that her skewed emotions had never been more doubtful. That disappointment preceded every other reaction to seeing Randall again after imagining their reunion for five years.

Too bad she couldn't enjoy the attachment she felt toward Garrett. Though, time was not a luxury she could waste. Her reason for coming to Asheville had stood in her aunt's living room this very afternoon and she had let him slip away.

"I don't know." Abigail shook her head. "It was careless and reckless of me to allow him to act in such a way in town earlier."

Her position was unique, and with it came an unwavering obligation. An obligation to prove herself capable of being independent and not becoming prey to the charms of any man. And even more so, to not allow herself to fall victim to unquestionable behavior.

Abigail crossed her arms. "I allowed myself to behave foolishly and now he will—"

"Do you love him, Abigail?"

Sorrow tugged at her lips for her answer was not at all what she had hoped it to be. She unfolded her arms. "I beg your pardon?"

"Randall Thorne. Do you love him?"

That was a question begging for a truth she was unable to give. So, instead she took a safer approach, hoping to obstruct her true feelings for the man standing before her. "What do you mean asking me such a personal question? That is none of your business."

"He was to be your husband? It wouldn't be so unnatural to still have feelings for the man."

A rumble of panic quaked deep beneath her ribs. Had her father betrayed her trust? Or had Randall told Garrett while she was acting as a child, hiding out in her room? She kept her head down as she navigated through her emotions. "How did you know that?"

"Your father told me."

Her brain worked desperately to secure a foothold. "He told you?" She closed her blurry eyes and shoved her hands against her chest to ward off nausea. Little panted breaths vented from her lungs. "How could he do that to me?"

"Abigail, surely you know that your father would have to give some explanation as to why you would want to spend time with the man."

"I never told him my intentions to…" She looked toward Aunt Louisa's house. Had her father known all along of her plan to reunite with Randall?

"I assure you, your father only had your best interests at heart when he disclosed those few minor details."

"Minor details?" Her breath reduced to an erratic wheeze. "They are not minor details, Mr. Barringer. It is the disgrace I have endured for five years. The very reason our family moved from this area. I brought shame on my family when Randall practically renounced his proposal."

He took her hand. "You must calm down. Surely, it isn't as bad as you claim it to be."

She jerked from his hold as outrage bolted through Abigail's veins, stealing all sensible thoughts. "How can you say such a thing?" She took a tumultuous breath. "You know nothing of the sorrow he left in his wake."

"There's something you should know." Garrett placed a hand on her shoulder, and she tensed at his touch. "Your father has given you permission to court Mr. Thorne."

Unable to believe her ears, she gripped the wood railing and drew in a sharp breath. "What?" she heard herself asking, her mind whirling in response to such a statement. "Why did Father not say anything to me?"

"Of that, I'm uncertain."

Abigail blinked as shock and disbelief left her speechless. She walked down the steps and along the cobblestone walkway. She wasn't offended by her father's lack of confidentiality. And not even that her privacy had been invaded. Although, a young woman her age was entitled to some secrecy. Yet that detail was the very thing that had cost her much. If only she had been more open with her parents. Honest about the warning signs Randall had revealed. Flirting openly with others, including her dearest friends.

Signs she had intentionally ignored in an effort to claim the man's heart. Signs she had conveniently pushed to the furthest corners of her mind. Signs that reared their ugly heads only moments after seeing him again.

Her family had to give up everything because of her decision to run off and marry Randall, and he had left her after one reckless night of passion. She could have righted everything by agreeing to marry William, but she couldn't bear to live all of her days married to the likes of such a man.

Abigail turned to face Garrett. "But what of William Arendell? I was certain my father expected me to marry him."

His focus landed somewhere beyond her. "Your father wanted to offer you the opportunity to see Mr. Thorne while you are visiting. As long as the man meets certain requirements. And of course, if that is what you wish." He spoke cooly, with a tone of practicality as though what he was saying was not of notable significance. "There's one more thing."

"There's more?"

"Mr. Thorne does not know of your father's wishes. He only meant to grant you the freedom to make your own choice in the matter."

Abigail closed her eyes for a moment, still reveling in the astonishing news. "If you knew this, why did you prevent me from speaking with Randall in town earlier?"

"I did not appreciate the way he looked at you." The creases of confusion above his nose crumpled into folds of impatience. "I thought it best to put some space between you before you said something in haste."

How long had Garrett been watching them? Her heart delivered a violent kick.

She considered him. "And how exactly did he look at me?"

"As if you were nothing more than a possession."

His voice had deepened, while her regret bore down, obstructing her judgment with dread.

Abigail slowly turned as the shocking statement drained the life out of Abigail's argument. For what Garrett spoke was truth.

Heat traveled in a slow wave as Garrett took a step closer and turned her to face him.

"And if you must know, that is the reason I stepped forward when I did. I will not prevent you from seeing Mr. Thorne or from reuniting with the gentleman if that is what you desire, but I will remain present until I am certain he has no intention to cause you harm."

Abigail blinked away the sudden warmth flooding her veins at his protectiveness. Her brain stirred with the abundance of information, struggling to find any coherent order of the facts laid out before her.

Her father was open to her possible reunion with Randall Thorne.

How could this be?

Did that mean if she chose Randall Thorne, she would be free of William Arendell? That choice would be easy. All she needed now was to convince Randall Thorne to ask for her hand in marriage.

Aunt Louisa walked toward them carrying several bags and Garrett reached for them. "Thank you, Mr. Barringer, but I can manage these," Aunt Louisa said, before turning to her niece. "Abigail, has Mr. Barringer informed you that the Vanderbilt's are hosting a small gathering at their new home tomorrow evening?"

"At the Biltmore? No." Abigail glanced between Garrett and Aunt Louisa. "He hasn't mentioned it."

"It seems as though Mr. Barringer has strong connections and you have received an invitation." Aunt Louisa took a few steps forward. "I will leave you two to discuss the details."

Garrett linked his eyes with Abigail's.

The revelation splashed a dose of cool water over her, yanking her ponderings from her newly found objective. "How did you hear of the gathering?"

"I had a meeting with George Vanderbilt's advisers this afternoon."

A new spark of interest ignited her thoughts. "And we were invited?"

"Yes. We were fortunate to gain the last two available seats for dinner. I also mentioned that your uncle works for the Vanderbilts. It seems as though Henry has made quite the impression."

Her uncle's accolade tugged at her heart strings. "Is that so?" she asked, though her unspoken question weighed heavy. What sort of meeting would Garrett have with George Vanderbilt's advisers? "An invitation to a dinner party at the Biltmore Mansion?"

Abigail stared into the distance as the earth expanded to form a blue summit embraced by misty clouds softening the sharp edges. The mesmerizing shades of blue shifted and posed at different points, creating a canvas of splendor. Her eyes drank in the scene as she inhaled crisp, wholesome air. She envisioned Rose serving alongside the Vanderbilt's and their staff. Upon her was an opportunity to witness the place for herself that would be gaining her dearest friend. She would never have believed such a thing were possible.

"Well, Abby?" A knowing smile adorned his voice. "Would you like to attend?"

Abandoning all restraint, she reached onto her tiptoes and offered Garrett a kiss to his cheek. "Yes, Mr. Barringer, I would, indeed."

Chapter Twenty-Two

At Garrett's arrival, Abigail was already waiting by the carriage, dressed in a gown similar to the first night he had met her. Though this one, a yellow ensemble of lace, brought out the gold specks in her eyes. The sight of her ruined the steady current of his pulse.

Abigail gave him a breathtaking smile. "Good evening, Garrett."

"You look lovely, Abby." Garrett reached for her fingers and brought them to his lips.

"Thank you." Her focus strayed toward his tie. "And you look splendid."

The beloved scent of her, that lingered to her gloves, nearly buckled his knees.

Did she believe Randall Thorne would be present this evening? Of course, Garrett already knew the man would be in attendance. A fact he had made certain to inquire of yesterday.

A fellow of Thorne's disposition didn't miss events such as these. But the real question remained. Would Mr. Thorne expect to see Abby here tonight?

It would be best to wait until things settled down before

Garrett explained to Abby in further detail what her father had meant by his proposal.

Randall Thorne courting her was only a small part of her father's plan. In truth, the man had hoped Abigail would see Randall's true character and decide for herself that he wasn't the best option.

Was she still in love with the Randall Thorne? That was the real question. One of which, Garrett had lost his opportunity to gain an answer. But in that moment, Abigail's feelings had been more important, and he had chosen sympathy toward her over his own desire for the truth.

Discerning her reaction to that first meeting with Randall remained hazy for he had been unable to steer his eyes from the man leering at Abigail as if she were a shiny new toy.

He had no choice but to allow Abigail to spend time with the man and form her own opinion before he approached her with his idea.

An idea that she did not have to marry Randall Thorne. Something he did not want for her. Unless, that is what *she* truly wanted. He wanted to share that there were other options. But she first had to come to terms with her own feelings for the man before she could ever begin to move forward. And Randall Thorne was something he wanted her to leave in the past. In his opinion, as far as Abigail Dupree was concerned, the past was the only place Randall Thorne belonged.

As they approached the magnificent home from the front walk, Abigail didn't dare blink, lest she miss a single detail. "I would never have imagined such a place could exist. And in the hills of North Carolina."

"It is something, is it not?" Garrett grinned, setting loose that irresistible sparkle in his eyes.

Abigail shifted her attention from the man who was sure to have left a string of broken hearts in his wake, and instead, drank in every millimeter of the house.

She formally folded her hands in her lap, warding off the breathless feeling of being in the man's presence after having been so close to sharing a kiss. "If only my mother were here to witness such a sight," she said, pleased with herself at having control over her voice.

"Perhaps your parents will be able to visit at Christmas."

"What a lovely idea!"

Whether or not the notion was to come to fruition mattered little. Garrett's consideration was the thing that held the significance.

Abigail stepped through the vestibule, and into an area surrounded by circular archways stretching from all sides of the reception space. She was scanning just past one of the arches when she caught sight of Randall Thorne.

A young woman stood across from him, clinging to his arm. Abigail blinked against the sudden pulsing through her diaphragm that took her breath. Though the scene itself was no surprise. Abigail had witnessed multiple similar occurrences. Memories she had conveniently pressed to the farthest corners of her mind. Until now.

Randall most likely had already secured a date for the evening long before their chance meeting the other day. Keeping some distance or at the very least giving the impression that he was not interested in more beyond an evening out with the lady would have been honorable. If, in fact, he intended to see Abigail again. But the atmosphere between the couple was anything but a mere friendship. In fact, they acted as if they had done this plenty of times.

What bothered her most was the way he looked at the woman. Entirely too similar to the way he had looked at her the other day.

Randall led his companion deeper into the home and Abigail turned in haste to flee her disgrace. But no escape materialized from her internal humiliation. Honorable had never been a word that would describe Randall Thorne. Something she knew all too well. Yet, still, she was here chasing the dream hoping that by some miracle the man had matured. Changed.

Turning, she found that Garrett's focus had been zeroed in on the same scene before he refocused and regarded her.

She could only imagine what he must be thinking.

That she had allowed Randall to caress her own hand in broad daylight the other day. That Randall bestowed the same attentions on the woman accompanying him this evening as he had bequeathed on her. And that most likely there had been and would be many others.

But still, that wasn't the thing that bothered her most. It was the surprising grief that swelled through her thoughts.

Abigail pasted on a smile for Garrett but quickly averted her focus toward a different arch. "What a lovely home!"

"Yes," the guide said as Abigail admired the greenery lacing the area. "Shall we move forward, then?"

"Yes, please." Leaving Garrett behind would be the better option for now. Leaning on him for support would not only be impudent, it would be dangerous.

Every stitch of each servant's attire was flawless, exposing yet another precise detail in the management of this home.

Catching the gaze of one of the younger maids was indeed an unexpected treat. To her knowledge, servants in homes such as these were to move carefully and quietly and to never make eye contact with guests.

As if knowing her place, the girl stiffened, offered a bashful smile, and skirted away quickly.

Rose. She would be leaving her. And very soon, as it would seem. Though heartbroken, Abigail could not be happier for her. There would be an opportunity for Rose to make many friends in a place such as this. Perhaps the young maid, who had already disappeared around the corner, would become one of Rose's closest friends.

As the guests were seated for dinner, Abigail had just expelled a breath of air when Randall Thorne and his date were placed at the opposite table, his back to her. Unfortunately, Garrett's place card was positioned for the seat next to her. Abigail looked about the room. It would be better to put some space between them until she could gather control of her feelings for the man.

The tinkling of metal against glass brought her awareness toward the front of the room.

"Dinner is served."

Garrett pulled out Abigail's chair. "I was beginning to worry you meant to abandon me."

A halfhearted laugh slipped from her throat. For that had been her exact motive, though it was opposite of her hidden desire. "I'm certain you would have made a new friend or two in my absence."

"A new friend." A chuckle rumbled from the depths of his chest. "I hadn't considered the idea."

Abigail forced herself to meet his gaze. "How could you? Especially under my father's influence."

"Yes, I have priorities to consider, but I do enjoy your company whether or not the feeling is mutual."

The conversation had swayed toward uncharted waters. Waters that could shift at any moment and drown her in depths of unbridled affection.

Abigail shook her head. "I do as well, though I have no desire to monopolize all of your free time."

Thankfully the staff rounded the table with the first course. And Abigail was content to listen to the others converse instead of having to speak.

As soon as the last course was finished, Abigail stood and edged past Garrett and withdrew to a corner.

Immediately, women swarmed toward Garrett, like vultures. He only seemed intrigued by one of them. A lady wearing a silver ensemble. If Abigail had not been so anxious to escape his presence, she would be the one obtaining all of his attention. Instead of the woman hovering much too close. But that was not fair. Neither to him nor to her.

Ignoring the prick of jealousy pinching her heart, Abigail spent the next half hour focused on the beauty of the magnificent home and the other guests and their partners, including Garrett and his lady friend.

Feeling no need to keep observing Garrett's facial expressions to ascertain his interest in the lady, Abigail stepped into a room brimming with tapestries. Garrett Barringer's and Randall Thorne's approaches toward the women hanging onto their arms tonight was incomparable. It was evident in Garrett's mannerisms that he made forth every effort to be a true gentleman in the presence of any woman. In her now vivid memories of Randall, he used an entirely different tactic. He toyed with a woman's emotions as if playing a game in his attempt to capture as many hearts as possible.

How had it taken this long for her heart and mind to uncover Randall's intentions? It was her own desire and sin that had kept her blinded to Randall's true character.

Making her fourth pass over the intricate designs of the tapestry exhibiting many scenes from the Bible, moisture gathered in her eyes. Nothing moved her to tears like God's Word. Especially when she was able to apply its truth to her own life. The detail in Jacob's ladder drew her in as she recalled the story of a young man evading his own unspeakable offense. Stealing his brother's blessing.

Running from his sin, Jacob settled in Haran for the night,

placed his head on a rock, and fell into a deep sleep. Then God approached him in a dream.

Even though Jacob had pretended to be Esau. Tricked his father, whose sight was failing. Stole a rightful inheritance from the brother to whom it belonged. Carried out the evil plan to gain his father's blessing all for himself. Though his sin was wretched, God, in His never-ending mercy, stretched out His hand, and saved Jacob from himself. Gave him the promise that Jacob's seed should be as the dust of the earth, and through his seed all the families of the earth would be blessed.

All the families blessed. Even her.

Jacob fell asleep a wretched man but awoke cleansed and consecrated by God Himself.

Garrett caught her by the arm, yanking her from her reflections. "I wondered as to where you had disappeared."

Abigail's heart leapt and her blood raced violently through her veins at his sudden presence. Her chin jerked toward him and she blinked several times, praying the moisture behind her eyes wouldn't betray her. "Good heavens, Garrett. You startled me."

"Please forgive me. But I have been looking everywhere for you."

Originating in her core, adoration swept over her like a soft breeze. "Why?"

"That is an answer of which I need not explain."

She laughed and forced her attention from him, worried he would no longer continue to stand there, but terrified he would. His presence gripped her thunderous emotions that were already set on edge of expanding into an unchained melody. Recalling her disgrace at the very reason for her presence in Asheville, North Carolina, this evening, she sighed.

Little difference likened her to Jacob.

If only she were free to choose her own fate. If only God would stretch out His hand and summon her in a dream. Give her a new beginning.

She gave Garrett a sidelong glance. "I envy you."

He offered no response as his eyes remained focused on the tapestries. Abigail allowed him to absorb the stunning displays of art before them while their close vicinity made it impossible to focus her attention on anything but him.

When he turned his head toward her, his stunned expression at her obvious admiration gave her pause.

"There haven't been many occasions where I was accused of being the envy of anyone."

She swallowed the moisture that had collected under her tongue. "I find that very difficult to believe." Careful not to make eye contact, she studied the freshly-shaven skin of his jaw. "You looked as though you were having an enjoyable time this evening."

"It has been agreeable enough. How about you?"

She averted her focus once again toward the tapestries. Witnessing the pleasure garnishing Garrett's features at his remembrance of the woman clinging to his attentions over the last hour would only serve to torture her even more. "I've enjoyed seeing all the grandeur of the Vanderbilts' home, but honestly, I am anxious for the close of this evening."

"Already?" He turned to face her, his eyes filling her with trust. "Are you not enjoying yourself this evening?"

Abigail caught a glimpse of Randall Thorne approaching in her peripheral vision and icy shards of memories rushed through her thoughts. "It has been lovely." At least the last few moments.

"I was looking forward to escorting you for a walk through the gardens."

Heat traveled through her veins, burning with unbridled desire to be held in the arms of the man standing before her. Abigail was no longer aware of whether Randall Thorne was resuming his way to the exit or advancing toward them.

She should stop this silly attraction now while she still maintained some of her senses about her. Garrett Barringer was not within her reach. Her gaze fell to his chest, the slow motion mimicking the lost feeling she'd experienced seeing his arm attached to someone else.

"I'm certain the lady you have been conversing with all evening will surely be honored to accompany you." Abigail winced, for her words sounded envious even to her.

Garrett's brows lifted. "The lady?"

"Yes, the one wearing the beautiful silver gown." With no effort to conceal her covetous heart, she continued in her most dramatic tone. "The same one who has been staring at you all evening with adoration." What was she doing? Why had she blurted that? Her mind skipped ahead to the repercussions of her admission. There was no denying it. She was jealous. And he had noticed.

He crossed his arms, the twinkle in his eyes mocking her. She closed her own, refusing to see the glimmer of victory in his. "You have been watching me?"

All the fight drained from her—weeks of fighting her attraction to him.

"I don't understand why you are still standing here with me? You're an eligible bachelor, Garrett Barringer. There are plenty of ladies who would line up to…" A hot flash of awareness coursed through her when she finally met his eyes.

He slowly combed her face, then lingered on her lips before arresting her eyes. "To what?"

Butterflies tumbled through her stomach, stimulating every nerve ending in her body. She cleared her throat, propelling all tempting sensations from her person. "I am a grown woman. I have no need of a babysitter," she said with a tongue that could cut, though a second round of butterflies emerged. "It isn't necessary to shadow my every move just because you work for my father."

Garrett's lips compressed in disapproval. "It's a wonder you haven't figured it out as of yet, but you, Miss Dupree, are my priority."

"Really, Mr. Barringer. I know my father means well, but I can take care of myself."

"I'm not sure that I agree."

Her anger rose at his audacity. He was here only out of obligation to her father. "I do not appreciate you accusing me—"

"I'm not accusing you of anything, Abby." He turned to face her, his features softening as his eyes sought hers. "I meant it as a compliment."

"Whatever do you mean? I find it impossible to glean a compliment from that phrase."

He took a step forward and in that one smooth motion, they were inches from each other. "You are a lovely young woman and perfect just as you are. But with your trusting nature, it would be too easy to fall into the trap of someone who would not have your best interests at heart. And I simply cannot allow that to happen. Whether you agree or not."

Speechless, Abigail clucked her tongue, even though she privately treasured his spirited scolding. And even more, agreed with him. If only her father had hired him five years ago, things might be very different. Very different, indeed.

"Now, please Miss Abigail Dupree, may I have the pleasure of escorting you for a walk in the garden?"

"If you insist."

Heat coursed through her veins as she slipped her arm through his and allowed him to lead her along the trail to the Italian garden.

Chapter Twenty-Three

The piercing in Abigail's chest did not belong there and was certainly unwelcomed. But as they reached the garden, Abigail blurted the question begging for release. "What is her name?"

"I beg your pardon?"

For heaven's sake, it was none of her business, but she was unable to impede her tongue. The accusation that had spoiled her evening lashed out. "The lady you have conversed with most of the evening."

"Ah, her. She's a friend from the past."

"A friend?" She must have been a very good friend to have so much to say. "Well, she must have been overjoyed to see you again. As you her."

He didn't respond. But gave her a look that warned her motives were trailing between a thin line of normal curiosity and full transparency.

Even then she couldn't control her dialogue. "What was her name, then?"

"Elizabeth Baxter."

Abigail clasped her hands together. "What a lovely name for a lovely young woman."

Garrett's brow furrowed. "Yes, I suppose."

"You surprise me, Mr. Barringer." Was it possible Garrett Barringer was not attracted to the woman? Elizabeth Baxter was certainly fond of him.

"Why is that?"

Heat crept up her neck but she snuffed it out, along with her own ridiculous visions of spending her entire life with the man. Keeping her smile in place, she inched forward. "I'm only teasing you, Garrett."

The water shimmered against the backdrop of the setting sunlight along a wall facing the ponds. Movement amid one of the lily pads scattered about the pools drew her attention and she took a step closer.

Garrett's arm stiffened at her motion. "Careful."

"Did you see that?"

He just kept staring at her, not saying anything. At least not with his mouth. His eyes were full of questions, scrutinizing her with such depth she had no choice but to take a step back.

"You missed it, didn't you?"

"Missed what?" he finally answered.

"There." She bent forward, and he grabbed her arm. The weight of his hand jerked her back onto her heels. "Will you quit worrying."

"I'm sorry. I did not mean…"

The notion enamored Abigail, and she smiled up at him. A faint splash brought her attention back to the water before her. "Look, there, don't you see it? That speck of orange swimming beneath the lily pad."

"Ah, yes." He grinned. A charming, full of effervescence smile. "That is a Japanese koi, if I am not mistaken."

"What a lovely addition to have an aquatic garden brimming with fish!"

Garrett crossed his arms. "Yes, it is lovely, indeed."

"You tease me, Garrett Barringer, but this is a treat you may never witness again."

"I do hope you're mistaken." Garrett snickered and uncrossed his arms. He leaned toward her, closing the span of space between them. "Because I would dearly love the opportunity to spend the evening here, again. And perhaps there will even be an occasion so that we may finish our dance."

"Finish our dance? Whatever would make you think such a thing?" His thought, however, brought about a surge of unbridled memories that created a storm of sensations through her core.

All playfulness evaporated from his expression. "Our last one did not end as I had hoped it would."

"Is that so?" She recalled strong arms leading her with a confident, yet gentle touch. "As I remember, you intervened at a most opportune time to save me from another painful dance because of those unforgiving shoes." And her partner. "I have not forgotten the kindness you showed toward me that evening. So, all was not lost."

His lips stirred with a taunting lift. "Are you giving me a compliment?"

"I suppose I am." She shared his smile and relished in the warmth that a friendship with Garrett Barringer had brought upon her. "Furthermore, I would be—"

He glanced away for a moment and exhaled an exasperated breath.

Her brow furrowed. Had she said something untoward? "What is it?" Abigail asked as she turned to look behind her.

Randall stepped forward. "May I have a few moments of Abigail's time, Mr. Barringer?"

Abigail winced at her own displeasure. She did not want to leave. She wanted to stay. Wanted to flirt with Garrett. Wanted Garrett to flirt with her. Randall had spent the entire evening with another woman. But then again, so had Garrett. While she'd wandered the great house alone.

Why did Randall have to seek her out now when she was finally enjoying herself? If she did not accept, Garrett may get the wrong impression and so would Randall. No point in prolonging the inevitable.

"Thank you, Mr. Barringer, for the lovely walk."

Garrett said nothing but searched her eyes. As if he did not want to allow it. Perhaps he wouldn't.

Heat crept up the back of her neck. "Do I have your permission, then?"

"If you wish."

Not expecting Garrett to toss the ball in her court, she locked her gaze with his. What was she to say to that? She couldn't very well tell the man she longed to remain by his side. And ignoring a perfect opportunity to spend time with Randall would be... well, it would be foolish, indeed. Whether or not the time would most likely be a waste.

"Thank you. I shall see you later, then." With one last glance in Garrett's direction, she took Randall's arm.

Randall led her forward and stopped near a bench beneath the cover of ivy and moss. "I was hoping you would make it tonight."

"I was actually wondering why you had not bothered to mention the event."

"Truthfully, Abigail, I wasn't sure you had received an invitation and didn't want to insult you so soon after your arrival. I truly am sorry."

"Please, do not apologize. I was only curious why you had not spoken of it. Of course, I understand perfectly, since you had already invited someone."

"The lady is a friend of the family, whom I was coerced into inviting."

Coerced? Not likely.

"Oh?" she asked, though she believed none of it. It wouldn't be the first time she had entertained that exact excuse. "Where is she?"

"I slipped away. When I saw you enter earlier, I knew I had to spend at least a few moments with you."

"Is that so?"

Leaving his unsuspecting date so he could spend time with another woman, did not impress her in the least. Her plan to attack him with harsh accusations fell away on the breeze of realization. Abigail hadn't seen Randall in over five years and spending time with him now made her suddenly aware of all his faults she had so conveniently forgotten. But more than that, none of his actions bothered her in the least.

"I presume you are feeling better then, since you have attended this evening."

"The long trip took its toll on me, but, yes, I am feeling more refreshed." Abigail glanced toward the water, hoping for another glimpse of a bright orange speck.

Randall placed a hand on her lower back. His touch brought on a rush of quivering apprehensions. Too informal. Too comfortable. Too intimate.

"I am praying you won't have to return."

At his statement and the placement of his fingers, she looked at him with astonishment but remained silent.

Randall glanced toward the house and the angst in his eyes didn't go unnoticed. Then he clasped his hands together, and she sighed with relief.

"I should take my leave. I have a big day tomorrow and need to gather some items for an important meeting scheduled for the morning."

Abigail shot Randall a sharp look. "So soon?"

"Please, forgive me, Abigail." He took her hand. "I do wish I would have noticed your presence sooner. Especially since I must now leave. Perhaps, we could meet for breakfast?"

"Breakfast?"

"Yes. There's a café on the corner in town where we met the other day. Meet me there at eight o'clock in the morning."

"But I will have to..." She glanced over her shoulder to find Garrett walking toward the house with the same woman wearing that silky gray gown. Her stomach tightened.

"I no longer believe Mr. Barringer will stand in our way. It seems he has found other things to occupy his mind."

Abigail supposed she couldn't argue, yet the critical statement still wounded her. "It would be in my best interest to gain permission—"

"Yes, of course. Please, forgive me. I meant no harm. My mouth tends to run awry when I am happy." He moved closer and took her hand. "And I am more than happy right this moment being in your presence. Only saddened at the same time for having to leave so abruptly. So, what of breakfast? Will you join me, then?"

"What of your meeting?"

"It isn't until ten in the morning." He leaned toward her and she took a swift step back. "And I—"

"I would love to." Abigail stopped him before he could continue with more false affections. "Are you certain you have to leave already?"

"Yes, I truly am sorry. It can't wait." He tightened his grip on her hand.

She sympathized with his inability to speak the truth. Another fault she had conveniently forgotten. For, she knew, his motives had nothing to do with a meeting, but everything to do with a certain woman who was in fact waiting on him this very moment.

"Will you be all right to find your way back inside? I would offer to escort you, but I had planned a shorter route for my exit."

Instead of confronting him about his lack of character, she felt an inner urging to be agreeable. "Yes, of course. I should like to enjoy the garden's scenery a bit more before returning to the house."

Randall brought her hand to his lips. "See you at eight?"

"All right."

And then he was gone.

She wandered around to the front of the house. Through the window she saw a few men gathered around with cigars and drinks. Thankfully, none seemed to notice her presence.

Garrett, who stood in a far corner, continued speaking with Elizabeth Baxter.

None of the other couples shuffled about along the front of the house so Abigail stepped beneath the portico.

The sun had painted streaks of orange amidst the blue. A cool, evening breeze caressed her and a few loosened strands of hair tickled her cheeks. A chorus of songbirds hummed from the trees surrounding the property.

She leaned against the rail beneath the first arch and looked across the vast lawn before her, Randall's invitation still buzzing around in her head. And even more, his restlessness.

Of course, Randall hadn't noticed her presence. Not with his full attention consumed by his companion. That Randall Thorne's actions this evening bore a resemblance to William Arendell's was inconvenient. William Arendell had no prior claim on her. Unfortunately, Randall Thorne did. Though none of those took precedence in her thoughts. Garrett Barringer claimed that role. And no matter how she tried, she couldn't shake the fantasies of having the love of a man such as he.

A young woman moved into the place next to her and pulled out a cigarette. "Can I offer you a smoke?"

"Oh, no, thank you." Abigail peered at the woman unsure if she was disappointed or pleased at the intrusion. "Aren't you —"

"The president's daughter, yes. But please don't hold that against me."

Abigail laughed at the woman's unusual wit.

"Miss Alice Lee Roosevelt." The young woman lifted her fingers in a casual fashion, the tip of her cigarette burning. "And you are?"

"Abigail Dupree. It is such a pleasure to meet you."

"The pleasure is mine. Please pardon my interruption but *we* needed to step outside for a few moments."

Not seeing any others standing around them, Abigail inquired of her use of a plural pronoun. "We?"

Alice lifted a green snake out of her purse. "Yes, my pet and I were both in desperate need of some fresh air."

Stunned, Abigail discreetly pivoted her head to the side and wheezed in two sharp breaths of air. "You carry your pet snake in your purse?"

"I do, since, I'm certain the other guests would not be thrilled to find him hanging around my neck." Miss Roosevelt regarded her. "I'm impressed. You didn't even flinch when I pulled him out."

Abigail quirked her brow. "You act as if that surprises you?"

"It does." Miss Roosevelt gave her cigarette a light tap, and a few ashes drifted to the ground. "I usually get a scream from most women."

"Then, I'm glad to know I stand out from the others." Abigail leaned closer. "Though, if I'm completely honest, it took me by surprise. Perhaps I am only skilled at hiding certain reactions."

"Much to my parent's dismay, that is unfortunately a skill I do not possess."

Abigail could certainly understand why. The president's daughter hauling a green snake in her purse was something Abigail would never have suspected.

Miss Roosevelt eyed her with curiosity. "Please don't mind

my bluntness, but it seems as though you were deep in thought at my approach."

Abigail exhaled a deep harrowing breath. "I, too, wrestle with my own need of disregarding my parent's wishes for my own desires. Though, unfortunately, they are usually right and I would be wise to heed their instructions."

"You must be speaking of a man." The woman leaned forward on the railing. "They seem to be the root of all our troubles."

Abigail chuckled. "In this case, there is more than one gentleman."

"Ah. That's interesting." Miss Roosevelt took a long puff of her cigarette and blew the smoke out in a perfect circular ring. "I have a simple philosophy. Fill what's empty. Empty what's full. And scratch where it itches."

An amused grin filled Abigail's lips. The woman was certainly unique. And bold. "They are very wise words from someone so young an age."

The woman stood taller. "I will soon be nineteen years old. Do you live here in Asheville?"

"I did at one time, but I currently reside in Charlotte. I'm here visiting my aunt."

"What a pity. For I feel as though, you and I could have been the best of friends if we didn't live so far apart."

Enchanted by the president's daughter, Abigail smiled. The woman was certainly unique. And bold. Admirable traits, indeed. "I feel as though I should like to be your friend no matter the distance. It is my hope to travel to the Northeast someday."

"Is that so?" Her eyes brightened. "You must come to the White House. I shall personally give you the grand tour."

"That would be lovely."

"If you are interested in travel, you must be introduced to Mary Cadwalader Jones. She is an American author who has just published a book on European travel. And she happens to be one of the guests this evening."

"How marvelous!"

"I will go now and leave you with your thoughts." An amusing sparkle ignited her eyes. "If you haven't got anything nice to say about anybody, come sit next to me."

As Miss Roosevelt walked away, a swallowtail butterfly coasted by and landed on the rail by Abigail's hands, evoking her thoughts back to that shared carriage ride with Garrett. To that almost kiss.

"Where is Mr. Thorne?"

At Garrett's sudden presence amid such luring thoughts, Abigail's breath caught in her throat.

"Did something happen? You had been in his presence no more than five minutes, before you approached the house." His questions hung in the air between them and Abigail was surprised by the concern framing his eyes.

"No. He..." Abigail swallowed the lump materializing in her throat. "Unfortunately, he had to take his leave."

"What was his hurry?" Garrett's hands perched on the rail before them. "I pray he escorted you back to the house."

She sensed Garrett's eyes on her as he spoke. She turned, not focusing on Garrett but the intricate design of the corner windows that appeared crooked. "There was no time for that."

"No time?" Garrett's incredulous tone matched her own opinion of Randall's hasty exit and gathered the attention of the other men surrounding them. "I find it rather difficult to believe that he would be in such a hurry that he would depart without the courtesy of escorting you back to the house. Especially after coercing me to leave the two of you alone."

Unfortunately, she had considered those exact thoughts. Though her desire for more independence dictated her reply. "As you can see, I have returned without a single mishap."

"That is not the point." He shook his head with a stern rebuke. "What was his excuse?"

"Some sort of important meeting for which he had to prepare. He gave his deepest apologies." Why had she defended Randall? It was certainly not deserved.

Garrett heaved in a long breath. "Still. He should never have left you by the water unattended."

That lifted her head. "The water? Are you referring to the ponds no more than three feet deep?"

The lines above his brows deepened as his face contorted with earnest concern. "I am."

Abigail's brow lifted at his melodramatic theory. "And you worried Mr. Thorne would throw me in?"

"No, but you could have tripped and tumbled in by accident. You have had quite a few spells of dizziness. If you had hit your head..." Vulnerability laced his words. "It takes very little water for a person to drown."

Abigail couldn't ignore the desperate plea for her wellbeing lurking within his lecture. He was serious. And sincere. "You have a wildly vivid imagination, Garrett Barringer."

His brows furrowed. "Yes, unfortunately, I do."

Abigail's heart swelled at his regard for her safety. "Well, as you can see, I am indeed dry and standing before you perfectly safe and sound. So, if you would not mind, I would love to finish our walk through the rest of the garden."

In her peripheral, Elizabeth Baxter appeared to be approaching.

Abigail pressed her palm against his arm, staking her claim. "If your proposal still stands, that is?" Proposal? Could she have not chosen a better word? One that would not reveal her true feelings for the man. Especially after assertively claiming hold to him in full view of the young woman who was also obviously interested in him.

He offered his arm. "It would be my pleasure. I would love to hear about your conversation with the president's daughter."

In that very moment all the expectations demanded of her suddenly seemed of little importance. What if she chose not to marry William Arendell or Randall Thorne? But instead chose to simply enjoy Garrett Barringer's sudden presence in her life. Would it be so wrong? She linked her arm with his. The affection brewing in his eyes lathered bubbles of bliss in her heart and presented her solution.

If for only one evening.

Chapter Twenty-Four

The rising sun's warmth likely had nothing to do with the heat radiating through Garrett's veins this morning, but everything to do with his beautiful charge standing before him on the front porch. The truth was, if Abigail had not accepted Mr. Thorne's invitation this morning, he would most likely have given in to his desire to kiss her as she approached him. Full of life. Full of love. Full of everything he craved in a woman. Yet, he would have a front row view over the next hour or more while the lady in question made another man fall in love with her.

Another man who did not deserve her.

Garrett regarded her. "You are very forgiving."

"Am I?" Vulnerability shrouded her eyes before she turned her face from him. "I should like to take that as a compliment since our heavenly Father expects that of us, if we are to be forgiven of our sins." She nibbled her lower lip. A nervous habit he had come to adore.

"As well you should." He only prayed she would be as forgiving of him when she learned the real truth of their visit to Asheville.

Her eyebrows drew together as she stared up at him, and

Garrett had to fight not to reach out to her. "Unfortunately, it is the forgiveness of myself that I find is the hardest."

"Sadly, that holds much truth for all of us." He had offered his protection before to no avail. He could not bear to fail Abigail, too.

Her gentle touch on his arm saved him from his condemning thoughts. "You have skeletons in your closet, Mr. Barringer?"

"Does not everyone?"

"I suppose." A trace of skepticism laced her voice as though she didn't truly believe anyone else suffered the guilt of their own mistakes. "I know you do not care for Mr. Thorne, though I am not certain I understand *your* reservations with the man," Abigail said, as if she had some doubts of her own.

"I have never admitted to having qualms with Randall Thorne. I simply cannot fathom a few of his qualities." Judging another often led to personal conviction. A place of which he was treading dangerously close. Though in this instance, he believed it was warranted. Garrett led her toward the carriage. "Leaving before seeing you safely back to the house has certainly not advanced his integrity in my view."

"Yes, well, being a man of law, you should not judge until given both sides of the story." Taking a step up into the carriage, Abigail took her seat and then promptly turned her focus to the open window.

"You are absolutely right," he agreed as he took his seat, his defensive shield wielded forward. "Mr. Thorne has some explaining to do."

"What I meant to say is, well I…" Abigail cleared her throat and met his gaze, those deep sapphire blues of hers imploring his for mercy. "It does not matter what I meant. Please do not embarrass me, Garrett. It is humiliating enough to have a chaperone escort me to breakfast."

His carefully disguised compassion for the woman was bordering exposure. And even still, his curiosity of what she intended to say occupied all thoughts to the point that he had no reply.

Abigail implored him with her regard. "You should have invited your friend from last night."

Garrett's mouth puckered into a hesitant smile. "Why would I have done such a thing?"

"We could have made it a double date of sorts."

While her romantic ideals were charming, her perceptions, and perhaps even Mr. Thorne, were lacking in the reality of the situation. Surely her father had no inclination of the extent of Randall's character. Thorne could indeed be an even worse pick than Arendell. And for Abigail's sake, he had to stay focused and remain diligent in his role.

"I would not have wanted to give Miss Baxter the wrong impression when I have no interest in courting her."

The slightest hint of relief softened her expression as the carriage came to a stop. Garrett took his exit before turning to assist Abigail.

"Perhaps you can agree then to be civil so as to not ruin my chances," Abigail said as she took his hand and stepped down from the carriage.

Perhaps he had been mistaken. "Randall Thorne would be the fortunate one not to ruin his own chances."

"Garrett Barringer?"

Garrett turned to see a woman approaching. A woman he could not place. "Hi."

She positioned both hands on her hips. "You have no idea who I am."

"I apologize, but I do not."

"Well, of course you wouldn't remember me. It has been years since we sat next to each other in Sunday school."

He had spent so much energy lately on escaping his past that the earlier, happier portions had somehow faded as well. "Sarah Thompson?"

"So, you do remember me after all?" Her eyes danced with humor. "I never expected to see you. I had heard you were in the Charlotte area."

"For a short time, yes. I traveled there for a job assignment."

Sarah lifted her brows and sympathetically cut her eyes toward Abigail.

"I'm so sorry. Sarah, this is Miss Abigail Dupree. We are only here for a brief visit."

"Ah, well, I am certainly glad I ran into you. And it is so wonderful to meet you, Miss Dupree."

Abigail reached for her offered hand. "Nice to meet you."

Time had somewhat changed since he had crossed paths with Sarah. As a childhood friend, he considered her one of his closest. Long-lost memories surfaced from their last summer of youth, before adulthood, jobs, and responsibility shuffled them into different directions.

"We were just going to breakfast." He glanced at Abigail. Perhaps it would make Abigail more comfortable having Sarah accompany them. Give him something to occupy his mind while Randall Thorne strived to win Abigail's heart. Something he dreaded immensely. "You are welcome to join us."

Sarah glanced from Abigail to him. "Oh?"

Garrett peered at Abigail's solemn face, discovering a touch of anxiety in the curve of her smile.

Even so, Abigail took a faint step forward. "Yes, please. We would love for you to join us."

"I would be delighted." Her focus bounced from him to Abigail. "Since you have not yet taken Garrett's name, I assume you have your wedding planned?"

Abigail's soft laughter spilled through the air. "No, we are not—"

"We are only friends." A proficient reporter should be more capable of hiding his emotions, but Garrett couldn't stop his heart from aching.

"Is that so?" Sarah cast a curious glance in his direction before touching Abigail's arm. "Well, Miss Dupree, any friend of Garrett Barringer's is a friend of mine. And I have plenty of stories to keep you entertained for hours."

"Yes, well, we should get to the restaurant. We wouldn't want to be late." The last thing Garrett needed was for Sarah to fill Abigail with outlandish stories from their past. With Sarah's exaggerated imagination, certain facts would be distorted to her advantage.

"Late?" Surprise brightened Sarah's eyes for a moment, before her brows lowered into a puzzled V. "You made reservations?"

"No, but we are meeting Miss Dupree's suitor and wouldn't want to keep him waiting."

"Of course not." Sarah gave him a look that warned him his invitation may have stumbled into a territory he had never intended.

He would undoubtedly cause them both unnecessary pain.

Randall had already arrived and motioned to them toward a table near the back of the restaurant.

Garrett extending an invitation to Sarah Thompson could mean only one thing. He was interested in courting her. Unlike the friend from the past at the dinner party last evening.

Abigail should be glad that Garrett had invited Miss Thompson to join them. After all, that *was* what Abigail had wanted. Thankfully, Randall did not seem to recognize Sarah. It would have been unbearable to sit through an entire breakfast knowing her date had wooed the same woman that was clinging to Garrett's attention.

After the waitress had taken their order and served coffee,

Abigail lowered her shoulders. Hoping to relax the stiffness. What was wrong with her?

Garrett had already proved to be a distraction. One she couldn't afford. She did not need more of his kindhearted impulses showering her with impossibilities. It only gave her false hope and muddied the waters even more against Randall's favor. How could it not? Garrett's every gesture exhibited warmth. Compassion. Loyalty.

Taking a sip of coffee, Abigail struggled to focus on the introductions going on around her.

Sarah locked Abigail in her gaze. "Did I understand you to say that your family is originally from this area as well?"

"Yes." Abigail cleared her throat. "We moved from the area just a little over five years ago."

"Funny that the three of us have never crossed paths until now."

Randall leaned forward. "Actually, Abigail and I go way back."

Sarah's brow lifted and her attention bounced between them. "Oh?"

Peering his way, Abigail forced a smile. "Randall is a life-long family friend." *Is,* was too strong a word. Too current. Never would be more appropriate.

"Much like Garrett was to my family." Sarah exchanged a glance with Garrett. "What a small world?"

"Yes. It is a small world, indeed." Abigail swallowed her displeasure. Their conversation only reinforced the notion that if Garrett Barringer had been in her past instead of Randall Thorne, Abigail's life would most likely look very different today. How, or more importantly why, had Sarah allowed Garrett Barringer to slip away? Instead, Abigail simply stated, "You were fortunate to have had Garrett as a childhood friend."

Sarah nudged Garrett's arm. "Yes, I should say I was truly

fortunate, indeed. But such a shame to have lost touch for all these years."

The waitress arrived with the entrées, cutting off Sarah's admiring look toward the man.

Unfortunately, Abigail was not the only one who recognized Garrett's qualities. Sarah Thompson, who had remained unmarried, posed an authentic threat to the comforts Abigail had found in Garrett's company over the last few months.

The notion throbbed through her heart, the entire duration of breakfast, and tugged all of her attention from Randall Thorne. Though Randall did not seem bothered in the least.

Not until they had all walked outside did Randall pull her to the side. "You hardly touched your food."

"I suppose I had enough last night," Abigail told him. Though, truthfully, it was more the untimely reunion of Garrett and Sarah that had stolen her appetite.

"It was a plentiful feast. Speaking of which, the Vanderbilts are hosting another dinner party next week. I would like for you to accompany me." Randall worded the invitation in such a matter-of-fact approach, Abigail couldn't tell if he looked forward to the evening or whether it would be an inconvenience.

Abigail glanced toward Garrett just as Sarah leaned away from him, her smile widening. Abigail turned her back on the couple, unable to hinder the frown forming on her lips.

"Do not worry. I requested Mr. Barringer's permission and he has granted it."

Abigail stood a little straighter and smoothed a hand over the waist of her skirt. "Is that so?"

"Yes, and he has invited Miss Thompson to join him for the evening."

Abigail offered a brief smile, even as she tried to conjure up how she had missed an entire conversation. It must have been when she excused herself to the wash-room. "Thank you for the invitation but I am—"

"Well, Abigail." Garrett joined them. "It looks as though we have been awarded another evening at the Biltmore. And Sarah has agreed to join us."

Abigail swallowed the lump in her throat and turned a strained smile on Garrett. "Yes, he was just telling me."

Randall's eyes probed hers when she returned his gaze, and she sensed he knew how she intended to respond to the invitation.

"I was starting to explain to Mr. Thorne that while I would like to accept, I wasn't certain the Vanderbilts would appreciate our presence again so soon. But if you are sure?"

"We were all cordially included in the invitation."

Thankfully, Randall overlooked her rebuff and spoke amiably about the upcoming evening as he led her toward the carriage.

"I must go. But thank you for meeting me for breakfast. And I shall be looking forward to seeing you at the dinner party."

Instead of responding verbally, she offered her warmest smile. Even though discomfort tinged her curiosity of the conversation between Garrett and Miss Thompson, she kept her focus trained on Randall. If her father was willing to accept Randall, Abigail couldn't afford to ruin her own chances with him.

At least not yet.

Chapter Twenty-Five

Things were slipping beyond Garrett's control.

He paused while Sarah walked away and then watched as Randall and Abigail said their goodbyes. Extending another invitation to Sarah had been essential in his plight to keep his promise to Mr. Dupree. He had no choice. And had done it simply to make Abigail happy. If accompanying Randall to the dinner party was indeed her desire.

Though, when he witnessed the small seed of doubt in her expression, he regretted his response instantly. Asking Abigail her desires himself would have been a more appropriate action.

He approached the carriage, blocking Abigail from moving past him and reached for her arm. "Where are you going?"

The tremble in her wrist commanded his attention, which led him to fasten his attention to her troubled eyes.

"I think I should like to walk."

"Walk?" He unhooked his grasp when she pulled away. "But I thought you would ride with me." He had hoped to discuss the dinner. To ensure she did wish to attend, though he hoped he had been mistaken.

Abigail rotated slowly until her gaze approached his in an

uncompromising manner. "If you feel I can be trusted for a few minutes, I prefer to be alone."

At her stern reply, regret washed over him. Something had happened to alter her disposition. But what?

"If that is what you wish." Garrett agreed as he registered the hidden sadness beneath her words. "Is everything all right?"

"Yes, of course. I have an abundance of energy in my excitement over Randall's invitation that I must exhaust. And a nice walk should do the trick."

Her reaction did not resonate as delight. Instead it seeped with gloom. But he felt he had no choice but to allow her to have these few moments to herself.

"All right, then." Garrett stepped back, allowing her to pass.

Heaviness sank to the floor of Garrett's gut. He fought against his desire to stop her.

Her brows lifted. "I will see you back at the house, then?"

"Yes, but I need to make a brief stop along the way."

Abigail nodded and moved briskly along the sidewalk.

He had no choice but to stand by and watch while Abigail allowed Randall to court her even though it made his stomach churn. To confess his reservations against the man would be a mistake. She had to witness his shortcomings for herself.

To learn beyond a shadow of a doubt that Randall Thorne was not the right man for her.

Abigail struggled to open the front door, tears clouding her vision.

Aunt Louisa pulled the door back and her eyes widened. "Abigail? What on earth? Did something happen?"

"No." Nothing except that the prospect of any future with Garrett Barringer had been completely crushed the moment she abolished her virtue, along with her heart. "It's nothing."

Aunt Louisa draped an arm around her shoulders. "Then why are you crying?"

"I do not know, exactly. I suppose I am wallowing in my own self-pity. The very thing God warns against." Abigail took a deep breath in an effort to stop the tears. "But is it so wrong to want a marriage built on love, trust, and respect?"

"Of course not. God would want nothing less for you." Aunt Louisa steered her toward the kitchen and steadied her while she took a seat at the table. "Now, tell me why you are crying. Something must have happened."

"Only the realization that I shall have no chance at a happy marriage."

Aunt Louisa eyed her skeptically as she lit the stove. "Why would you say that?"

"I am certain you were well aware that it was my hope to reunite with Randall Thorne?"

"I knew your plan to spend time with the man, though I was not fully clear of your expectations."

Another round of tears welled in her eyes as she recognized the truth. "My expectations have been unreasonable. I hardly know the man."

"It takes time to build a friendship, and so much more to develop a relationship." Aunt Louisa spoke with conviction as if from her own years of experience. "And it is certainly not something to be rushed."

Abigail nodded in agreement. Heaven knew she would benefit from that luxury.

"Unfortunately, time is an advantage I do not possess," she said lethargically, wearily. For each day that passed brought her another day closer to her time with Garrett Barringer coming to an end. And another day closer to realizing her hope of an affectionate reunion had been nothing more than a nonsensical dream. "With what little I have gained from the brief moments spent with the man, I am beyond certain that a marriage to Randall

Thorne would be no better than a marriage to William Arendell. That perhaps it would be even worse."

Aunt Louisa grabbed two cups from the cupboard. "I tend to agree, from what little I know of the man, but that is nothing for you to cry about."

"How can you say that? I only have two choices. And neither one is agreeable."

"Why do you have to choose either of them?" Aunt Louisa set the porcelain dishes on the table before she reached for the heated kettle. Eyes narrowing, she filled both cups. "They are not the only two available men."

Of that she did not need reminding. It was the very essence of a particular man that had her heart writhing in pain. "I am ruined. No one else will have me."

"That is not true." Aunt Louisa challenged as she settled a tea bag into each cup of steaming water and set one in front of Abigail.

"But it is." It was a truth her mother had infiltrated into her soul from the moment Abigail had confided in her. Even if Garrett Barringer did accept her, her sins and reputation would follow and extinguish any promises he may make.

Another bout of tears flooded her eyes as she aimlessly stirred the spoon from side to side. Then Aunt Louisa cleared her throat and focused on the doorway beyond her. Abigail released her spoon and wiped at her errant tears.

"Mr. Barringer?" Aunt Louisa smiled up at him from around the brim of her tea cup and took a sip as if their discussion had been nothing more than a light subject. "I did not hear you come in."

Thickness clogged Abigail's throat as charged silence filled the space. How long had he been standing there? Had he overheard their conversation? Abigail's chair scraped against the wood floor as she pushed it back and stood.

Abigail turned slightly to face the man, then rattled off the

223

first thing that came to mind. "That didn't take you long at all."
Garrett met her eyes, no doubt seeing the moisture still encasing
them. "I thought you may take advantage of your time alone,"
she said, her voice carrying a teasing pitch.

Garrett's eyebrows hunched sharply. "I hurried through my
errand, wanting to make sure you arrived safely."

Of course, he did. That was the essence of his character. One
of the very things she loved about him. Heavens. Of all the times
to think such thoughts. She had enough trouble constantly
realigning her feelings. A tiny shred of admitting such things,
even internally, would only crush her spirit more.

She nibbled her bottom lip as she reached for her tea cup and
instead took a safer route. "It must be exhausting for you to have
to see to a woman uncapable of caring for herself. As you can
see, I made it here safely and without a scratch." Regretting her
condescending voice, she added, "I do, however, appreciate your
concern."

He must have heard the apprehension in her voice because
the sound of his boots shuffled closer. Being present at any sign
of her distress was something he had always done, without fail
every single time. It was likened to an invisible wire instinctively
pulling him toward her in her moments of distress. But how did
he always know?

"I was hoping to speak to you for a moment if I may."

The scraping of chair legs brought Abigail's eyes up and
toward Aunt Louisa in a skittering glance.

"If you will excuse me, there are a few things I must attend
to," Aunt Louisa admitted as she stood.

Garrett did not acknowledge her aunt's departure. And
neither did Abigail.

Abigail returned her cup to the table and glanced toward
Garrett. "Can I offer you a cup of hot tea?"

"Yes, please."

She stood and moved to the counter.

His presence brought about whirling sensations that heightened her awareness and exploited hidden desires she had not known existed. Delightful palpitations pirouetted across her heart as she selected another cup and reached for the kettle. She had to stop this nonsensical musing immediately.

"Is everything all right?" Concern escalated in his softening tone.

She took a much-needed breath before she carried his cup to the table and took a seat. "Yes, of course it is." Abigail deliberately kept her voice light and cheerful, hoping to camouflage her turbulent emotions. Bringing her cup to her lips, she glanced up at him. "What did you wish to speak to me about?"

Something altered in Garrett's eyes. "I plan to visit my family tomorrow."

"Tomorrow?" Her heart thumped against her chest in anticipation.

"Yes, and I hoped you would accompany me."

His eyes pleaded, but his voice resonated with such struggle and torment, it alarmed her. Then in the next instant, his smile returned and she wondered if she had imagined the entire thing.

"That is, if you are still interested."

Thrilled at the possibility of being invited to join him, she unleashed a full smile, feeling lighter than she had in months. Abigail fixed her eyes to his in anticipation but something was terribly wrong in his expression. Raw, conflicted sorrow suddenly shrouded his face.

"Yes, of course. I am looking forward to meeting your family. Especially your sister." It was as if her reply physically pinched him. But then just as quickly the vice that seemed to crush him slackened, and he leaned forward and offered a breathtaking smile. "Good. Then it's a date. Let's plan to leave here right after breakfast in the morning."

His efforts most likely had more to do with her father, but still, it was touching. Encouraging. Advantageous. Three things she should not center her focus where Garrett Barringer was concerned. A fact she knew too well.

Unfortunately, it would take numerous attempts to convince her heart.

❧

Unease filled Garrett's chest with a weight heavier than he could lift. Still, he had shoved the invitation from his throat. It had conjured up all the terror, fury, and grief he'd experienced as if that horrifying day was being replayed in slow motion.

Shame coiled around his neck, choking him. What must Sylvia be feeling? Lost. Lonely. Abandoned.

As the horses trotted along the trail, pulling the carriage, an occasional buzzard would startle at their approach and break from devouring what was left of a carcass that had at one time been full of life.

Sylvia had been spirited, animated, full of life. Until the accident. From that day forward, all that was left was the exterior of what his sister had once been. And it broke his heart, seeing that she had rejected everything. Everyone. Watching her withdraw into her own shell was the very thing that had driven him away.

He had put off seeing his sister entirely too long. Leading the carriage down the country lane toward his family home, Garrett calculated how many weeks had passed and tirelessly toiled to formulate a strategy for how to explain his distance. Somehow, he hoped Abigail's presence would soften his guilt. His pain.

Abigail clasped her hands together. "I have looked so forward to meeting your family. Especially your sister."

He couldn't see Abigail's face but could hear the sparkle in her voice.

"Has she married?"

The very essence of Abigail's question quickened his guilt. For she would most likely never wed.

"No," he replied quickly, because up until now, his silence had been the easier path.

At his answer, her chin lifted a fraction. "Oh?" Her focus strayed to the road before them. "Well, then. That is certainly something we shall have in common."

Redirecting the conversation would be the wisest choice for now. Though, he had to know what she'd meant by that. "You seemed surprised."

"I most certainly am." Stretching out her legs, she shifted in the seat. "She will be the third woman my age, whom I have met on this trip, who has remained unmarried."

"What is so wrong with that?"

"Nothing at all. In fact, I find it quite refreshing." She took in a shuttering breath. "I only wish my mother were here to witness the anomaly herself."

Thinking more on her words versus his own distress and guilt over his sister, he pressed on. "You are not looking forward to marriage, then?"

She twisted in her seat to face him. "As a matter of fact, I am not."

Garrett glanced her way, hearing her muddled answer. She bit her lip as if trying to conjure up an explanation.

"Especially given my current circumstances."

His heartbeat quickened. "Your current circumstances?"

Did that mean she did not find Randall Thorne a suitable match? If not, what did she mean then? As he stared at the open road, his vision blurred with images of a life with Abigail Dupree.

"Look!" Thankfully, the flock of geese gliding across the sky in a V had captured Abigail's attention and her delighted reaction shackled his ponderings. "There has to be at least twenty of them."

He grinned as a picture of Sylvia before the accident sprang to mind. If things were different, he could imagine Abigail and Sylvia becoming the best of friends.

As they drew closer to his childhood home, his grin slowly fell away. Abigail's disillusionment added another layer of regret. After parking in front of the house, he took several long moments to find the right words, before facing Abigail. He needed to explain. To prepare her. To prepare himself.

"Garrett?"

The familiar voice of his mother startled him and he turned. "Mom?" The endearment was all he could manage through the thickness in his throat. Seeing her standing there in her flour-coated apron funneled in countless memories. And along with them a renewed dose of regret.

"You're here. I can hardly believe it."

If his mother was anything, she was strong. Something she had demonstrated his entire life. Even now, she wore a wide smile as if everything in her world had never been altered. A faith so big, she found the light in every circumstance, no matter how much the darkness attempted to claim her joy. A trait he had not inherited. For, he was nothing more than a coward. Concerned only for his own needs.

Her bright smile faded into a subtle frown. "We have been worried sick over you."

The unpardonable statement hit Garrett like a punch to the gut. How could he have added more grief to his mother's load? He should have stayed. Should have never left them.

Still clinging to the reins, he hunched forward, unable to look another second into her eyes, wearied and tired from countless, sleepless nights she had surely endured. An apology would do nothing to right all the wrongs of his departure, but it was all he had to offer.

"I'm sorry."

A touch to his shoulder startled him and he leaned back.

Garrett caught Abigail's worried glance and knew she felt sympathetic toward him though she knew not why.

"I'm so happy to see you, Garrett." His mother reached for his hand. "And there's much to tell you. But first, how long must I wait before you introduce me to your lady friend?"

He really looked at Abigail then. Her long lashes fluttered twice as her troubled expression morphed into pure delight. "This is Miss Abigail Dupree." He matched her smile with one of his own. "I am working for her father and have escorted her here to Asheville for a brief trip from Charlotte."

"I see," his mother said, breaking his trance. "Well, Miss Dupree, it is a true pleasure to meet you, and I am so delighted you have joined Garrett today."

"Thank you, Mrs. Barringer."

Garrett shifted in his seat and cleared his throat before once again looking toward his mother. "How is she?"

Her gentle hand squeezed his. "Why don't you see for yourself."

Garrett looked toward the house at a sudden motion. There, on the porch, stood his sister. Alone. No one escorting her. "Is she—"

"Come along. Sylvia will be thrilled to see you and meet Miss Dupree." His mother turned, expecting him to follow.

After helping Abigail from the carriage, he felt her take his hand and tenderly pull at him, her eyes probing his with questions. But the answers would have to wait. He offered her hand a gentle squeeze before he reached for his mother and brought her into his arms. The three of them made the short trek to the house.

"It's about time you came home." Sylvia walked toward him, missing his gaze by a millimeter. She then wrapped her arms around him. "I missed you fiercely."

Before he could gather his wits about him, she pulled back.

"Well, Garrett?" She looked just past him to where Abigail

stood by his side. "Aren't you going to introduce me to your lady friend?"

How did she know someone accompanied him?

Not waiting for Garrett's response, Abigail stepped forward and took both of Sylvia's hands into her own. "Hi, Sylvia, I'm Abigail Dupree. It is such a pleasure to meet you."

Sylvia looked toward her face, not quite focused on her eyes, and beamed with her sweetest smile. "It is lovely to meet you, Abigail."

"I must confess, I was thrilled to learn that Garrett's family lived in this area, and have looked so forward to this day. And to meeting you all. I do hope you will forgive me for imposing on his visit. I practically begged him to bring me along." Abigail's confession flowed from her with unhurried confidence. As if she had known about Sylvia's handicap all along.

Enthralled, Garrett stared at Abigail as she conversed with his mother and sister, but he wasn't absorbing the core of the context. Abigail's communication skills were unpredictability inspiring.

Some people would abandon the idea of chatting with someone with a handicap. Unfortunately, it was the manner society had taught folks. Instinct demanded it. But Abigail forfeited her own comfort without hesitation. Instead of focusing on his sister's disability, Abigail offered grace by treating Sylvia in the same manner she would anyone.

With each passing moment, his admiration of the woman deepened and so did his attraction.

Snapping his attention from his charge, he returned his focus to his sister.

As they walked inside, shame hit him hard. Why had he stayed away? If it had not been for Abigail's nudging to visit, he may not have come today. He wasn't sure how he knew, but somehow he suspected that Abigail's presence would soften the blow. And he had been correct.

Distracted by his own thoughts, Garrett simply went through the motions of entering the house and did not notice when Mom stopped at the doorway and turned to face them. "It isn't often that Garrett brings a lady-friend home."

"This is actually a first for him, Mother." His sister smiled. "Are we to assume there will be a wedding to plan?"

"A wedding? Oh, no. We are not engaged." A deep hue of pink tinted Abigail's cheeks. "Though it goes without saying, your brother would most certainly be quite the catch," she said, shocking him at the bold statement and closing her argument with a breathtaking smile.

A statement and action that lingered long into their visit.

Chapter Twenty-Six

A bigail's chest nearly overflowed with unbridled emotion. In truth, the only thing that would have made her happier was if Garrett Barringer was not out of her reach. But today, even that fact didn't matter, for she had spent the entire morning in Garrett and his family's company and the day was far from over. Not with his mother's invitation to join them for dinner that evening.

Garrett placed a hand on her lower back as he led her out the front door. His darkened expression took precedence over his affectionate touch. Raw pain etched every line of his face as he released her hand.

What could have happened between him and his sister that would bring such devastation upon him that he would keep any distance from the beautiful family who had showered him and her with an abundance of love from the moment they had arrived?

Garrett's family had been so much more than she ever dared dream. She loved them instantly, and if she was not sorely mistaken, they loved her as well. An onslaught of affection mingled with a hefty dose of regret. For by her own burdens, Garrett's family would never be her own.

She shot a glance in his direction as they drew closer to the carriage. Garrett walked next to her. Tall. Confident. Accomplished. Yet there seemed to be a lingering sadness hidden deep within all that poise.

"To leave out the pertinent details of my sister's condition before our arrival was more than unfair to you. And a cowardly action on my part."

She slowed. "You are far too hard on yourself, Garrett. Though, I did wonder why you chose not to tell me."

He stopped and his hands moved with a nervous twitch as he faced her. "I do not know why. I wanted to. I tried." Garrett then resumed walking and led her to the other side of the carriage.

"It would not have mattered. But I would like to think that my knowing may have helped you somewhat in seeing your sister again."

"Your presence helped more than you will ever know."

"I'm beyond happy to hear that." Logic told her to leave it be, but curiosity wrestled the statement right out of her mouth as she followed him to the passenger side. "She made it sound as if losing her sight had been a recent occurrence."

His focus had settled somewhere above her head, far beyond them. A deep sigh left his throat before he glanced down at her. "She nearly drowned."

"Oh, no." Abigail shook her head, the action doing nothing to soften the vivid imagery of the young woman struggling for air. Struggling for her life.

"And it was my fault."

Filled with instant regret for having asked such personal questions, Abigail gasped and placed her hand on his arm. "Surely not."

Her memories raced to Garrett finding her by the water on their property. His anger at Randall leaving her alone by the pond. The undeniable fear in his eyes. His actions were beginning to make sense.

Garrett's dark eyes clouded with deep-rooted guilt. "I didn't cause her to go blind, but I didn't protect her when I should have."

"Seeing the two of you together gave me no indication that she blamed you for anything." Abigail squeezed his arm. "Except perhaps for staying away too long."

The lines of his forehead softened and his eyes roamed her face as if caressing her. The deed was subtle, but the notion invaded the very depths of her heart. "She was so different after the accident. As if the life had been completely snuffed from her. We have always been so close. She told me everything. Well, almost everything." His head lifted again. "Then she stopped talking. She did nothing but stare into the darkness. Became angry if anyone encouraged her to do otherwise."

Afraid of doing more harm than good with careless whispers, Abigail stared at the broken man before her.

Garrett blinked. "Of course, I took her side and told them to leave her alone. Seeing her that way…there was nothing more I could do. And what could she accomplish, really? Without her sight it would be impossible. A waste. But even my support didn't help. It was as if she hated me all the more. Couldn't stand to be in the same room as me."

At that moment, Abigail wanted nothing more than to hold Garrett in her arms and take his pain from him. But such an act would be neither appropriate nor wise. "I am so very sorry, Garrett. It must have been devastating. For all of you."

"My parents made the decision to send her to a school for the blind. She didn't want to go. When she begged me to help her convince them to let her stay and I failed, she stopped talking to me." He shook his head. "So, I left. I took any job that was offered that would keep me out of town."

Abigail suppressed a shiver. "How long have you stayed away?"

"For nearly a year."

Her stomach tightened. His pain mirrored her own, for she too believed that she had destroyed her own family.

"None of that matters now. When I saw her today, it was like seeing her again as she was before the accident." His reflective smile nearly took her breath. "At first, I thought by some miracle she had regained her sight."

"She is an impressive young lady."

"Somehow I knew deep down if the circumstances had been different, you two would become the best of friends."

Abigail's heart swelled with gratitude at such a compliment. "I should hope that to be true regardless of the circumstances. I simply adore her."

"I promise you, the feeling is mutual. Speaking of which, there is something I must confess."

"Oh?" The vulnerability in his eyes gave her pause. "And what is that?"

"I had not planned to come here." He took her hand and pulled it to his lips for a tender kiss.

The action scattered a million butterflies in her tummy.

"I have you, Abigail Dupree, to thank for my visit today."

Her pulse drummed and her breathing quickened. "I only wanted to not be your excuse for staying away."

"It was your insisting that changed my mind." Warm tingles jetted across Abigail's arms as Garrett continued holding her hand, his long fingers stretched beyond the length of her own, the feel of his lips still grazing her skin. "I would most likely have continued to put it off had you not suggested it. And I have you to thank for that."

"My insistence? Hmm. Perhaps, I should be more demanding, then," she told him, in a teasing tone.

"Yes. You most certainly should."

That stole her attention.

"Especially things concerning your heart." In that instant, Abigail saw his determination. "Abigail, you have the freedom to choose. And as long as it is in line with God's will for your life, there is no reason you should not have…whatever it is that you want."

His words were meant to encourage her, but they only reverberated void in Abigail's heart. Abigail tucked her head toward her shoulder. If only things were that simple. If only she could erase that one blemish staining the hope standing before her. If only.

"What is it?"

Explaining her situation was not possible. So instead, she lifted up onto her tiptoes and gave him a peck on the cheek. "Thank you, Garrett. You are absolutely right."

"I realize you haven't had much opportunity for courting. So, if you would prefer to spend the evening with Mr. Thorne, instead of joining me and my family for dinner, I will completely understand."

"No, I would very much like to join you and your family this evening. There is still plenty enough time for that." More time than was needed, she thought with a trace of bitterness. But she was determined not to allow her depressing thoughts to settle in her soul. Not tonight.

Even though Randall Thorne had not made clear his full intentions toward her, Abigail was more certain than ever before.

If things were different, the man standing before her would be her one and only choice.

Chapter Twenty-Seven

As Abigail put the final touches to her hair, her thoughts traveled to Rose. Her sweet, beautiful friend. Had mother already sent her away? Would Rose be at the mansion tonight? Working among the others down stairs?

She stepped into the parlor and found Aunt Louisa waiting by the front window, her hand pulling the heavy drape to one side. "Henry's pulling the carriage around now."

"Is he?" Abigail questioned with a smile though she had dreaded this evening. And then wondered why the object of her affliction wasn't present. "Surely he did not need Garrett's help to obtain the carriage?"

Aunt Louisa released the curtain. "Garrett is not here. Did he fail to mention that he would be going on ahead of you?"

"No. I hadn't realized…" Abigail swallowed the lump in her throat. "He must have decided to escort Sarah, then?"

"Yes, I do believe he confirmed that before his departure." Aunt Louisa's brows furrowed. "Randall has come for you, though. He walked out with Henry."

Abigail smiled in an effort to hide the pang of grief. "Wonderful. We shall have a lovely evening out."

No decisions had to be made tonight. Though her time in

Asheville was drawing to an end, she had come no closer to choosing her fate or whom she should be more inclined to marry. William Arendell or Randall Thorne. Nor had she advanced toward her cause of winning Randall Thorne's heart. For in truth, she was not certain his love was something she wanted to attain.

"I do hope you have enjoyed your time here."

"I have enjoyed it more than I can say," Abigail said truthfully as yesterday's events had been one of her most memorable days.

And Abigail pondered those memories for the entire duration of the carriage ride to the Biltmore.

Randall led her inside the mansion, and Abigail's eyes drank in the now familiar rooms garnished with polished, cherry wood. Strokes of color on tapestries and area rugs. A spill of light dancing along smooth marble. It stirred memories of her first visit to the Vanderbilts' lovely home. Her time with Garrett by the water garden. His protective stance solely toward her.

As they stepped into the dining area, Abigail searched for two of the people who mattered most to her. Rosalind Whitmore and Garrett Barringer.

Abigail was scanning the room when she caught sight of his transfixed brown eyes. Eyes that were focused on her. She whipped her focus from Garrett just as his generous lips widened into a smile. Sarah Thompson was standing next to Garrett, wearing a lovely dress in a soft shade of purple. The extravagance of the design made Abigail's own gown seem plain by comparison.

The woman's brows lifted with a spark of recognition when she glanced in her direction. With a swift peek at Garrett, something in Abigail's chest stuttered. A touch of genuine adoration flickered in his smile as he took Sarah's arm and led her toward Abigail and Randall.

"I'm happy to see that you and Mr. Thorne made it safely this evening," Garrett said, aiming his focus at Randall.

Sarah reached for Abigail's hand. "You look just lovely, Abigail."

"Thank you." Abigail did not want to like this woman. It would be much easier to dislike her. "You do as well. I was just admiring your dress."

Sarah leaned toward her, a light blush pinkening her cheeks. Making her even more charming. "It's one I have been working on for weeks."

Abigail's smile faded quickly. "You made this yourself?"

"Yes. And I worried I would not finish in time. But I stitched the last hem at half past twelve this morning," Sarah admitted, as if it were a normal occurrence.

Abigail absorbed the intricate details. "Well, I am certainly impressed. You are incredibly talented."

Sarah lifted a hand to her cheek. "That is a wonderful compliment since you have such marvelous taste."

In truth, all of Abigail's pieces were styles her mother had chosen. Not her own. But this conversation brought to light a notion Abigail had not considered before. Her mother only wanted the finest things for her only daughter. Had that been so horribly wrong?

"I would love to have you visit my shop. It isn't officially opened, but I would truly value your opinion on some other pieces that I have in progress."

Shop? Sarah had a shop here in Asheville?

"I would be honored to visit before my time here comes to an end." Abigail couldn't quite keep the skepticism out of her reply.

"When are you to leave?"

Before Abigail could stop herself, her gaze traveled once again to Garrett. "I'm not certain."

"Would you be available to come by in the morning?"

"Tomorrow?" Abigail glanced at Garrett, but thought better of asking for his help. "I suppose I could have my aunt drive me over."

"Wonderful." Sarah glanced up at Garrett, her cheeks blushing. "I shall be looking forward to it."

As harshly as the sentiment resonated within her, this was the kind of woman Garrett deserved. A woman of noble character, clothed in fine linen and purple.

A Proverbs 31 kind of woman. An impossible to disapprove kind of woman.

She was a woman who sets about her work vigorously, work that brings a profit, and her lamp burned well into the night. Midnight seemed late enough to Abigail. *Sarah.* Even her given name was biblical.

Not knowing what more to say, Abigail glanced over at Randall who had been abnormally quiet. Then hesitantly, Abigail projected her attention toward Garrett.

A line creased Garrett's brow, but didn't slacken the intensity of his eyes that were aimed directly at Abigail.

Then Sarah broke the awkward silence. "Perhaps we can visit more after dinner."

Why would Sarah wish to spend time talking with her when she had Garrett Barringer as a date for the evening? It was certainly an oddity. Though one she would be most willing to overlook since it would allow her to be in Garrett's presence as well. As for the obvious conflict of watching the two of them fall in love, she would have to cross that bridge as it approached.

Randall disrupted her thoughts with a squeeze to her shoulder. "Shall we?"

Abigail glanced between Garrett and Sarah. Two people who, by chance, had reunited after many years of separation. Very much like her and Randall. Although, she was certain her feelings for Randall were in no way equal.

Garrett and Sarah were the fortunate ones, indeed. If only she had the privilege to choose her own fate.

"You are in love with her."

Garrett's pulse accelerated, and his mind spun at Sarah's allegation. "What in the name of heaven are you talking about?"

"*You* are in love with Abigail Dupree." Sarah raised her hands to his chest and gave him a playful push. "And don't you dare try to deny it, Garrett Barringer. It's a wonder we all did not feel the effects of the sparks flying between you two."

Garrett pulled slightly back and averted his focus in order to hide the play of emotions upon his features that Sarah's statement had surely revealed. "I am uncertain how you came to that conclusion since, while in Miss Dupree's presence, you spent the entire time conversing with her about dresses and your views on them. And not once did you ask for my opinion."

Sarah eyed him suspiciously. "You would have given your thoughts, then?"

"I would like to think so," he said, hopeful he had succeeded in averting the topic. He most certainly needed to avoid Sarah's speculating about his feelings for Abigail. He had enough trouble convincing his heart that voicing his feelings for Abigail Dupree would only lead to a painful conclusion.

"That's impossible. Since your eyes and thoughts, I presume, have remained attached to Abigail Dupree from the moment we arrived."

Garrett absorbed the truth of her blow. He had been completely unaware of anything else in the room since Abigail Dupree's arrival. Of that he could not argue. Sarah had cornered him with no visible way out. And he opted to plead the fifth by keeping any fabricated excuses to himself.

"The question is why did you not invite her to join you this evening? Instead of using me to camouflage your true intentions."

Garrett's jaw tightened, for he was unable to deny the truth of her statement. "Sarah, I am truly sorry if I—"

"Heavens, don't be ridiculous. We were childhood friends.

Do you not think I would have been less willing if you had outright asked?" There was no accusation in her voice, only encouragement. "In fact, it would have broadened the excitement of this event."

"It would not have mattered." Garrett grimaced, not intending to voice his thoughts aloud. But spending so much time with Abigail over the last month had accomplished only one thing...losing his entire heart to the woman.

Sarah's enthusiastic smile wavered. "Why would you say such a thing?"

Garrett laughed then, for it was the unlucky draw of his fortune. To meet the woman of his dreams only to never have the chance to shower her with his love. "She is determined to reunite with Randall Thorne."

Sarah's eyes widened. "Yes, I remember that *was* the story I was told when I was first introduced to Miss Dupree and Mr. Thorne. But to reunite?" Sarah stared off in the aforementioned couple's direction with a slight shake of her head. "I don't believe it. I honestly would never have taken them as old acquaintances."

"It has been many years since they parted ways."

"As with us. But it seems as no time has passed." She touched his arm. "Abigail acts if she has only just met the man. As if she's almost wary of him."

And with good reason. Garrett clinched his jaw. "I have said too much."

"I do not understand all the circumstances nor do I need to. However, there's one thing of which I am certain. There is no love lost between Abigail Dupree and Randall Thorne." Sharp images of Abigail's aloof responses to Mr. Thorne ebbed through his memory at Sarah's observation. "But she is most certainly in love with you."

His knees nearly gave way hearing Sarah's opinion. "But I am her guardian."

"Yes, a charming, considerate, and might I add, very handsome guardian." Sarah nodded her head toward the dining room. "Just look at her. Anyone observing Abigail Dupree would agree that she has no sparks for Mr. Thorne, whatsoever. However, it seems she has wooed Mr. Thorne into submission. Even though it is obvious that was not her intention."

For that, he could hardly blame the man.

Garrett's attention was compelled across the room to the woman. At that same moment, Abigail glanced at him. He smiled. Abigail bit her lip, her cheeks darkening, but she did not look away. Her brows lifted in question and then she tilted her head toward Sarah. As if she were sending him a secret message not to ruin his chances with the young woman standing next to him. And he couldn't help but laugh.

"Why don't you tell her?"

A smile curved his lips as he recalled their first meeting. How, even in her distress, she expressed her opinion. "She is in fact worried I will ruin my chances with you."

"Admirable." Sarah cast Garrett a telling glance. "Yes, it is as I thought."

Garrett frowned. "What is as you thought?"

"You must not let her go, Garrett Barringer." Sarah's mouth lifted as her eyes brightened with mischief. "And I ought to see to it that you don't."

Garrett smiled, graciously tolerant of her impossible scheme. For he was privy to the entire story behind Abigail's motive to reunite with the man. And that was the one thing with which he could never compete.

"I see the way you look at her."

That was something over which he had no control. Abigail Dupree was so different from any other woman he had ever met.

"What I don't understand is why she is here with Randall Thorne. He acts as though he may be hoping for a future with her, but she most certainly does not care for him."

The latter part of Sarah's words gave him a morsel of hope. Though the first portion of the statement had him worried. For he knew Abigail would say yes to the man only to right her wrongs.

"How can you be so sure?"

"No woman in love with another looks at a man the way Abigail Dupree looks at you."

If it weren't for the bridge that connected Abigail to Randall Thorne, Garrett would undoubtedly make his true feelings known. But Abigail intended to choose the man, and even though it was in no way truthful, if she believed marrying the man would set her free mentally and spiritually, he could not stand in her way. He loved her too much.

It would be best to stop this imprudent talk before his heart forced him to do something foolish.

Abigail's father had intended for this trip to Asheville to give his daughter a full view of Randall Thorne's true characteristics. Hoping to turn her feelings away from the man for good. Unfortunately, there wasn't quite enough time to display all of the man's undesirable qualities. Though, Garrett could not fathom how Abigail's father would allow her to choose either Randall or William.

But what if they were not Mr. Dupree's only reasons for sending them on such an excursion?

Chapter Twenty-Eight

R andall led Abigail through a series of turns then steered her into a large room to the right. The crackling of fire in the hearth captured her attention first. But then her gaze rose to the books lining the shelves from floor to ceiling. Why, there must have been a thousand or more that surely included all genres. Multiple styles. Countless authors. She wanted nothing more than to explore the variety of stories with full abandon. Running her fingers over a few spines within reach, Abigail imagined Rose's reaction should she to ever witness such a wonder. A gentle smile filled her lips as a thought occurred to her. Perhaps Rose would see this magnificent room after all.

Randall stood motionless by her side, regarding the room with the intensity of a young boy awaiting punishment.

The magical fragrance of volumes and smoke was only dimmed slightly by the look that crossed Randall's face.

Abigail glanced over her shoulder. "Should we be here?"

"There was something I wished to discuss with you." Randall seemed more unsettled than she ever remembered seeing him. Then he glanced over his shoulder. "And I was hoping for privacy."

Abigail could not fathom what on earth had put him in such a state. She moved toward him. Perhaps he would tell her he had fallen madly in love with someone else. "Well? What is it? Please, don't keep me in suspense."

He led her to sit on a velvet cushioned settee, and then he dropped to one knee, and Abigial's heart stuttered. His eyes turned sultry. No doubt he was going in for the kill, but her defenses had been forged, and all that was left was pity for the man. She wasn't sure when or how that had happened. And it would certainly make things more difficult.

Her fingers stretched across the pearls dangling around her neck. She should be shouting from the rooftops with joy, yet the act brought about a disturbing spell of nausea.

"Abigail, I know we have just recently reacquainted, but I am certain there is nothing I want more than to correct my wrongs that I committed against you by asking for your hand in marriage."

Correct his wrongs. It certainly wasn't the most romantic way to present a proposal, but she couldn't fault the man for his honorable deed. Even if it was five years too late. Pressing her hand to her heart, she took a much-needed breath. "I don't know what to say."

"Say yes."

A yes to Randall was the last thing she felt in her heart, even though she had come to Asheville for that very purpose. Garrett Barringer had compromised the entire visit with his...well, with everything about him. But throwing Randall's proposal into the dust could be a mistake. Perhaps it would be better to only put him off for a bit.

"Well, how long must I wait for your answer?"

Being unable to explain the ordeal of her pending marriage to William Arendell only caused her more grief. "I'm afraid it isn't that simple. You see my father..." she started, hoping to satisfy his yearning.

"Of course, I intend to ask your father for your hand. I only knew our time together was drawing to a close, and I wanted to share my intentions should you leave before I had the opportunity."

"Were you planning to visit Charlotte to speak to my father, then?" She questioned him. "I am not certain when I am due to return home. Though I am certain it will be soon."

"If that is what I must do, then yes." He took her hands. "Though, I do wish you could stay."

She couldn't say the same nor could she admit the truth, so she simply inched closer and kissed his cheek. "I am honored by your proposal, Randall. And perhaps, my father will be as well."

He then lowered his hand to the hem of her skirt and slid his fingers up her calf.

Abigail stood quickly, forcing his hand to fall as the sensation of her chest wall squeezing nearly choked her.

"There is no need to worry," he said. "We are alone here."

Fear sucked the moisture from her throat. Why were they alone? Where was Garrett? "It is not proper for us to be alone. Nor are your actions." Her gaze zeroed in on the doorway. Dead silence hovered as if they were suddenly miles away from everyone. Why hadn't she noted that earlier? She'd been a fool to allow him to lead her here. "Someone may happen upon us."

Randall dropped his hands by his sides and blew out a frustrated breath. "I presume, you speak of your chaperone, Mr. Barringer? The one who is always lurking around and never ceases to give me some much-needed privacy."

At least she had diverted Randall's attention. But that nagging pang in her chest only worsened. She had no one to blame but herself for being put in this position.

Randall stood and took several steps closer. "I do believe his date has preoccupied his mind elsewhere. If I had to guess, they have wandered off and found their own private quarters."

Abigail's stomach sickened at such a notion, and she turned

from the man who was forcing such despicable thoughts on her. "You shouldn't speak of others in such a way."

"What is it, Abigail? You act as if you have some claim on the man."

Hearing Randall's allegation of her feelings toward Garrett heated her cheeks. A mixture of grief and despair overcame Abigail. "I have never insinuated such. It is improper to speak against my—"

"Your what?" he asked, drawing out the word, his pitch criticizing.

"To speak against anyone," she argued. The commanding tone she'd meant to convey into her words fell flat. "It isn't proper."

"If I remember correctly, you were not so concerned with propriety in your younger years."

"Well, it seems I have matured a great deal."

Randall eyed her in an inappropriate manner. "Yes, you have, indeed." He then clasped his hands, and a full grin widened his cheeks as if the two of them had not gone rounds over her chaperone. As if he had not insulted her greatly. "I have an excellent idea. Why don't you send a telegram to your father for permission to prolong your visit?"

Abigail set the troubling reflections aside and turned her attention back to the man still waiting for her reply. "I am beyond certain that would do no good. My father expects me to return and it would only put others at a disadvantage as well." She had no choice but to ignore the accusation, not trusting her own voice. "As well as my aunt and uncle. I could not expect to impose on them much longer."

"I do not wish for you to leave. You do not know how often I have thought of you." He grinned vindictively. "And as for your father, given our history, I am not concerned in the least. I do believe your father would willingly accept me. Seeing as how it would release him from a precarious predicament."

"Whatever is that supposed to mean?"

Randall heaved an exaggerated sigh. "Your remaining unmarried at your age, of course."

"My age?" Abigail hissed through her bruised ego.

"As well as your state of virginity." He rested his hand on her waist, his fingers slowing rising with each breath. "How I have reminisced about our last night together."

Her cheeks flamed.

"You are just so beautiful. Even more so than I remembered. And I have longed to hold you in my arms as I please."

"Mr. Thorne!" Abigail lurched away from him. "I cannot believe you would speak such a thing out loud."

He inched closer. "It isn't as if we have never…"

Her blood boiling, Abigail took a step back, but a wall blocked her from moving as far from Randall as she would have liked.

"It's that Garrett Barringer fellow, isn't it?" With narrowed-eye scrutiny, Randall watched her. "Have you and he—"

"What? No." She stared at the man she hardly knew, his crooked grin accusing her. When had she heard such blunt cruelty?

"I certainly wouldn't blame the man for trying."

Abigail sucked in her breath.

"There must be something amiss about him to pass up an opportunity to have you all to himself."

"How dare you suggest such a thing?" Abigail squeezed her hands in tight fists to prevent herself from slapping him hard. "I must go. Now."

He took a step back and in the brief moment she found her escape.

"Don't be sore. I meant no harm."

Not stopping, she continued toward the exit. "I need to return to the main hall."

She started to glance back toward him, her last hope slipping through her fingers. But what good would it do to stay? She had seen all she needed to see. Randall Thorne was not the man she wanted or needed.

Not only had he disrespected her with his callous words, but his eyes had veered more than once to other women while in her presence. Though he thought to have concealed the glances, Abigail had caught his gaze dipping to inappropriate levels on more than one occasion. A trait Randall unfortunately shared with William Arendell.

Garrett, on the other hand, had a respect for women that was unmatched against her long list of male acquaintances. Garrett was more like her own father in that regard than any other man she had ever met. He possessed many admirable qualities. Though the problem remained. She did not deserve Garrett Barringer, and she never would.

The sound of his footsteps drew nearer as she reached the room's exit.

"I would have never left had it not been for Lydia and the baby."

Abigail slowed. *The baby?*

"She didn't give me much choice, as you well know." Randall took another step toward her. "I believe she fabricated a plot to lure me to take her as my wife, knowing you were the only one I wanted."

If that were true, Randall would have returned for Abigail. But he had not.

Horrified for having been so blind, she felt regret expel through her essence and lodge in the pit of her belly like a fever-borne infection.

"Goodbye, Randall," she said without looking back.

Abigail preferred to remain unmarried all of her days and to become an old maid, over tying herself forever to the likes of him.

Chapter Twenty-Nine

A bigail had said her goodbyes to Randall Thorne last night, her heart certainly not breaking for the man, but for the idea that he could have been an answer to her prayers in more ways than one. Not even the unfavorable option of a marriage to William Arendell awaiting her when she arrived home was not the thing that was crushing her spirit.

It was the idea of knowing Garrett Barringer would never be hers and absorbing the fact that she would have to bury her true sentiments for the man.

Garrett entered the room and Abigail suppressed her inner thoughts.

"Good morning, Ladies." Garrett moved toward the entryway instead of joining them in the dining room. "I pray you ladies will enjoy your day."

Abigail looked up sharply. "Are you leaving?"

Garrett looked at her and the effect he had on her was instant and pathetic. Her heart flapped madly like a bird's wings.

"Yes, I am actually on my way out, now. And will most likely be absent most of the day."

She scraped a dry tongue across her lips before fashioning a charming smile, though deep down her insides were gathering for a great storm.

A half hour later, Aunt Louisa was driving Abigail toward the shop of the woman who would surely claim the very thing she wanted more than anything in this world. Garrett Barringer's heart.

The sound of Sarah's voice greeted them before they even reached the portico. "Welcome to my humble abode."

They all exchanged pleasantries, then Sarah led Abigail inside the store nestled in the middle of downtown Asheville.

Abigail absorbed the details of the quaint shop complete with a table and small chairs for tea. "What a wonderful, charming place you have!"

"I'm thrilled that you like it," she said as she raised her slender fingers to fidget with a button at her collar.

"And it is in the perfect location," Aunt Louisa added.

Sarah's gaze traveled to the front floor-to-ceiling, windows. "Yes, as long as we don't get an abundance of rainstorms."

"Oh?" Abigail inquired. "Why is that?"

"The roadway turns into an oversized mud hole and it is impossible to navigate until the weather dissipates and road crews have an opportunity to clear the pathway."

"Well, we should hope we get only enough rain to water our crops, then," Aunt Louisa stated, as she stared up at a few gowns hanging from the wall. "These dresses are just splendid."

"I have been working hours, hoping to have everything ready for my grand opening the first of the year." Sarah waved her hands in the air as if adding more excitement to the event.

As she chatted, Sarah led them into another room of the shop. "I have quite a few ladies who are already working on domestic dresses we will be selling, but my heart and soul adores designing the more fashionable attire. And with the Swannanoa Hotel, there's always a need for a ball gown. The dances there seem to be endless."

Abigail shoved her conflicting emotions about this woman from her head. They were an unwelcome beast and the woman before her was not deserving of her jealousy. "Well, I must say, you do it very well."

"Yes, indeed," Aunt Louisa added. "You are very talented. If ever I am in need of a new costume, I will most certainly retain your services."

"Yes," Abigail said, "and I shall do the same. I would love for my mother to see your designs. She is very particular about such things. And I can guarantee she will love your work."

Sarah brought both hands to her cheeks. "That is so kind of you."

Aunt Louisa turned to Abigail. "Since we're in town today, I was hoping to visit some other shops."

Sarah touched Abigail's arm. "Oh, would you mind if Abigail stayed a bit longer? I was hoping we might chat a bit."

Abigail looked toward her aunt, who had a drawn brow.

Still, Aunt Louisa wasted no time in giving her answer. "Of course, I do not mind at all. Shall I meet you back here then when I am finished?"

"Yes, that would be fine," Abigail told Aunt Louisa, though she worried over Sarah's true intentions.

As Aunt Louisa made her departure, Sarah slipped her arm through Abigail's and led her toward the back of the store. "I hope you won't think me pushy, extending an invitation in that manner, but I have so longed to talk with you privately."

"Is that so?" Did Sarah intend to confess her love for Garrett? Abigail wasn't sure she could stomach such a sentiment.

"Yes. But I knew your time here was short."

Ducking away from the woman's penetrating stare, Abigail toyed with the lace of her sleeve.

"You see, I have found myself in a bit of a predicament."

The announcement brought Abigail's head up.

"There is a specific dress that I have promised a young lady coming all the way from New York and she's scheduled to pick up the gown next week."

Abigail's anticipation escalated as her fear waned. This wasn't about Garrett. She gave a little laugh. "That's wonderful."

"Well, it would be, except for the fact that I'm worried about the fit of the dress."

"Did you not have the lady's measurements?"

"Yes, but I still need to know how the piece will look on a human subject. These dress forms can only show so much. And I realize this is an odd request, but I was hoping you would be willing to try on the dress so that I can get a better idea of whether I need to adjust some of the pleats or leave them be. Perhaps, make it more appealing in certain areas."

"Me?"

"If I had to guess by looking at you, you are her exact size."

Abigail couldn't be certain, but it sounded very much like Sarah had just paid her a compliment. "Well, then. If I am, it would be my honor to oblige."

"Oh, thank you, Abigail. You are an angel of mercy." Sarah's face brightened with her smile. "I'll fetch the dress and we can use the dressing room to the left."

We? The thought had not occurred to her that Sarah would assist in dressing her. Though, it couldn't be much different than Rose.

Sarah returned with the full-length golden gown bursting with intricate details of lace and silk.

"Heavens! I have never seen anything so beautiful."

"I am delighted that you like it," Sarah said as she led Abigail to a closed-off room in the back. "We shall have plenty of privacy back here. Tell me, have you enjoyed your visit to Asheville?"

"Very much so."

Sarah unfastened the buttons from the vibrantly colored silk and set the dress aside. "I can hardly wait to see you in this,"

Sarah stated, thankfully changing the course of their conversation.

Abigail turned at Sarah's suggestion and Sarah unlatched the first of Abigail's buttons.

"Did you need to take my measurements?"

"I do not believe that will be necessary. We will see how it works first and then proceed from there."

Abigail lifted the gown out as she once again admired its features. "I do hope it fits."

"Oh, it will."

Abigail stole a glimpse at Sarah. "How can you be so sure?"

Sarah tilted her head. "I fortunately have a keen eye for such things."

Abigail stared at her reflection in the mirror while thinking how advantageous it would be for Garrett to gain such a woman, even though her heart ached at the thought.

Slipping off her own dress, she reminisced about her time spent with his family. Oh, how she wished to see them again. But it would most likely never happen. They would all but forget about meeting her when Sarah entered the picture in a more permanent fashion.

Then at the awkwardness of having Sarah there and lifting the bulk of material over her head, and then helping her into the new gown, Abigail's thoughts drifted into a different direction. To her dearest friend, Rose. And how grateful she felt at the countless times Rose had been there to help her into her dresses.

Sarah buttoned the last hoop and then glanced at the full length of the dress in the mirror. "Let's go out front so I can see it from a different angle."

Abigail stepped from the dressing room, and the dress swished from side to side with each movement.

"How does it feel?"

"It fits perfectly."

Sarah hooped the few buttons on each sleeve and adjusted

CINDY PATTERSON

and tied the bow more securely at Abigail's lower back. Then
Sarah proceeded to inspect and pull at the material, starting at the
neckline and working her way to the floor.

"It is just as I thought." Sarah took a step back and surveyed
the dress from head to toe. "You were made for this dress."

Abigail waited, unsure how to reply to such a compliment.

"And I knew it would give me better insight into exactly
what is required to make it perfect. But now seeing it on you, I
believe the dress is complete."

"I agree. It is perfect just as it is." Abigail turned at an angle
and looked at her reflection in a mirror. "I have a friend who
enjoys needlework. She was always helping me out of precarious
situations."

"Oh? She sounds like a gem of a friend."

"She is that." Abigail felt a frown fusing to her lips. "And I
certainly miss her."

"It is rare indeed to find a trustworthy friend." A slight
grimace, graced Sarah's mouth. "I assume she is from the Charlotte area?"

"Yes, she is."

"Well, have your friend look me up should she ever be in
Asheville. I may have a job to offer. And who knows, she could
be a perfect fit."

"I will." Abigail wanted to explain that Rose would most
likely be removed from her home by the time she returned, and
would most certainly be moving to this area and had already
secured a job, but she was confident it would be wise to say
nothing more. Especially since Abigail knew more of the situation than she should.

"When will you be returning home?"

"I'm uncertain. But I had thought to remain through the
summer." Though her visit may be cut short. And the reasoning
behind it, had her stomach in knots.

"Is that so?" Sarah asked, still fussing over the intricate

details of the dress. "What will happen to poor Mr. Thorne? Surely his heart will be broken to see you go. Or, does he plan to accompany you?"

"Oh, no. That shall never happen," Abigail said, almost regretting it instantly.

Sarah was much too easy to talk to and Abigail was talking entirely too much.

"Oh? I thought the two of you were hoping to reunite, or was Garrett mistaken?"

"The mistake was in allowing my memories to lead me in such a direction." Abigail had to change course of this conversation before she could blurt out more excessive chatter. "It's a rather long story, which I am certain would bore you to tears."

"All was not lost, though?"

If only Sarah knew Abigail's skeletons, she would never have asked such a question. Nevertheless, what was not lost was her time spent with Garrett Barringer. However, she could never admit to such a thing.

Abigail tucked a stray strand of hair behind her ear. "Not all, indeed. For, if I had not come, I would not have had the privilege of meeting Garrett's family."

"Oh, yes." Sarah smiled and her brow crinkled a bit. "They are wonderful people who I have missed terribly."

Abigail couldn't decide if there was resentment in Sarah's voice or not. Perhaps her expression stemmed from concern over Garrett's sister.

"I imagine Sylvia must be awaiting your return."

"Unfortunately, I doubt there will be another opportunity for me to visit." Abigail's brow creased at the depressing thought.

Sarah's smile was substituted with a look of curiosity. "Surely not."

"I'll be heading back to Charlotte, and not sure when or if I'll be back."

"I was hoping...well." Sarah paused. "Garrett had mentioned

that he may be returning to Asheville as soon as this particular job was completed."

Abigail's throat seized and knotted.

Sarah brought a hand to her mouth. "Oh, heavens. I should not have said anything."

"No, it's perfectly fine." The ache moved down Abigail's throat. "That isn't something that he would share with me. It only took me by surprise. I guess I hadn't realized—"

"I keep forgetting that you and he...well, to be perfectly honest, I would have thought the two of you were a couple before I could envision you and Mr. Thorne."

The statement brought a rush of awareness that nearly took her breath.

"Heavens, no. Garrett is nothing more than my chaperone," Abigail said, overly conscious of her true feelings for the man. "Though, I'm still not exactly sure why my father had him escort me."

"From what I can remember of Garrett Barringer, and from what I've seen during our brief visits, I would imagine your father a very wise man to entrust his only daughter to his care. At any rate, I do wish you could stay. Especially now that I have spent time getting to know you better." The intensity in her eyes left no doubt of her sincerity. Then Sarah cleared her throat. "Speaking of Garrett, there was one other thing I had hoped to discuss with you."

Angst bottomed out in Abigail's stomach.

"You see, he—"

"Oh, dear." Air wheezed through the thorny ball of emotion forming in Abigail's chest when she glanced at the entrance and saw her aunt approaching. "My aunt has returned, and I'm still wearing your dress. Perhaps we will have another opportunity to finish our chat."

Abigail didn't miss the disappointment that shrouded Sarah's countenance.

"Yes, perhaps we will."

In Abigail's opinion, Aunt Louisa had returned precisely on time, before Sarah had an opportunity to pour out her heart about Garrett.

That would have surely ripped her own heart to shreds.

Chapter Thirty

Garrett whistled quietly as he trekked to the main entrance of the Biltmore. He may not understand the exact reason why God had brought him back to Asheville so soon, but God had a purpose and he'd been given a front row seat to all His wonders. If it hadn't been for his visit to see Sylvia, he would have missed out on the beautiful blessing of seeing his sister's blooming.

Something he had never expected to see again. And it was all because of Abigail's urging.

His Abby.

At least he wanted her to be his. More than he had ever wanted anything. The woman had stolen his heart and taken his ordinary life to another level of living.

Vanderbilt's head adviser opened the door at Garrett's arrival. "Mr. Barringer. It surprised me to hear from you again so soon."

"I do appreciate your taking the time to see me." Garrett's neck tensed as he followed him inside the magnificent home. With each step, his pulse quickened. His job with Dupree had nearly come to an end and the time had come to make a decision that would impact the rest of his future.

"I thought to have our conversation here in one of George's

favorite rooms. This is Vanderbilt's cigar room." He offered one seat to Garrett while he took the opposite chair. "Very well, then. What did you have on your mind?"

"I have a proposition for you," Garrett told the man, even though his plan was not warranted with a guarantee.

"Do tell."

"When the *Asheville Gazette* contacted me with an offer to accept an editorial position, I refused. But it seems as though I will be remaining in Asheville and will be taking the job after all. With that being said, it is imperative that I bring my own ideas. And that's where the Vanderbilts and this magnificent home come in.

"I would be honored to run an ongoing story about the new additions to the Biltmore. And in exchange, I have a proposal for an idea I would like to see come to fruition. One that has the potential to bring another great opportunity for grand publicity."

"Oh?" The man crossed his arms. "What exactly would that be?"

"A wedding on the grounds of the Biltmore."

His brow lifted as if Garrett's suggestion had fashioned favorably. "What a splendid idea. It is one of which I believe Mr. and Mrs. Vanderbilt both will embrace with open arms." The man clasped his hands together. "Might I inquire, who is the fortunate groom?"

Foreboding pierced him. What if things didn't transpire as he hoped? Still, Garrett forged on, determination padding his tone. "I am."

Abigail prided herself for controlling her reaction to hearing of Garrett's plan to return to Asheville. But now that she was alone, the sorrow of his plan to return to Asheville nearly strangled her.

Once she returned to Charlotte and her father no longer needed Garrett's services, she may never see him again.

Tonight though, she intended to enjoy every second in the man's presence. Make enough memories to last her a lifetime of living without him.

And since her aunt and uncle had already turned in for the evening, it would be just the two of them.

Abigail set about her tasks of preparing her favorite supper recipe from their dinner left overs. One that Mabel had taught her as a young woman. A time before her mother deemed it unagreeable for Abigail to learn anything about cooking or baking.

Over the course of the evening, a growing sense of apprehension swelled within Abigail, making it progressively harder to take a full breath.

To make matters worse, her last conversation with Randall had replayed numerous times throughout the day.

Abigail paced the kitchen and looked through the window pane. A storm brewed outside that resembled the turbulence strengthening within her. All while pondering Lydia's secrecy of such a tragic ending to her own love story. And what of the baby? Had she lost the baby? Abigail's stomach turned at Randall's nonchalant attitude of Lydia and his unborn child.

Abigail looked toward the front door. Garrett should be back by now.

For the hundredth time, Abigail adjusted the silver settings. Repositioned the fresh wild flower assortment in the vase. Listened for the sound of an approaching carriage.

Where are you, Garrett Barringer?

A crack of thunder exploded and she gripped the edge of the table. Had something happened to him? Was he on the side of the road with a busted wagon wheel? Or worse? No, she would not allow her brain to venture there.

She instinctively bowed her head. *Heavenly Father, please keep him safe.*

Any other time, Abigail would have welcomed the sound of rain pelting the tin roof. Would have enjoyed reading a book or lying in bed being comforted by the gentle rhythmic drumming. But tonight, it only produced distress and caused her to visualize every worst-case scenario.

The sound of the door opening brought her head up. Blinking away the sudden moisture that distorted her vision, she turned. There, standing in the doorway was Garrett's alive, breathing body. The most welcomed sight she'd seen all day.

Thank You, Jesus.

After taking a deep, relieved breath, she stood, walked into the front room, and propped her hands on her hips. "Garrett Barringer, where on earth have you been?"

Garrett peered at her oddly, slanting his head at an angle, as if unable to quite fathom her reaction. "I had a meeting."

"It must have been mighty important to keep you out this late? I was ready to send out a search party."

His eyes widened slightly, then creased at the corners as he removed his wet coat. "I do apologize. I would never intentionally upset you."

Only then did she realize how affectionate her words must have sounded. She gave off a slight laugh to disguise her embarrassment. "All is well. You are here now. Safe and sound. I hope you are hungry?"

"I am, indeed."

"Good. I have everything ready."

Abigail thought herself a foolish woman as she led him into the kitchen and glanced at the table. The setting was romantically prepared for two. Foolish, indeed. Perhaps he wouldn't notice.

"Everything looks lovely."

To that she had no response. Instead, she moved toward the

stove and retrieved two plates and filled them with a helping of beef, potatoes, and carrots.

"Here let me help you with that." Garrett took both plates and set them on the table.

"Thank you," Abigail offered as she took her seat.

After Garrett finished a prayer of thanksgiving for the food before them, he looked at her. "I received a telegram from your father this morning."

Abigail's heart clenched at the news. "A telegram?"

Garrett reached for a roll as if the statement was nothing but ordinary. Yet, she could not fathom her father sending a telegram only to say hello. And why would he send it to Garrett instead of her? Something dire must have happened. "What did he have to say?"

"Your parents are to come here."

"What?" Her head whipped back. "But why? I thought I would be staying for another few weeks."

"Apparently your father has some business here in Asheville of which he needs to attend."

Abigail chewed her bottom lip. "Those were his only words?"

"Yes, it would seem so."

Even though her father traveled for business often, it was indeed better news than what she had anticipated hearing. Though, her mother never accompanied him.

"Good heavens. I cannot imagine my mother outside of her own home." Though, the thought of the Biltmore and the opportunity to witness her mother's excitement at such a sight brought a smile. Then Abigail sat taller as the thought of seeing her dearest friend leapt to the forefront of her mind. "I wonder if Rose will be attending her?"

"Of that, I am not certain."

Abigail poured them both a glass of water from the pitcher. "Oh, I do pray she is. I searched every face of the Vanderbilts' help at the dinner party, hoping to see Rose, but praying I would not. I can only assume she has not arrived as of yet." Abigail stiffened her shoulders at the grievous mistake of breaking her promise to Rose to keep silent about the opportunity.

"Whatever do you mean? Why would your maid be serving at the Vanderbilts'?"

"Oh, but I should not have said anything. I gave Rose my word." Tension radiated through Abigail's shoulders and spine. Rose could not lose this position over her blunder. Abigail would never forgive herself. "Please, Garrett, I beg you not to mention this to my father and especially my mother. Could I implore of you to forget everything I have just spoken?"

Garrett's eyes narrowed, but he nodded. "Of course. Anything you wish."

Moisture cloaked her vision. "Though, since it is now out in the open, I do wish to tell someone. It has been weighing so heavy on my heart since we left, and it has been pure torture keeping the news to myself." His answer emerged from the warmth in his eyes, so, Abigail continued. "Rose is to leave me. Perhaps, even before I am to arrive home."

"How did you hear of it?"

Abigail's shoulder's wilted as their last conversation replayed in her memory. "She confided in me the night before our departure."

"And she was to be employed by the Vanderbilts?"

"Yes. And it's such a wonderful opportunity for her." Yet that knowledge did little to soften her own pain of losing her most cherished friend. "It is more than selfish of me to not want to let her go."

Garrett's chair scuffled as he shifted his weight. "You must miss her very much."

"Dearly. She is my best friend. Perhaps more like a sister." Abigail grinned at the recollections of Rose, bubbling up in her memories. "You must think me a silly, immature girl admitting such things."

"Not even a little. I admired your relationship with Rose from the first moment I met you."

Her cheeks heated at his affirmation. "I took her presence for granted. And I regret that now, immensely. Knowing she will most likely be removed from my home before our return has nearly devasted me."

She ached for her friend. Their extensive talks. Sharing their long-lost hopes and dreams. If only Rose could see her now. Sharing her heart with the man of whom she had fallen in love. Abigail could almost envision the woman's eyes twinkling with happiness at Abigail's admission. And she would most certainly squeal with glee and say, "Well, it's about time."

Abigail's eyes were pooling again. Blinking away the moisture, she snapped out of her thoughts and reached for a roll. "Thank you for your generous toleration of my blabbering."

"There is no need to apologize." Garrett took a sip of water. "It is obvious in the way you treat Rose and speak of her that God brought the two of you together for a reason. And from what I can see, she was a very special and important part of your life and blessed to have you as well. There is nothing wrong with loving her and grieving her departure."

"There are certainly worse things a person must endure. And even though it hurts, I am so very happy for her." Abigail glanced at her plate, which she had yet to touch. "However, I do hope our distance over the last few weeks will make it easier to return to an empty home."

"Since the trip may be extended at your parent's arrival, it will give you additional time to visit with my sister. And Mr. Thorne if that is what you wish."

"I hadn't considered that." Even though, she had no desire to spend more time with Randall. "What I don't understand is what on earth could be so important that my mother would leave home now, when I was certain she was anxiously planning my wedding. Either way, the longer I am out of Mr. Arendell's reach, the better." Abigail touched her mouth. "Please forgive me for speaking out of turn."

"Perhaps then, a wedding is not of the upmost importance to your parents."

"It would seem not." She shook her head in wonder. "Whatever the reason, if it has taken my mother's attention away from my unattached state, I welcome it wholeheartedly. Unless she has convinced my father into some other fiasco of which I am none the wiser." How many times had she scolded herself for having no control over her tongue? Yet, her own reprimand did nothing to steer her to use a softer dialect, and her gruff statement did not go unnoticed.

What must Garrett think of her?

He cleared his throat, his gaze holding hers. "There is something else I wished to speak to you about."

The genuine empathy in his tone took her by surprise. She had expected condemnation. Or, at the very least, disapproval.

Perhaps she had no reason to worry. For she could almost see anticipation in his eyes. Giving her hope of what he might say. What she wanted so badly for him to say. What if he offered a confession of his love? Abigail peered at him more closely. Good heavens! But his rugged charm was impossible to resist.

"Oh?" She schooled her features. "And what could that be?"

"With your parents' arrival, my position with your father will end. And I have decided to stay in Asheville."

Her concentration suspended mid-course, and she was unable to process fully what he was saying. Knowing Sarah had spoken the truth...that he had confided in Sarah...that he would be leaving her, brought another round of agonizing heartbreak. Abigail thought she would have additional weeks or even months to say her goodbyes.

He reached for her hand. "After seeing my sister and my family. I don't see how I have any choice."

She trembled at his touch and a tiny gasp escaped her lips.

"Abigail, I have you to thank for that. Your encouragement gave me the strength to face them again."

The surge of disappointment took her breath. She couldn't speak. Couldn't concentrate. Of course he would be staying. How else would he maintain a relationship with his family? A courtship with Sarah?

Fighting the urge to cry, she sank deeper into her seat. Their hands slipped away from each other. Just as he was slipping away from her.

He continued eating and speaking, but nothing else he said registered. Every word became a blur of syllables. Twisting, squeezing the very life from her.

What if she never saw him again? Why would she? He would more than likely marry Sarah and there would be absolutely no place in his life for her. She would be nothing more than a woman he once knew.

Then he smiled. "Thank you for dinner. It is delicious. But you have hardly touched yours."

"I'm glad you enjoyed it." Sorrow tore through her. "It seems that my appetite has diminished."

Garrett finished another bite. "I'm sorry to hear that. I hope you're not feeling unwell."

Abigail's palms shoved against her stomach as she struggled to find a breath. His words finally registered and echoed in Abigail's mind like a boulder rushing down a hill aiming straight for her. Intent on crushing her.

I have decided to stay in Asheville.

That he would be staying could only mean one thing. She would be returning to Charlotte with her parents and would not even have those last few days with him.

"No, it's nothing," she assured him before making the mistake of glancing his way.

How would she go on about her life having known him? Her heartbreak over Randall's leaving her behind after receiving her most precious possession held no comparison to the sorrow consuming her now. Abigail's mind twisted in anguish. It wasn't as if she would be able to visit with Garrett. Take long carriage rides. Enjoy other dances with the man. Allow him to hold her in his arms.

Abigail stood. "I'm terribly sorry, but I need to…if you could please excuse me for a moment."

"Abigail, what is it?"

"I'm sorry. But, I must…"

She took off for her room. Only then could she allow her pent-up sobs to escape. Closing the bedroom door behind her, Abigail slid to the floor. Somewhere deep inside, she had hoped, had prayed that Garrett would pledge his undying love to her. That perhaps her father would give his blessing on such a union. It was foolish to harbor hope, especially with her stained past.

With her father's permission to court Randall Thorne, Abigail knew what she had to do and that choice nearly choked her.

Abigail's chest heaved at the heartbreak devouring her. Harsh, uncontrollable sobs broke loose, expending every emotion that welled within her.

Chapter Thirty-One

G arrett ran a hand over his face, the stubbles of his recently trimmed beard rubbing against his palm. He leaned against the wall that led to Abigail's bedroom.

What had he said to receive such an emotional reaction? He had thought Abigail would be pleased to hear he wished to remain close to his family. His sister. That she would even be happy about his decision. But it was the exact opposite. It was as if a barrier had been raised and she alone held it in place.

He should have waited to tell her his plans. Sarah had assured him it would be easier to gain an honest reaction of her opinion of his staying instead of waiting until after her parents' arrival. With the likelihood that their presence would muddy her response. Though it had not mattered, since he had been unable to finish. Now, he was rethinking his decision.

When Abigail learned the truth of her mother's illness, she would be devastated. And would most likely hate him for keeping his knowledge of her mother's fate from her. But he had promised her father to not say a word. Perhaps his knowledge of her mother's difficulty would remain untold. Yet, starting a future built on lies would lead to ruin.

Finally, after several minutes, Abigail exited the confines of the bedchamber.

"You must think me a silly woman." Her shoulders loosened from their stiff position. "Please forgive me for leaving so abruptly amidst your important announcement."

"I think no such thing. And there's no need for an apology. In fact, I'm the one who should be asking for forgiveness because I have not been completely honest with you." Her eyes narrowed but she said nothing, so he continued. "I was hoping..."

She blinked, then tilted her head. Her brow drew into a curious point. "Yes?"

He wanted to go to his knees and ask for her hand in marriage, but now was neither the time nor the place. Not with fresh tears welling in her eyes and threatening to spill over at any given moment. Only he could not understand why.

Garrett touched her shoulder. "Have I said something to upset you?"

"Good heavens, no." Distress, if not outright sorrow had dimmed the light in her eyes. "I think all the excitement of my parents' arrival tomorrow and you...well, believe it or not, I will certainly miss you, Garrett Barringer."

"You will miss me? No, there must be some other reason." Something deep down told him to ask the question and wait for her answer before saying anything more.

Abigail smiled. "I had planned to break the news to you earlier, but I was uncertain how you would respond."

He raised a brow at her, all while bracing himself. "What news do you have?"

"Mr. Thorne has asked me to marry him. My father's plan worked, so there seems to be an opportunity for us both to remain in Asheville."

Garrett flinched. He had been mistaken. When Abigail hadn't responded directly to spending more time with Randall, but had instead skipped to her mother's arrival, it had given him hope.

Garrett shoved his hands into his pockets and dipped his head slightly, trying to hide his heartache. A kick to his ribs would have hurt less.

"You wish to marry him, then?" he asked, his tone sharper than it had been.

She frowned at his question before she walked away from him and to the kitchen. "My father must approve the man if he gave me his permission to spend time with him."

"Your father only wanted you to have the opportunity to put your past behind you."

It did not go unnoticed that she had avoided his pointed question all together. Garrett worked to keep his expression discreet, though his heart felt as if it were being ripped from him.

Her tears gave way and spilled over, fracturing the unyielding mask she had adorned since returning to the kitchen.

She shook her head and lifted a smile at him. "I apologize. It seems that my emotions have taken me beyond my control."

Before his brain could register what was happening, Abigail took both of his hands. "I wanted to thank you for this opportunity. Without you, I am certain my father would never have allowed me to come to Asheville. Our time together..." She tilted her head, just enough to conceal her eyes, but not enough to hide the tears dripping down her cheeks. "It has been a time I will never forget, Garrett Barringer."

He must not betray Mr. Dupree's trust, but he could not let this woman go without telling her his true intentions. "You did not answer my question."

Abigail glanced up at him sharply, and her eyes revealed how harsh he must have sounded, all while ignoring her tears.

She took a few dishes from the table and carried them to the sink. "I'm not certain of what question you speak."

"Do you intend to say yes to the man?"

"You know as well as I do, that I am unable to give him an answer until he has spoken with my father."

"And if your father approves?" He lifted his chin. "Do you mean to accept him? Do you love him?"

"I do not see how that is of any relevance." She wiped away the moisture clinging to her cheeks. "I am not sure what else you expect of me—"

"Only for you to be completely honest with yourself." Garrett frowned at the direction this conversation was headed, but he had to gain the real truth of her intentions. "And your yes to the man is not the only answer for which I am searching."

"Well, what then?" Only a touch of rebuff amplified her words. "William Arendell is certainly no prize."

"Will it make you happy to spend the rest of your life with Randall Thorne?" Garrett continued talking in an even tone, though his stable, mental state felt just out of reach.

Abigail looked at him long and hard until something that felt like awareness materialized in the space between them. "I alone, discarded any choice in the matter or my happiness some time ago."

"I do not believe that for one second."

"Unfortunately, your beliefs are not relevant in this matter. Besides, you base your assumptions on distorted facts. You do not know my past, Garrett Barringer." Garrett shifted slightly to the left as she pushed past him and returned to the kitchen as if facing him was too hard.

But he did know, though he was not at liberty to admit such details. "I know you well enough to know that you deserve happiness."

"It sounds as though you are trying to dissuade me from marrying Mr. Thorne." Busying herself with washing the dishes, she kept her back to him. "Surely you do not believe Mr. Arendell is a better match."

"I am only concerned for your happiness." He took a clean plate from her hand, grabbed a towel, dried the dish, and placed it on the opposite counter. "And you are correct. I do not believe William Arendell is a worthy candidate."

"Yes, well, if that is the case, we should hope that in the end, Mr. Thorne will make me happy after all." Upon cleaning the next plate, she handed it to him. "He is certainly a better choice than William Arendell."

Abigail was an expert at convincing herself. But she would never persuade him to believe Randall Thorne deserved her.

"And what if Mr. Thorne is unable to make you happy?"

Lowering another dish into the water, Abigail glanced at him. "That is my burden alone to bear."

Unable to pass up the challenge at such a statement, Garrett pressed forward. "Are you implying that you do not believe what the Bible says?"

She stopped mid-scrub of the next bowl and met his gaze. "Mr. Barringer? What on earth would compel you to ask such a question?"

"Do you or do you not believe the Word of God?"

She resumed running the cloth over the bowl as the gentleness in her features returned to normal. "Of course, I do."

He angled a sidelong glance her way. "And you are familiar with Romans 3:23?"

"I am." The answer was a jagged whisper on her tongue.

"All have sinned and fall short of the glory of God."

"I know the verse, Garrett." Her gaze slammed into his, her eyes awash with unshed tears, shimmering in the candlelight. "Unfortunately, my sinful nature reminds me daily of that misfortune."

"As it does to us all." He regarded her for a moment as a brief inner review of his own regrets plagued him with insecurities. How was he to convince Abigail of anything when he understood fully how guilt could hold someone in bondage? By reason of his own disgrace, Garrett believed she too deserved the freedom that Jesus offered. "God wants us to give Him our burdens. Yes, some burdens are meant for us to carry. But not alone. It is His desire to lift most of the weight from our shoulders."

"I *am* aware of that."

"Are you, truly?"

She didn't answer, so he continued.

"It seems to me you are willing to carry the weight of your past—whatever that may be, and no matter how heavy—all on your own."

"It's not that simple," Abigail said in a quiet voice.

"God is the light of the world. And He says, whoever follows Me will never walk in darkness, but will have the light of life." Locking his eyes with Abigail, he implored courage into her, then urged her to listen to God's voice. "He wants you to have a life of joy, not of pain and suffering."

"You do not know the mistakes I have made." Her chin tilted as she looked up into his face, her words a hoarse whisper.

"Nor do I need to. But you need to accept that God forgave you the first time you repented, Abigail. No matter your sin."

The competitive flicker in her eyes finally waned a bit as her smothered laughter ended in a stutter. "You confuse me, Garrett Barringer."

He bit the inside of his cheek to keep from grinning. "In what way?"

"I'm having a difficult time ascertaining the intent of your speech." Her words challenged him, but the drooping slant of her shoulders attested to her defeat.

His duty and desire for Abigail had muddled into an unrecognizable pile of slush. "I do not think it is wise for you to marry William Arendell or Randall Thorne."

A hint of a smile quivered on her lips. "Tell that to my mother. And father."

God had a future husband designed solely for this woman, and God help Garrett, he wanted to be that man. Though, great care would need to be taken to keep things in their proper order.

He turned her to face him. "I wish to discuss that very thing when your parents arrive tomorrow. In fact, I intend to give your father my thoughts on the matter."

He could almost see her eyes swimming in disbelief. "You will do no such thing."

"Why ever not?"

"From where is all of this foolish talk coming?" Confusion distorted Abigail's lovely features.

For a moment her pursed lips diverted his attention. Restraining his thoughts from the untimely urge to kiss her, he yanked his focus back to her eyes. And his ears to her voice.

"My father, or heaven forbid, my mother, would conclude that I put you up to the task."

"And it would be best to take the easier route by marrying one of these men."

Abigail's expression fell, sorrow creeping back into her weary eyes. "You do not understand."

The muted statement wrenched his heart. "Then, help me. I cannot for the life of me comprehend how your father or mother would allow such a thing."

The inquiry, naturally, drew her eyes to him. "You must not think harshly of them. It is my fault alone that I am in this predicament. My father and even my mother have been more than gracious to me, given the circumstances."

"There. Can you not see it?"

Her brows furrowed. "See what?"

"Your concern for others above yourself. It is a God-given attribute. There is nothing in your character that would convince me that you should suffer the rest of your entire life in an unhappy marriage. That God Himself would want that for you."

As he finished making that statement, she leaned forward into his chest, her hands covering her face. It was a force that staggered him, and he had to set a foot to his side for a more balanced stance.

Then, without hesitation, Garrett took Abigail into his arms, like a man hungering for a bite of food after going without for days. Her hands slipped from her face and attached to his shirt at his waist, clinging to him. He had made a promise to himself that he would keep his feelings for her neutral. Yet, he had broken that pledge within his heart, almost from the very beginning. He should not have held her so close, not while wanting to bestow his heart to her.

Abigail chuckled. "You have this strange way of making me feel better even amidst my circumstances."

He'd been only a heartbeat away from tilting her head back and kissing her with all the longing he'd restrained many moments since their first encounter.

"It is, indeed, an admirable trait, Mr. Barringer. One of which I would desire to hold possession." Her sobs eased to an occasional breathless whimper, the last of them cinching around his heart like a tightened vice. "It would be a weapon you should use often in your profession. If in fact, you are planning to take the route of law. You would certainly have the capacity to make unaware jurors trust you. Of course, that would be unethical."

"Perhaps."

"Think of me as no different, then. After all, you are employed by my father." Abigail twisted around as if in a dance, her full skirt spinning. "I wonder. Would you see me then as a case that must be convinced? Or would I be convicted?"

He allowed a smile of his own to answer her.

"Well. What is your verdict, then?"

"Hmm."

"Mr. Barringer, that is not an intelligible answer," she insisted, a charming shade of pink rising to her cheeks. "After all, if you are to be a lawyer, you can certainly never use that tactic when speaking to a jury."

He looked at her long and hard.

"For heaven's sake, stop staring at me like that. What is your verdict, Garrett Barringer?"

He read the admiration and respect in her eyes, and that conveyed the most important element to him at the moment.

"This." Garrett enclosed her jaw gently within his fingers and lowered his lips to hers.

For a brief moment, she stiffened in surprise. Then her palms rested against him and delightful quivers skipped across his chest as he closed the distance between them. She clung to his shirt as if her life depended on it and kissed him back with an exhilarating fusion of timid hesitancy and fierce hunger. Lifting his other hand to cup her face, Garrett drew her closer and deepened the kiss. Craving even more, yet needing to restrain, he softened his hold.

"You should be treasured. Adored. Cherished," Garrett whispered, tendering tiny kisses to her lips, her nose, her forehead. "And I am in love with you."

Her breath caught, and she trembled. "What? No. We shouldn't have done that."

He lowered his arm and wove his fingers between hers. Gently, he stroked the soft skin just beyond the curve of her knuckles. "I love you, Abigail Dupree."

Abigail pushed back and frowned up at him. "I am so sorry if I gave you—"

"I have longed to do that for months."

Her eyes darted around the room as if she had forgotten where they were standing. "For months. No, Garrett. I'm not—"

"But, you are, Abigail. You are everything to me."

Abigail took a step back. "How will Sarah feel about you making such a confession?"

His own brow puckered. "Sarah?"

"Yes, Sarah is in love with you, and I—"

"Sarah and I are friends, but nothing more."

"No. You don't understand. She started to share her feelings for you but we were interrupted."

"If she meant to tell you anything, it was of my feelings for you."

"What?"

He simply nodded.

Abigail's eyes darted around the room. "She knew?"

The Abigail Dupree who'd ignored his offer to see her to safety that first evening was a far different creature tonight, with shimmering tears still glazing her eyes because of her worry over him.

"I thought you intended to stay in Asheville so that you could remain close to her."

"I never said that." He captured her fingers and lifted them to his lips. "If I remember correctly, I said it was my family of which I wished to remain close. And though I was not free to say, I wanted you to remain in Asheville as well."

"Me?"

"Yes, you." He lowered himself onto one knee. "I am speaking out of turn, but this is my closing argument. I can no longer hold my tongue. I do not want you to marry William Arendell or Randall Thorne not only for the reasons mentioned earlier but also because I want you to be my wife, Abigail Dupree."

Chapter Thirty-Two

Abigail awakened to early morning sunbeams dancing across her eyelids and dreams of Garrett professing his love. Sparks of delight flickered around her brain as she blinked away her drowsiness and sat up.

It hadn't been a dream. It had actually happened. They had shared a kiss. More than one. Warmth flowed through her but just as quickly was replaced with apprehension.

As soon as Garrett found out the truth of her impurity, he would revert his proposal. Who could blame him? He deserved a woman who had saved herself for her husband. Not someone who had given in so easily just to win a man's affection. The discouragement of her own foolishness seeped through Abigail, assaulting her all over again.

Her father would have no choice but to be completely honest. Especially with this man. Garrett was a gentleman and deserved to know the truth.

But God had forgiven her. Abigail had searched her Bible and discovered numerous verses in multiple chapters. Truths that she had devoured well into the night. And that meant He wanted joy for her. Just as Garrett had said. Even if Garrett renounced his proposal after learning the truth of her past, at least she knew now what she had to do. And only had to convince her parents.

Abigail heard voices in the parlor.

They're here. She jumped to her feet, her back stiff, her arms dangling at her sides. Good heavens. What time was it? How could she have overslept today of all days?

She glanced in the mirror. The hair of a wild woman swept around her face in a disorderly fashion. Not to mention the sleep matted in the corner of her eyes.

Going out there in her unsightly appearance would be a disaster. It would cause an immediate argument with her mother. Nor did she want to face Garrett. Even if God did indeed bless her with a marriage to Garrett Barringer, her disorderly state would run him off for sure.

Her parents would just have to wait.

Ten minutes later, Abigail rushed toward the vanity. Shoving a dangling hairpin into its proper place, Abigail opened the door to her bed chamber and walked down the hall. A breath of laughter escaped.

Garrett Barringer had only hours ago declared his love to her. A moment she would never forget.

Abigail craned her neck inside the parlor in anticipation of seeing her parents and Garrett. But only her aunt was present.

"Good morning." Abigail joined Aunt Louisa on the settee. "I thought I heard voices. Have my parents not yet arrived?"

"No, dear. It was only a telegram delivery." Aunt Louisa reached for the envelope and offered it to Abigail. "It was addressed to you."

"Me?"

Abigail opened and scanned the contents quickly all while her lungs constricted at the news. Father had made his decision. Despair severed her brief moment of happiness.

"What is it, dear?" Aunt Louisa stood. "I pray it isn't bad news."

Abigail's hand trembled as she reread the telegram once more.

COMING TO ASHEVILLE. WILL SEE YOU UPON ARRIVAL TO DISCUSS ARRANGEMENTS. LOVE WILLIAM

Aunt Louisa touched Abigail's arm. "What does it say?"

"He's coming." Drawing her eyes from the words, Abigail looked up at her aunt. "He's coming here." Shakily, Abigail handed her the message. "There is only one thing he can mean by 'arrangements'." Especially with the timing of her parents' arrival.

Before Abigail could explain further, the sound of another presence, closed her lips. "My darling."

Abigail startled, every nerve ending standing on edge as she turned to find her parents in the doorway.

Aunt Louisa stood. "What a wonderful surprise it is to have you here."

Abigail noticed her mother first. Catherine Dupree never had even a single strand of hair out of place. But Mother's bun had loosened, and her makeup had not been applied as liberally as usual. She looked even more beautiful in her state of disarray.

Abigail kept her expression solemn as she moved toward them, though the news of William's arrival had her on the verge of tears. "Mother, how marvelous it is to see you. You look beautiful."

Catherine Dupree lifted a hand to her bun in confusion and fussed over the loosened pins as if she had only just realized something were amiss. Then she dropped her hand not bothering to fix anything and once again attached her gaze on Abigail.

A gasp escaped Abigail's throat as her mother wrapped her arms around her and held her tightly. Something her mother had, for years now, believed improper.

"My sweet Abigail, I have missed you so very much."

"I have missed you too." With a drawn brow, Abigail glanced

at her father. But he gave no hint of an explanation in his features. Instead, he held her in much the same way her mother had.

Father cleared his throat. "We pray you enjoyed your visit."

"Yes, I have enjoyed my time here very much." Though, Abigail's heart was crushed, she held no harsh feelings toward her father.

Mother turned her attention to her sister-in-law. "Your home is just lovely."

Wrinkles bridged the span of Louisa's forehead. "That is so kind of you, Catherine."

"I hope you don't mind us dropping in on such short notice," her father said.

"Not at all," Aunt Louisa replied. "We're more than glad to have you."

Abigail glanced about. Where was Garrett? Then another thought occurred. Abigail had been so worried about the unexpected arrival of her parents, and Mr. Arendell's telegram, she had almost forgotten about their maids. "Did Mabel and Rose not accompany you?"

"We thought it best to bring only one of them."

"I see." Abigail wanted to ask the question but wasn't sure the best way to approach it without giving away her knowledge of Rose's new position. "I suppose Mabel came along then, and Rose stayed behind?"

"Mabel joined us, yes."

The news nipped at a bruised area of her heart, but another dreadful image shoved its way through to the forefront of her mind. The image of William Arendell's telegram. Abigail shook the vision free and sucked in a much-needed breath. "Where is Mabel? I should like to say hello."

"Most likely unpacking our things."

Abigail was anxious to see her mother's maid. To hear the truth from her lips whether Rose had already left for her position at the Biltmore. Though, she wouldn't dare ask the question and could only hope Mabel would feel able to confide about Rose's whereabouts.

Father cleared his throat. "Perhaps it would be best to allow Mabel to finish seeing to our luggage. There will be plenty of time to see her later."

The rebuke stung, but Abigail agreed. "Of course. As you wish, Father."

"Shall we?" Her father pointed to the table, quietly requesting she take a seat. "There are some things I wish to discuss."

The unexpected statement made Abigail's throat convulse with a swallow. She watched her father's expressions with rapt attention, making her pulse fire haphazardly through her veins.

Mother took Aunt Louisa's hand. "Why don't we leave them for a few moments."

At her father's command, and her mother's curious behavior, Abigail's stomach pitted into tight coils. The news was for her ears only? It all sounded so serious. And that could mean only one thing.

Her attention was focused on the door when her father cleared his throat. "Your mother and I have decided to return to Asheville."

The words that came out of her father's mouth banished any assumptions she might have had. "Permanently?"

Her father's eyes darkened a shade. "Yes."

"That's wonderful news." Wasn't it? Her father's features were enhanced with agony instead of joy. A storm of panic welled in Abigail's middle. "Is everything all right, Father?"

"There have been some developments in your mother's health."

"What kind of developments? I pray there is nothing amiss."

"Her memory fails on occasion but over the last few months it has become increasingly worse."

Abigail recalled how her mother had often referred to her as a child in certain instances. "Now that I think of it, there have been times I witnessed a small difference. What is causing her confusion?"

"They're not sure. Unfortunately, the traits are very similar to a senile person. We have seen several doctors, but because they don't have any another explanation, they want to label her as senile and send her away."

Torn between encouraging her father and fighting back tears, she simply held her breath while asking the grave question. "The doctors want to admit her?"

"Yes, but I will not allow it."

Out of fear that if she permitted her emotions to take root, she may irrevocably break, she tucked them tight into a protected corner of her heart. "Of course, you wouldn't."

"There are times when she seems normal, and it is hard to ascertain when a spell will arise."

"You knew about this before sending me here?"

"I prayed the doctors would be able to help or that her healthy mind would return." Father took her hand. "We hoped we would never have to tell you."

"I should have stayed." Guilt quivered through her chest. "I should have been there to help you, Father."

"It was one of the main reasons I sent you away."

His response kindled regret. What must her father think of her, a woman who cared only for herself? Her eyes shuttered. "Forgive me, Father."

"No, sweetheart. You have been a blessing. The brightest light in your mother's world."

That wasn't true. What had she been doing while her poor mother had suffered with a silent disease of the mind? Criticizing. Complaining. Shame enveloped her, submerged her chest in grief.

"I needed the time to ascertain our next step."

Blinking away hot tears, she took a deep unbalanced breath and lectured herself into remaining strong. "You should have come to me."

"I'll admit, the thought occurred to me several times. But it has been difficult, and I didn't want you to have to carry any of the burden."

But that was just it. She should have been more sensitive to her mother's needs. If only she had been a better daughter. Not added unnecessary stress to her mother's life. Perhaps none of this would be happening.

"The hardest part of all is when she drifts to a different place in time. At times, she doesn't recall moving to the city and seems confused about why we are in our home."

Neither her mother nor father deserved such a fate. What of his work? His life?

"Does she understand what's happening?"

"To a certain extent, but not fully. Her short-term memory seems to be growing worse all the time."

Abigail covered her mouth to restrain her cry. "Oh, Father. What will we do?"

"I have found it best to comply with her state of mind at the aforementioned times. It seems to settle her mood."

"How though?" Her voice grumbled with defeat.

"Tell her the truth of her surroundings but with gentleness. Try not to argue. Even when she gets agitated. And answer her questions over and over. No matter how often she forgets that she has only just asked me."

A troubled sigh left her throat before she even suspected it was on its way up. "How long have you known?"

"I first noticed the changes less than six months ago."

"Six months?" So, that hadn't been the reason they left Charlotte as Mrs. Lewiston had spoken. But had her mother told the ladies that to spare Abigail's embarrassment? Had all the quarrels with her mother been initiated by this...this ailment? She glanced toward the parlor, searching for a glimpse of the woman who had reared her.

How had she not recognized the changes in her mother? She should have known. All the signs had been there. Abigail bit back a groan as regret swept over her. The way her mother spoke of past things often as though they were presently occurring. The way she spoke to her as if she were once again a young girl. How her mother greeted her just today as if she held no grievances toward her.

He stared straight ahead toward the parlor. "I thought it best to move her back here to the home she remembers well. And to a place where fewer eyes will be watching her every move."

"Where will we go?" she asked, fighting to maintain a steady voice.

"Our former home remains unoccupied."

For one quick second, Abigail's hopes quickened. Then in the next, her stomach churned as she considered her question begging for release. Was that the reason for William Arendell's telegram?

Had Father invited him to come as well? Had Garrett misunderstood his intentions?

Terror at the thought of William Arendell coming here with an objective to wed her constricted her chest. But if her marriage to William Arendell was her father's wish, and her mother's, she had no choice but to comply. Especially in light of these new developments.

A proposal from Garrett Barringer had been one of the greatest gifts she had ever received, but she could never accept it. Not now.

"I thought you would be pleased."

Abigail adjusted her frown. "Returning to Asheville is wonderful news, indeed."

"Your long face reflects deep concern over your mother, but

try not to worry, my darling girl. She is in God our Father's hands."

In the safety of her own thoughts, Abigail lamented. For it had not been her only thought. "Are you not worried that Mother will only worsen with time? What if she loses all of her memories and no longer even remembers us?"

"Nothing true or real can ever genuinely be lost." He took her hands. "I intend to care for her to the best of my ability for as long as we both shall live."

The loss of her mother's health and the sentiments of devotion from Garrett Barringer were still brimming through her heart, but she needed to say something before she changed her mind. "I will marry William Arendell if that is what you and Mother wish."

She would attend, toss her hopes into the air, then attempt with all her heart to find some good in her future.

The pounding knock on the front door startled them both.

Then, in the next few moments, William Arendell was standing in the doorway of the kitchen. All the blood rushed to Abigail's head and she reached for a chair to steady herself.

"Arendell?" Her father's voice demanded. "What on earth are you doing here?"

"I feel as though I should be asking you the same question."

Her father stood. "You, sir, are not privy to such personal information."

"I do believe I have waited for our arrangement to come to a close long enough."

The idea made her stomach turn. Only by God's grace would she survive such a union.

Her father grunted. "Is that so?"

"Why, yes." William Arendell stepped forward. "In fact, it is the very reason for my arrival. When I learned you would be traveling to Asheville, I thought to accompany you."

"So, it should seem. However, I do believe, sir, that the arrangement is something to be discussed in private."

Thankfully, William Arendell had barely looked in her direction. Could it be that there was some other reason for his visit that did not concern her?

Her father touched Abigail's shoulder. "Darling, if you will excuse us, I need to speak to the man in private."

"Of course, Father." Without a glance in Mr. Arendell's direction, Abigail scurried from the dining room to find the parlor empty. She did not miss the first of her father's hushed words. "Some unusual developments have occurred."

Then suddenly Garrett walked in through the front door. Had it only been mere hours ago that he had bestowed his love upon her? And now within minutes all hope of ever having a life with such a man would be snatched away forever. She should break the news now before he had any opportunity to talk to her father. Losing Garrett's respect would surely kill her.

"Has William Arendell arrived?"

Had Garrett known he would be coming?

"Yes," she said, glancing over her shoulder toward the dining room entrance. "He is speaking with my father. Perhaps you and I could take a walk."

He took her hand, and leaning forward, he brushed his lips against her fingers. "I would love nothing more than to take a walk with you, but first I must take care of something."

"But, I'm not certain this is the best time to interrupt."

"I, however, believe this is perfecting timing." His eyes riddled with confidence as he offered a calm smile. "Do not worry my love."

"But, no, please—"

She was too late. He was already gone.

Chapter Thirty-Three

A bigail took a shallow step forward as her father's voice broke through the silence.

"It seems there will no longer be a need for your services."

The solitary sentence interrupted the sorrow enveloping Abigail and she entered the dining room against her own better judgment.

Expecting her father to flinch at her presence, she was surprised when instead he stretched out an arm, inviting her to join him.

Though the angst in Garrett's expression was telling. He did not in the least bit agree.

"I do believe my daughter has something to say."

Confounded, Abigail glanced at her father. Regretting her entrance immediately, she frowned.

"Go ahead, dear. Tell Mr. Arendell what you were saying just before his arrival."

Abigail swallowed the bile rising in her throat. With desperation, she pleaded for more time. "I apologize, Father, but I cannot seem to recall my exact words."

"Then if you will allow me, dear," her father said, before turning to face William Arendell. "If a marriage to you are the wishes of her mother and me, then my daughter has agreed to the arrangement." As her father finished the sentence, she glanced at Garrett. His face was ashen. Stoic.

"Very well, then." For once, William Arendell's surprise matched her own. "That is what I was hoping to hear."

Her father cleared his throat. "But unfortunately, for you, Mr. Arendell, that is not the wish of my wife or me," he said with a tongue that could cut. "So, I must now ask you to leave."

William drew his head back. "I will do no such thing. You well know there are other reasons for such a union and no one will have your daughter when I am finished slurring her name."

Garrett yanked the man by the collar, bringing them face to face. "You are mistaken, sir. For you will do no such thing if you wish to see the light of day again or to have any future dealings or work of any manner. And I would also have you know that no matter Abigail Dupree's past circumstances, if her father approves, I intend to have her as my wife."

Abigail gasped and bit her lip, her emotions sprouting.

Still clinging to Williams shirt. Garrett averted his focus toward her father. "Please forgive me, Mr. Dupree, for speaking out of turn.

"Apology accepted. Now, Mr. Barringer, would you mind escorting Mr. Arendell to the door?"

"Of course not, sir." Garrett complied as he pulled the man by his collar through the exit.

Abigail turned to her father, her emotions still blooming and scrambling for coherency. "I thought you meant to give Mr. Arendell my hand in marriage."

"He should have to find another hand, I suppose."

Her heart was so full of joy, it felt as if would burst. "Oh, Father! Do you mean it?"

"Yes, dear. You never have to spend another moment in the presence of William Arendell."

"And Mother feels the same way?" Abigail asked, her voice scratchy.

He frowned. "Actually, she has never cared for the man."

Abigail stilled as she recalled countless conversations over the man. "What do you mean?"

"The day of our first meeting, she spotted him in town, but he had not seen her." Father took her hand. "Let's just say, his motives were less than honorable toward the woman your mother saw standing before him."

Abigail lifted her chin. "When was this?"

"Before you were even acquainted with the man."

"Good heavens." A year of the man pursuing her flashed before her eyes. "Why would Mother force me to spend time with him, then?"

"We had to convince William that we both wanted this union." Her father squeezed her hand. "Your mother wanted nothing more than to protect you."

Every word drizzled a healing salve over every intricate element of her heart. All this time, she had been wrong in thinking her mother wanted to be rid of her. To marry her off to any interested man. Instead, her mother had sacrificed her own comfort to protect Abigail's name.

"My dear, how would I ever allow you to marry a man who did not deserve you or whom you did not truly love?"

She swallowed the urge to squeal with thanksgiving and turned toward the sound of footsteps behind them. Exhilaration shot through her at Garrett's sudden arrival.

Abigail just stood there, suddenly unsure how to act in his presence. "Miss Dupree."

Garrett looked at her with so much compassion, heat raced up her chest and neck, and didn't stop until her cheeks burned with longing.

"Mr. Barringer." Father stepped toward him. "How good it is to see you again!"

"Mr. Dupree." Garrett reached for her father's outstretched hand. "I hope you had a pleasant trip."

"We did, indeed. The train is certainly improving with time."

Abigail suppressed a smile. It was as if their conversation with William Arendell had not occurred only moments ago.

Thankful for the distraction, Abigail recalled Garrett's proposal. A mixture of delight and sorrow welled up in her. Even if Garrett chose to have her, her father would have no choice but to tell Garrett everything. And even if by some miracle, he chose not to spill her immorality, she would never allow Garrett to marry her not knowing the disgrace of her past. Garrett would never look at her in the same way again. Was a marriage proposal to the man worth losing his adoration and respect?

Garrett cleared his throat. "I do apologize for not waiting to speak to you in private first."

"The timing was perfect, in my opinion, young man." Her father wrapped an arm around Abigail. "If you will excuse me and my daughter a moment more, I should like to get a detailed account of her visit and to discuss her wishes in the matter."

Abigail bit her lower lip. *Her wishes?* Could this truly be happening? She watched Garrett walk away, her heart longing for a future with him.

"Well, my dear, I haven't had an opportunity to ask, but how is Mr. Thorne these days?"

Her face heated with accusations against herself. "If I may speak bluntly, he has not changed in the least."

"I would have figured as much." There was no surprise in her father's eyes. "He never was a man of which I felt I could fully place my trust."

That was a generous description. But her father was an honorable man.

"You knew my reasons for coming here, yet you never said a word." Abigail folded her arms. "Why would you allow it?"

"I knew your heart was broken when he left. But I hoped

with time it would heal and you would forget him and all that had been taken from you."

But that was just it, he didn't only take it, she had offered. "I hold most of the blame, Father."

"Yes, and you believed that reuniting with the man would somehow redeem you. I was afraid that if you did not realize that it would not, you would never be able to move on with your life."

A familiar prayer resonated—a prayer for full redemption. "But no man will have me."

"William Arendell was ready and willing to take you with full knowledge."

Abigail flinched. "He knew? But how?"

"To that, he did not disclose, but if I had to guess, Mr. Thorne."

Randall? How could he?

"That was my reasoning for keeping Mr. Arendell close for so long. I needed him at arm's length until I could settle things."

Abigail darted a glance at the doorway. "But how? Will he not go about blurting my disgrace because you have refused him?"

"Not with the information Mr. Barringer has gathered and threatened to use against him just as he told the man earlier."

Abigail's heart froze. "Mr. Barringer?"

"My dear, Mr. Barringer has been a godsend in this matter. I do not know what I would have done without his help."

Abigail soaked in all her father was saying, still unsure how Garrett had any part in the matter.

"And now I must ask of you, what are your feelings toward Garrett Barringer?"

Abigail looked at her father. "I love him."

Her father spawned a smile of quiet confidence. "Thank heavens."

Abigail laughed in delight. "It was your hope that I would fall in love with him?"

"Guilty as charged. For all has transpired just as I had hoped."

"What of my past, Father?" Abigail's smile faltered. "He will have to be told before I can accept him."

"It was a detail I had no choice but to articulate, though I did so in the most prudent manner possible."

"He knew of my relationship with Randall Thorne the entire time?" Abigail swallowed the bitter news. "But he treated me with such respect."

"Why shouldn't he have? You are a precious daughter of the King." Her father nudged her chin up with the tip of his finger. "I know in my heart Garrett Barringer will cherish you."

Abigail nodded, though her heart was not as convinced as her mind. "But I do not deserve it."

"None of us are deserving of the Grace of God, yet He gives it freely. My darling, you have suffered long enough and carried the weight of your sin without truly believing your Father in heaven has forgiven you."

"I have tried." Abigail had thought to have succeeded this morning. "But it is an irreversible, despicable thing I have done."

"We all have a story we wish not to be spoken aloud. You have repented and are no longer living in the sin, so why should you spend all of your days living in regret? Your heavenly Father does not want that for you and neither does your earthly father."

"Oh, Father, I love you so much," Abigail said as she wrapped her arms around him.

"And I love you, my darling girl." He pulled back slightly and looked down on her. "Should we let Mr. Barringer in on the news that there's a wedding to plan?"

Abigail unleashed her overjoyed tears.

While her father stepped away to retrieve Garrett, Abigail

relished in her undying love of the two men God had benevolently given her.

When Garrett returned without her father, Abigail looked just past him.

"He left us to speak alone."

"What did he say?"

Abigail bit her lip, her heart pulsating so quickly she felt wobbly. "He gave us his blessing."

"Is that so?" Garrett took her into his arms and whispered closed to her ear.

Shivers pirouetted across her skin as his heated breath grazed her cheek.

"Can I presume that was because of something you may have said?"

"You can." Abigail wrapped her arms around him, her hands resting in the small of his back. "There is nothing more that I want than to be your wife."

He then lifted her chin up and drew her into a passionate kiss. After several long moments, he pulled back and took her hands into his with an unspoken promise of more to come. "You have made me the happiest man on earth."

Garrett loved her. Abigail drank in the exhilarating moment of her prayer answered.

"Are we free to enter?" It was her father's voice.

Abigail laughed. "Yes, please."

Her mother stepped forward first. "I understand that congratulations are in order. And what wonderful news. My darling daughter is to be married."

Abigail pulled her mother into a warm embrace. "Oh, Mother, I have never been so filled with joy."

Her mother beamed. "I must admit I am rather fond of your Mr. Barringer."

Abigail didn't have adequate words to express her gratitude —not to her amazing mother, or to the father she adored, or to her God who in His great mercy had saved Abigail from herself. Just as He had done for Jacob through a timely dream.

Then Abigail shared a tender glance with Garrett. He was truly going to become a permanent fixture in her life. A life she could hardly wait to begin. Perhaps eventually, her shame and gut-wrenching regret would completely dissipate with the gentle healing from her Father in heaven and with the love of such a man.

A man God had designed solely for her.

The End

About the Author

Award-winning author, Cindy Patterson, believes in captivating romance and happily-ever-afters that start with Jesus. In her stories, she loves to give glimpses of how God can use brokenness and make them whole. She reads a lot, drinks too much coffee, and wishes she had more time to write. Author of Chasing Paradise, Broken Butterfly, and Shattered Treasure, she loves to connect with her readers and you can find her at cindypattersonbks.com and on twitter @cpattersonbks

SIGN UP FOR CINDY'S NEWSLETTERS!

Keep up to date with Cindy's news on book releases and events. Click on the link below.
www.cindypattersonbks.com

amazon.com/stores/author/B00QNXPWLA

bookbub.com/profile/cindy-patterson

facebook.com/cindypattersonauthor

instagram.com/cindy.patterson

Acknowledgments

I have a vivid recurring déjà vu moment of being in an elementary classroom on a cold rainy day holding a first grade reader, with big bold letters and bright, colorful pictures. This vibrant memory was the beautiful beginning of my journey with reading. There is also a strong connection within this same musing of the close bond I felt to my mama.

As a young adult, she was my biggest inspiration for reading since she was always reading something and would share her books with me. She first introduced me to Historical Fiction through her collection of Janette Oakes *Love Comes Softly* and multiple series written by Lori Wick.

When the *Left Behind* series by Tim Lahaye & Jerry B. Jenkins came out, we would take turns buying the next release and gobble them up quickly. Since she was the faster reader, I'd allow her to read first. I, on the other hand, have always enjoyed taking my time and savoring each word. And I still do.

Twenty-four years ago, my mama and I took a trip together with our choir group to Lancaster County in Amish country, and that brought a whole new world of fiction into both of our lives. It is also the thing that sparked my interest in writing.

She was always the first to read any of my work. I couldn't wait to share some of this book, so I sent her the first five chapters to read.

But then, I unexpectedly lost my mama to a severe case of Pneumonia two years ago. So, this is my only book that she did not finish.

The grief I have endured is something I've been blessed to have never experienced, until now. I miss her terribly and sometimes feel it will never get easier.

I found I could not depart with any of her books. Especially the ones we shared.

But as I sorted through her things, I found countless notes and reflections from her own Bible reading and studying of God's word. It has been one of the most precious gifts I have found since Heaven received her.

I am so thankful for my mama, for her Godly influence, and for her love of reading that has poured out and into my life and has made me the reader and writer that I am today.

All of the words that pour out of me, would not be possible without my Jesus.

I also want to thank my husband and children for all of their support of my writing.

And you. Thank you so much for giving my books a chance. I am forever grateful for your support.

Also by Cindy Patterson

Chasing Paradise

Broken Butterfly

Shattered Treasure

PRAISE FOR CINDY PATTERSON'S BOOKS

Booklife Editor's Pick

The novel's overwhelmingly hopeful messages surrounding acceptance, faith, and second chances are sure to delight aficionados of light, clean, inspirational romance and have them eager for more.~*Booklife*

Author has a gift for emotional description, that pulse-pounding realization that escape is needed, and the physical. Author also gives us rounded settings with plenty of sensory details to add realism, and author brings our attention to some details that can be revealed, while others require our patience for well-crafted story structure. Revelations are very authentic for an injured, fearful character who must unspool slowly, and the author's empathetic writing forms great logic in that.~*Writers Digest*

"This lesser known author captured me completely with her words, her complex characters, and a plot line that will blow you away from the start. Her words are captivating, pulling the reader into the heart of the story instantly." ~*Readers Favorite (Molly Edwards)*

"Author writes movement especially well. There's a nice interplay between characters in dialogue scenes, and author has a good instinct for describing how they move together, angles, contact, along with excellent inner dialogue.Story structure is strong, the pace moves, making reader cares about these characters. The author knows how to do this well! We get real flutters and our own quickened breathing when author uses realism-building in the story line. Well done." ~*Writers Digest*

"A superbly written Christian romance. Patterson has created an engrossing and believable plot with a multitude of conflicts that keep things interesting throughout, and a group wonderful characters who tremendously enhance the plot. A story rich in setting and depth of character, *Shattered Treasure* will be a treat for fans of Christian romance, character-driven romance, and dramatic contemporary fiction." ~*Self-Publishing Review*

An emotionally complex and ultimately moving romance. ~*Kirkus Reviews*

Shattered Treasure by Cindy Patterson is a God-driven romance that is top in its class. I found this book to have everything and more than the description offered and I had a hard time putting it down. I was sad to have come to the end. Shattered Treasure is about love, compassion, forgiving and God's grace all wrapped up in a perfect story.~*Readers Favorite Review*

An inspirational novel about hard-won love finding its truth path.~*Kirkus Reviews*